THE FIFTH HORSEMAN

THE FIFTH HORSEMAN

A COMIC FANTASY THAT RIDES ROUGHSHOD
OVER THE RULES OF LIFE... AND DEATH

JON SMITH

THE FIFTH HORSEMAN

Published by Balkon Media

Paperback edition ISBN: 978-1-8384529-4-0
E-book edition ISBN: 978-1-8384529-5-7

www.jonsmith.net
www.balkon.media

ALSO BY JON SMITH

CHILDREN'S FICTION

Toytopia

NON-FICTION

The Bloke's Guide To Pregnancy

The Bloke's Guide To Babies

The Bloke's 100 Top Tips To Surviving Pregnancy

The Bloke's Guide To Baby Gadgets

The Bloke's Guide To Getting Hitched

Be #1 On *Google*

Dominate Your Market With Twitter

Web Sites That Work

Get Into Bed With Google

Google Adwords That Work

Smarter Business Start-Ups

Start An Online Business

Digital Marketing For Businesses

For those who fear Death...
Know that he's coming for you and he's rather grumpy

CHAPTER ONE

E mma reached out to steady herself on the copper base of
Bella, the magnificent Liver Bird that stands sentinel atop a
white dome, looking out over the River Mersey and across to the
Wirral and North Wales.

Her legs shaking from both effort and fear, she stopped for a
moment to try and catch her breath. She ran a hand through her
long auburn hair, gulping in oxygen and regretting cancelling her
gym membership earlier in the year. A strong and sudden gust of
wind hurtled in from the Irish Sea, its elemental tendrils clawing
at the exposed skin of her hands as the cold sting brought tears to
her eyes. Whilst she rued her choice of the landmark building, real-
ising that not for the first time she'd let form take precedence over
function, she paused to appreciate the stunning waterfront vista –
forged in blood, sweat, and tears by the city's maritime and
cultural history, both old and new, good and bad.

Why the clowns at UNESCO had stripped the city of its
World Heritage Site status would forever remain a mystery.

However, with typical scouse nonchalance, she parked that train of thought and tried to focus on the task at hand.

Everyone was out and about – on Pier Head, on the Strand, on their phones – busy with their day. Busy with their lives. Not many people looking up, which suited Emma just fine. She was used to being ignored. Used to just blending in. It was a learned behaviour that had started when she was a child, living under the strict rules of her parents, who firmly believed that children should be seen and not heard. She had trained herself to remain quiet, remain small, and remain in the background. It made for a lonely childhood but a peaceful one.

But much to Emma's chagrin, once she'd left for university, she found it difficult to unlearn, and thus difficult to make and maintain friendships. Or to be noticed by lecturers, even if she had her hand in the air. Or to be noticed by boys, despite being single and very much ready to mingle.

However, what wound Emma up most was not being noticed at work, no matter how diligent she was or how many new accounts she brought in. It was never Emma who was celebrated in the company newsletter, and it was never Emma who was put forward for promotion. Emma was just... there. A safe pair of hands at the back of the room. Reliable Emma. Wouldn't say boo to a goose Emma. The same Emma who'd just been handed a P45 and a beautifully written termination letter with her last and middle names mixed up. That's how well management and colleagues had got to know her in eighteen months.

For once, standing next to the symbol of Liverpool, over three hundred feet above the city, she was grateful that no one noticed her. She didn't really feel like looking back at them. She wasn't there to be gawked at or be made into some kind of sideshow on the street.

Not until after she jumped, of course.

At thirty-one years old, online articles all tried to convince her she was in the prime of her life. In reality, her happiness scale was registering an error; the reading was so low. She was neither playing the field nor settled with a significant other. She couldn't afford to rent her own apartment, never mind become a home-owner, so she was flat-sharing. She worked long hours at a thank-less insurance company full of dull, grey people. She made enough money to get by but not enough to actually *live*. She never broke through that ceiling to join those who are 'doing well enough to plan for a future'. Thus, she never thought she had a future – just a series of past mistakes and present dreads.

Someone finally looked up and saw her, squinted to make sure they were right, shook their head in disapproval, and walked off. She sighed. Was she really that unremarkable? She thought she was pretty in an understated way. A heart-shaped face, button nose, and two little dimples when she smiled – which, to be fair, hadn't been all that often recently. Her breath got caught on a shift in the breeze and blew back in her face. She smelled coffee and a bit of sick. All she'd had for her final meal was lukewarm coffee earlier in the morning. It wasn't fair to go out with such an unpleasant smell lingering in her nose. Nothing was fair.

"Emma!?"

Someone called her name as a hand slammed onto the dome, trying to find purchase. An arm and then a head of shaggy black hair soon followed. Mark, her tall lanky flat-mate, looked up at her. His puppy-dog eyes were wide with fear, both for himself and for her.

"Shit." Emma sighed. He'd found the letter and clearly ignored the instructions to open only after seven p.m. She should have known he would; his childlike curiosity was both endearing and infuriating – and predictable. Now she had to do what she had to do with an audience.

She took a step towards the edge.

"Don't come any closer, Mark."

He pulled himself up onto the dome, gauging how far it was to Bella's leg. He couldn't believe what he was seeing. His best friend and flat-mate with nothing behind her but a grey sky to catch her fall.

Another strong gust rattled the metal struts supporting the Liver Bird statue, blowing Emma's hair into her eyes. She angled her face away, as much to avoid Mark's judgemental frown as the wind.

"Don't turn around," he pleaded, and she remained steadfast where she was. "There's a... nothing behind you."

She turned slowly to see what he meant.

He winced. "No, don't look!"

"I know there's nothing," she said.

"Well, don't fall into it!" he exclaimed. "This high up – you'll die."

She put her arms down and sighed.

Mark looked at her critically. "Really?"

"I'm done, Mark," she said. "You know how long it'll take me to pay off everything? Years from now, I'll still be stuck in this same rut. I'll be old, incontinent, and already dying, and I still won't have saved enough to put down a deposit on a small one-bed flat in need of major renovation. I may as well..." She turned, and Mark gasped again. "I may as well not bother."

She lowered herself calmly and sat on the dome, legs kicked out casually in front of her, and immediately regretted it, as the frigid metal sucked away what little warmth she had left in her body through her thin cotton skirt and tights. She had to keep her balance as she swayed. Too relaxed, and she'd fall or slide down, and she didn't want...well, she didn't want to do that *yet*. Mark couldn't be there to see it. She had to make him go. Her teeth started to chatter as a trio of seagulls circled them, clearly wanting to set down, cawing their frustration at the presence of humans on their favourite perch.

Mark fought off every primal instinct to lower himself down to safety and instead cat-crawled *up* the dome, wrapping his arms around the Liver Bird's legs and hanging on for dear life. He peeked with one eye over the edge, just until he could see the ground below and no further. Staring down at the pavement from this height... he was shivering too, but not from the cold.

"Come on. Let's get down, have a drink at the Albert Dock, and talk about it."

"I haven't done my hair."

"You look great."

"*Please.*"

"We can work through this," he persisted.

"Work," she scoffed. "We can't, actually, because I got laid off. Again."

"That's constructive dismissal. You'll have a case," he guessed, floundering for options to keep her talking.

She shook her head. "I'm out, case closed. Less than two years, so they can do what they like. They wouldn't even let me say goodbye. Or take my stuff out of my drawers. Just confiscated my key card and marched me out of the building."

"Oh," he said in shocked disappointment. "Then that means — What'd you leave behind?"

"Nothing important, it's just the principle," she said.

"No, wait, what'd you leave?"

"Nothing!" she insisted.

"I know you left something," he said, snippier, "because it's still not back yet."

"What's not back yet?"

"My two-compartment container. With the red lid."

She groaned dramatically.

"Long enough for a banana, remember?" he asked.

"Yes, I remember."

"With the clip top?"

"Yes."

"It's part of a set of four I've been using—"

"Mark, I got fired! Now I'm here. The plastic tubs don't matter!"

"That's fair," he said, hands up in surrender. And then he quickly grabbed Bella again. "I just— I've just been wondering where it is... Was it empty?"

"Oh, God." She shook her arm in frustration. "I'm here to end it all, and you want to know if I ate your Thai green curry?"

"Well... yeah," he said. "It was a new recipe. If I do it again, I want to get it right."

Emma gestured to her predicament, being one wave of her hand away from teetering over the edge to her death. "Again?"

Mark was in denial. He smirked at her. "Well, I mean... y-you're not gonna, right?"

"What other option do I have?" she asked. "No, really." She turned around and sat with her back to the Mersey, which was somehow worse for Mark to watch. "You tell me what I should do, aside from killing myself? No job, no savings, I'm over sixty grand in debt and—"

"We can get through this. I'm working. My mum and dad could help, maybe enough to cover your rent for a few months."

Emma got increasingly tired of his delay tactics and slowly turned towards the river. The ferry had just docked at Pier Head, bobbing up and down on the swell. She watched as the commuters and tourists poured across the gangplank, glad to be back on firm ground.

"It's not impossible!" Mark continued. "Nothing is!"

"You sure about that?"

"Yes!"

She turned and gave him a cold, teary stare. "You think I might survive then? If I drop? Is that not impossible?"

"No, that's unlikely and not worth the risk. Please don't." Mark dropped to his knees and tried to reach her. He couldn't stand – at such a height, it'd be so easy to waver off and die in a silly way – but he could shuffle over to her on his knees, and he did. "Please."

"At least you'll get the insurance money. I put you as my beneficiary."

"Actually, they don't pay out if you take your own life."

"You serious?"

"Deadly. Deadly serious... How do you *not* know that? You sell insurance for a living."

"Not anymore," she scoffed. "Sorry." And she really, honestly, bottom-of-her-heart meant it.

She bit her lips together, making them flush red, then she reached over and hugged him around his neck, a big strong hug. She made sure to use up all her strength, every ounce she had left, because she didn't need it anymore.

"You can live without me. There must be loads of cool flatmates out there. Cooler than me at least. And able to pay their half of the rent," she said.

"N-no."

"It's not impossible."

"It's... unlikely."

Emma smiled, chewing the inside of her cheek as she tensed her arms, ready to push herself up. Mark reached out, grabbing her wrist.

"Wait. There's something I need to say," he pleaded.

"Don't, Mark. No more talk. You're not going to change my mind. I'm angry you came, but honoured at the same—"

"I love you."

Mark really hadn't meant to say it. Not now, not ever. But the words climbed up his throat like a lump and forced themselves out with brute force.

"You what?" Emma scrunched up her face, not sure she'd heard him right.

Here was his chance to apologise and laugh it off. A pressure-induced *faux pas*. She'd understand; he was always saying daft things.

"I love you, Emma. I have done since the day we met. I love you and I've loved every minute you've been in my life. Please don't do this."

"What the fuck?" Emma was incredulous.

Not quite the reaction Mark had been hoping for.

"Don't do this," she said. "Not now. Not here."

"Then when? There is no tomorrow, not if you go ahead with this. There is no perfect moment. All you've left me with is now."

"What do you want me to do with that information?"

"Changing your mind would be a good start."

"That I can't do. You're a good friend, Mark. Thanks for trying. I'm sorry."

"Best friend?"

She smiled. "The bestest."

She kissed him on the cheek before they parted. She stood up while Mark stayed kneeling on the dome, unable to get onto his feet. He was frozen to the spot with cramp and despair.

"Okay," she said. She took in a deep breath, let go of Mark, and put her arms out.

The people on Pier Head looked up with a bit more alarm. Apparently, putting her arms out was the signal that she was about to jump, rather than just standing limp-shouldered in a morose state as before. Her street-side audience had really noticed her now, and some of them actually rushed to do something. One man ran into the Liver Building, but he'd be a fair while traipsing up all those stairs, so there was no way to stop her. A few mobiles came out. Some were filming, some were taking selfies with Emma as the background, and others actually used the phone function for the first time in many, many months to make a call.

"Emma, wait," Mark insisted. He fought through the pain, pushed himself up with his hands, and stood behind her. He was just one slip away from certain death, and knowing that made him woozy. His legs shook, and he wavered a bit as he reached out to hold her back.

"Let me go, Mark," she demanded.

"Absolutely not," he said. "I won't—"

She cranked an arm back and slapped him across the cheek. She immediately felt bad.

"Oh God, I'm so sorry!"

"Ow!"

He lifted her just enough to get her away from the very edge. She turned and tried to nurse him while he held his face.

"You're not supposed to stand behind a suicidal person. You might get hurt," she said.

"That's an old wives' tale," he replied, still stroking his sore cheek. "Also, it's about horses. Though, it is true." He tried to grin, but his face muscles were so tight, it was more of a grimace.

"This is why you need to leave. You'll just complicate things if you stay."

"Well, good! I'd rather you be alive in a complicated way than complicating yourself all over the ground down there!"

"Oh, you're really helping."

"I'm helping you stay alive! That's as helpful as an unrequited lover can be!"

She managed a smile. "It'd be more helpful if you somehow summoned gold to rain down on our heads from above. About sixty grand's worth. Or, cash preferably, it's less likely to pummel us."

An impasse. Their situation was unchanged. Mark realised that saving her wasn't what she wanted, no matter what he said or did. He didn't like her situation any more than she did. It wasn't fair. And she was right, her misfortune had no easy exit. But he was sure they could work it out together. Share, and thus halve, the burden.

"I'm going now," she said adamantly, and stepped forward again, arms rising. Mark lunged to stop her and wrapped his arms around her waist. She resisted him and was sent into a bit of a twirl as Mark twisted himself to pull her back up the side of the dome.

"STOP!" a voice cried out.

The man on a rescue mission bounded up onto the roof. His abrupt appearance was so shocking that it made Mark jump back.

For a moment, he teetered on the edge, Emma still in his arms.

Then he fell off the dome.

CHAPTER TWO

A gnarled hand balanced a glittering coin upon its knuckles, surrounded by a void filled with an unshaken quiet. Only the clatter of the coin across bony fingers could be heard. It resonated in the emptiness. Robes fluttered in the windless air, the only movement in the stagnant space.

The coin was pinched between the fingers. The thumb tensed, and then gave it a flick. It spun in the air with a whining sound, then landed in a palm of taut, aged skin. A flower of parting, a bouquet of mourning, graced the side that faced up – a side of leaving. Tails. A bony mouth grinned with long, ivory teeth. The figure set the coin into another twirl, another spin.

It flew up into the air once more, glistening momentarily. A whirl and a turn, and then a landing. What would it be? Tails, the flowers lining the river of the dead, or Heads, the skull, the greeting of the reaper?

The coin slipped from the grasping hand and tumbled away.

"Oh, shit."

It fell clean off the boat and cast the first ripple in the silent waters, breaking the illusive quiet with a distinctive syrupy *plop*. The boatman crouched down with a rickety posture and leaned over the edge, eyes rheumy with age and resentment, trying to locate the lost treasure. The deep water rippled with an inky dark and then faded back into a placid white.

"Hmm," he groaned.

The ferryman looked to the back of his boat. All he had were his oars, a lantern, and an empty sack. No more coins to play with...

"Damn it."

He grasped the handles of the oars and let the blades drop just below the surface of the water. He began to row. With gentle, steady strokes, the ferry disappeared into the heavy mist.

Mark beheld the sky as he fell. It was grey and everywhere, and for a moment, he mistook it for the ground in the winter of his youth. On the rare occasions it had snowed, council snow-ploughs would mix a slurry of slush and road grime into a grey mound on every pavement. He once played in it and threw rotten, fag-ash coloured snowballs at his brother until his mother shouted at them both for even touching the dirty, filthy stuff. For the longest time, he thought she was talking about snow in general, and thus he came to hate it.

Until one day, he met a girl named Emma, who loved the snow and taught him to love it again. And they lived happily ever after together. Through thick and thin, they had met challenges head-on and survived all kinds of awful events. Like the time he had blurted out his true feelings for her and then accidentally suplexed her off the roof... That was when he came to, as the sight of the rapidly approaching flagged pavement snapped him back to reality.

Emma screamed. She had been lucid and awake the whole time. Nothing flashed in front of her eyes. She'd spent all morning contemplating, mentally preparing herself for this very moment. She had gotten it all done and out of the way beforehand, leaving her with no numbing, comforting memories to distract her as she zoomed towards her death.

She blamed Mark, just slightly, but then it passed. She was mournfully terrified of death. Yet she still believed what she was doing was the right thing. It was the only way out. The alternatives were poverty, meaningless work that would enslave her to a life not worth living, or the shame of returning to a home that was obliged, but not proud, to accept her back. To be a burden on her parents, a burden to her flat-mate, a burden to herself – with everyone treading on eggshells around her for years – and yet, there was no one there to carry her burdens for her. It wasn't fair. Especially not on Mark.

He, on the other hand, hadn't prepared for this moment. Not at all. And that was a problem. He was an organiser. A list writer. It wasn't on his radar if it wasn't scrawled on a Post-it note. Plunging off a tall building and hurtling towards the street whilst embracing his roommate wasn't even on this month's additional goals – the mental list of bonus tasks he created to push himself to greatness, be it eating less carbs, lifting more weights, or reading at least two chapters before bed.

Today had begun much like any other. He'd gone to work and come home again and, given that it was still a week until payday, tried to spend as little money as possible during waking hours. Then he'd noticed the letter, stuck to the fridge door with a chipped *Visit Cyprus* magnet – he'd never visited; it was gifted to him along with other used but still usable kitchen essentials by his parents when he had first moved into the flat.

He scanned the letter and ran. Just ran as fast as he could towards the Liver Building, all the while cursing himself for taking the scenic route home from work and not finding the letter sooner. Asking himself if he would reach Emma in time, or if he would be just in time to witness the aftermath.

As he hurtled towards his end of days, he was proud of all he'd achieved but remembered there was so much more to do – not least, the three incomplete items from today's list. Deep down, he wished he'd spoken up sooner and told Emma how he felt. But he hadn't. He was too afraid of rejection. And now the moment where he was finally truly connected to the world, and especially to Emma, would be his last. It was not fair.

The pavement got closer. They passed by the sixth, then fifth, then fourth-floor windows. It all seemed to be taking a bit longer than it should. The lowest floors whizzed by, the windows they passed offering a little glimpse into the offices behind. A potted plant. A grey-suited man in a private room. A lady in a red cardigan. Someone giving a presentation in front of a big screen.

Mark and Emma shared the same thought just as the steps to the main entrance came into view: they would have been much better off if they'd done things differently.

When they could almost reach out and touch the flag-stoned pavement, they both instinctively closed their eyes, braced for one final and fatal crunch.

And then they were falling... sideways.

They should have hit the ground. Hard. Bone and flesh smashing into the street. But the catastrophic impact Emma and Mark were both expecting simply didn't happen. Instead, they flew across the building's grand front entrance and along the series of windows to the ground-floor co-working space. Then they were rising up again in the air, past the first, second, and third-storey windows, and away from the Liver Building entirely.

All Mark could think of at that moment was why on earth there was a such a distinct smell of grass – of the lawn, rather than narcotic variety.

A thin, bony arm reached around and under both their waists. Mark kept his eyes fixed on the ground as it sped by far below like he was being dragged by an aeroplane. Emma regained her faculties a bit quicker and turned to look at what had caught them. Over the whipping sound of air rushing through her flowing hair, she heard the clopping of hooves and the haggard breathing of a great horse.

"Up you get."

A deep, bellowing voice bored into their heads as they were hoisted and secured on the back of the horse. The thin arms stretched back and were rolled into shoulder sockets with two noisy, bony clacks. A robed figure rode in front of them on the saddle of the pale, white horse in the sky. Mark hung onto the steed's rear for dear life while Emma struggled to hike her leg up and around to mount it properly.

"Ow! The devil's clutch," the voice said. "Move back a bit."

"What?" Emma called.

A skeletal arm poked out of the fluttering black robe and pointed to her lap. "You're sitting on my robe."

Emma scooted back to release the fabric from under her, which caused her to bump into Mark.

"AGH!"

"Oh, sorry."

"That's better," the rider said as he turned to look at his passengers. "No reason for discomfort, short trip or no."

"Jesus Fucking Christ!" Mark exclaimed.

"No," the rider announced. "Not exactly. Not the weirdest

guess I've ever heard though." With a tap of his booted heel and a pull on the reins, the horse turned sharply and rose higher into the sky.

Emma had questions. Lots of them. Some were obvious, albeit strange, even if they turned out true. She knew the rider was Death. It had to be. A skeleton in a black robe astride a pale horse, with a distinctive voice that seemed to bore into your skull and makes your eyes hurt. And they were flying, which might not have been real. But why hadn't they hit the ground? Had they hit the ground? She was sure she would have remembered if they did.

"Are we dead?" she asked, settling on the most pressing hypothesis that remained untested.

Death tilted his head and shrugged. "It's complicated."

"Can we please go back down?" Mark begged.

"Did we already hit the pavement?" Emma asked. "Is this the last flash of our consciousness as our brains go splat on the steps?"

"No," Death confirmed. "But... well..." Failing to offer a proper explanation, Death's right hand produced, from thin air, an ornate hourglass. Emma turned and pulled Mark up. Like before, he clung tight to her, though with far less chance of swinging her off their only safe purchase in their dizzying climb into the sky.

Death shook the hourglass. Some sand appeared to be stuck to the inside of the top bulb. The last few granules held fast, just a tiny scab against the clear glass. Death tapped the glass to try and free it. He shook it and quaked the bottom mound out of its place. But the sand was firmly stuck, and he murmured at the stubborn sight. "See? Too late."

"Too late for what?" Emma asked.

"For you," he said. "Damned glass fogged up on the inside. Your final moment was meant to pass already. His is the same, but now that you're here... I don't know what I'll do with you."

"Well, this is hardly our fault," Emma said. "No need to be rude." She reached out to the small brass plaque secured to the bottom of the hourglass – her full name and date of birth etched in Comic Sans.

"Please!" Mark said. "For the love of God, make it stop! Just drop us off down there, in Sefton Park. We can walk back. Anywhere, really. Just... drop us gently. Like at ground level. Or just park the... horse and let us climb down, so we don't fall at all."

"No," said Death, and the hourglass vanished. His hand reached out and a handle sprouted from it. As he turned, it grew into a spiralled gnarl of wood, and at the end was the great curved blade of a scythe. He raised it back over his shoulder, giving Emma and Mark a good, full view of the implement before he swung it dead ahead. A fissure opened in the air, which crackled with indigo lightning. The fissure widened into an inky black hole, the lightning arcing across it with sudden bright flashes.

Emma wrapped her arms back to embrace Mark.

"This is," he said, "the least likely thing that could have happened."

"It could be worse," she said. "It's unlikely we live through this part now."

"Yeah, but it's not impossible."

The horse dove through and they were away. No one saw them come or go before the portal closed behind them.

Death took them, body and all...

CHAPTER THREE

D eath. The final ending, the insurmountable obstacle, the last moment of any life.

The figure of Death, the robed skeleton with a scythe, was the eternal visage of a human's last and greatest mentor. He was inevitable. Every part of him was meant to elicit a fear ingrained in and inherent to all human life. A body without flesh was, without any question, dead. The understanding of that resonated through various fields of human psychology as a way to explain the nearly universal personification of Death as a figure in myth.

He came in many forms, but nearly all of them were faceless, skeletal, and so often on a horse as pale as the skull hidden beneath the dark cloak or as bony as its rider. And the scythe, his tool, was the sublime lesson of man's finality. To be raised up, grow strong, bloom, and be harvested at their peak – a scythe slicing them down. In Death's hollow eyes, man was no more than fronds in the field, undulating like a sea of amber.

That Death, the very same, lived in a quaint white pebble-dash cottage.

The front garden was full of flowers, scattered among reeds and wheatgrass stuck in perpetual sprouting greenery. They were just in view of a great river of iridescent colours, as though oil had been carefully cultivated to form a film over its current, and thus every ripple sent out a rainbow of reflected light. Further in the distance was a storm – eternally brewing over a darkened place full of mountains and valleys covered in permanent shadow.

Like a light aircraft, the pale horse galloped down and slowed into a nose-up landing. It clopped along the ground towards a stable at the side of the house. Emma and Mark took a moment to behold the majesty and strangeness of the new world they had just been thrust into. Upstream, to the left of the river, there was an endless void, where it seemed nothing at all existed. Along the riverbank were other homes of various sizes and architectural designs, some on Death's side and others across the bridgeless water.

As their pale mount clip-clopped into the cobblestone paddock, Emma felt thoroughly confused. Sharing a saddle with Mark had not been on the itinerary. Nor was having one arm draped around Death's waist. Despite spending all day – and, in truth, most of the week – thinking about her death and its execution, she'd never once thought about the possibility of an afterlife. She felt decidedly unprepared and underdressed.

The pale horse sighed as it came to a stop at a stable door, immediately dropping its nose into a granite water trough, gulping noisily. Mark relaxed his white-knuckled fingers, which he realised were still clamping the creature's rear end in a vice-like grip. He apologised silently to the horse, fearing that if he spoke the words aloud, the old girl might just respond. And discovering Mrs Ed right now might just send him over the edge, for the second time today.

He tried to make sense of their surroundings. The cottage, the paddock, the river framed by dark mountains, and what looked like a brewing tempest to the west – none of it was a far cry from his Duke of Edinburgh Award expedition to the Lakes.

"Must be Cumbria," Mark said. "Look, see? It's like a huge campsite. Bet they've got water sports."

"We can't be in England anymore," Emma disagreed. "I don't think anywhere in England has a... void."

"Birkenhead town centre comes pretty close..."

Death groaned as he dismounted the horse. Emma and Mark followed and tentatively tried to pet the horse as thanks for not bucking them off. Death, meanwhile, used his scythe as a cane to start walking up the path to his home. He had a hobble in his step.

Mark stood close enough to Emma to whisper. "You know what I said, just before—"

"Not here, Mark," she whispered back, taking a first step towards the cottage. "I'm still processing... well, everything."

"It's just... I hope it's not, you know, awkward between us now."

"It's not," Emma replied.

"Well, that tone kind of indicates that it is."

"What tone? Look, I..." Emma stopped and waited for Mark to catch up, leaning into his ear. "Don't take this the wrong way. But you professing your love for me, on any other day, would count as the weirdest thing in the world. Ever. But, given what else happened today. What *is* happening... I think we park that conversation, and we'll say no more about it. Agreed?"

"Fine." Mark tried to smile and gestured zipping his lips with a finger, but try as he might, he couldn't hide the hurt from his face.

Death was almost at the front door of the cottage.

"Do you know how to ride a horse?" Mark asked, changing the subject.

"I took lessons once," she whispered back, "as a child, but we only ever went around in a circle on a tether."

"Is flying a horse much different, do you think?"

"I'm not stealing Death's horse!" she whispered. "If that's your suggestion..."

Mark looked around them dramatically. "I don't think we can wait for a bus."

"You two!" Death bellowed. His voice, ancient and commanding, shook the very air and rattled around in their skulls for a moment, just in case those at the back weren't paying attention. He was impossible to ignore. "Don't dither. Come inside."

"Yes, sir!" Mark called. Death headed in and left the door ajar while Mark brought Emma in close. "What's the protocol for entering Death's literal home? Should I genuflect or something?"

"Just be well behaved," she said. "We don't know where we are or what's going on. We don't know what we're dealing with here. Could be *Meet Joe Black*, could be *Beetlejuice*. Got to tread carefully."

"Yeah, but if we hassle him, and he kicks us out – will that mean we go back to Earth? Will we have to stay here if we're too docile and polite?"

Emma considered this. She had wanted death. She hadn't banked on an afterlife but was willing to play along. All of the pain, the fear, and the crippling loneliness that had haunted her thoughts for years was suddenly gone. And it felt good. So far, this whole death lark was a giant leap in the right direction. And she knew she wanted to stay dead without a shadow of a doubt. Mark, she was sure, would be thinking the exact opposite. He was the master of the small print, and he'd be focussing on the detail, the get-out clause, the Article 50 he could trigger to somehow wind back the clock and get them transported to their shitty flat in Liverpool. She had to play this carefully. Keep Mark on side but ensure that he didn't find a way to shuffle them *back on* the mortal coil.

"We play it by ear," she said. "If he wants us to stay, we act stupid until he kicks us out. If he wants us gone, we act polite and try to stay."

He gave her a thumbs up and led the way into the living room. It was quirkily decorated. Some ornaments hung on the walls, mostly skulls and paintings – there was definitely a theme. Death had a Last Supper variant over his hearth, where everyone was a skeleton. A portrait of a gold-inlaid skeletal man hung near a window. A bust of Apollo, but skeletal, took pride of place on top of a bookcase. Every book was a great chronicle of death. Many of them were books about war; the only exception was a dog-eared copy of *Fifty Shades of Grey*.

"Kinky." Mark sniggered.

"Shh," Emma hissed as she urged Mark to stop staring at the décor and keep following their host.

Other than those decorations, the home was made up of pretty standard – if a bit niche – furniture. All of it dated from around the seventies, some wavy designs with psychedelic colours which had clearly withstood great periods of fading. The carpet was plush but beaten down by trodden feet, and only soft with thick fronds in the corners, near the walls. The ceiling was surprisingly high for a cottage, plenty of room for a voice to echo.

There was no sign of Death in here, so they continued into the hall and through to the kitchen.

"Ohh, exposed brick, very on trend." Mark nodded his appreciation, rubbing his finger along the breakfast bar and then checking it for dust. "Clean and tidy too."

"We're not on a flat viewing," Emma quipped, before immediately opening the doors to the oven and washing machine and having a nose in the cupboards.

There was no shortage of appliances but they all seemed to be of the same era as the furniture – old but functional, like a time capsule of post-war Britain, with the occasional splash of seventies disco.

"No way! A Marathon." Mark was almost bouncing with excitement at the discovery of the pre-cursor to the Snickers bar. "Fifteen pence. I feel like a millionaire. Look how big it is!"

Mark and Emma were having more than a sneaky peek through the cupboards at this point. To a casual observer, which Death was, as he considered the pair from the kitchen door, they looked like a couple of very hungry burglars. All the cans and packets of food were things of death, defunct brands that were no longer available from dead companies in the real world that had found their way to Death's simple manor.

"Ahem." Death beckoned them from the doorway to the hall.

He turned on his heel and Mark and Emma quickly closed the cupboard doors and followed him. Death hobbled around the house quite comfortably as he led them past the staircase and through a set of double doors into his study.

He reached for his leather smoking chair, then fell back into it, brushed his hood off, and let the air into the holes of his skull. His jaw opened when he made any vocal noises. It didn't jiggle like he was talking; it was simply either closed and quiet, or open and loud.

"Veronique!" he called.

"Coming!" a chipper French accent responded from the top of the stairs. Shortly after, a girl no older than eighteen, with long blond hair tied in an intricate braid and wearing a black mourning dress, came around the corner and into the room. She exclaimed when she saw the additional company. "Oh, my, monsieur. Guests?"

"Don't be too excited," he said. "They won't be here long."

Mark and Emma nodded at each other. The act was on, but for very different reasons.

"So pleased to meet you," Emma said, extending her hand in greeting. "I'm Emma. This is my flat-mate, Mark."

"We're just passing away," Mark said. "I mean, through."

They both smirked at the bad joke. Veronique laughed with them sincerely and took Emma's hand. Emma could feel the bones under her gloves. She was herself, just a little bit deader than them.

"Very nice to meet you," she said. "I am Veronique. Death's assistant. His second hand. His— Oh, monsieur?"

"What?"

"Were you planning to return to reap more souls sometime soon?"

Death groaned. "No. This has—"

"And did you forget the shopping?" she asked. "And the copy of *Heat* I requested."

Death facepalmed. "I did."

Veronique sighed. "If you permit me to do so, I can go and get it myself. But I did ask you, so kindly, and you did agree, as you often do—"

Death smacked the leather arm of his chair. "I have considerably more important things to worry about than what celebrity has ruined their life this week!"

"Well, I don't," she complained.

Death groaned again; another argument worthlessly begun and ended without advancing any agreement.

"Er..." Emma said. "About us?"

"You said our hourglasses got stuck?" Mark prompted.

"Hmm, yes," Death said. He produced two hourglasses, conjuring them into his palm with a mere twiddle of his fingers. The mostly empty bulbs were on the top. When he turned or tilted them, all the sand stayed stuck in place. "Cheap, plastic knockoffs. Gets a little humid around here – the river, you know? I must've left your hourglasses out on a walk or something and some moisture was trapped on the inside."

"Rice might help sort that," Emma suggested. "When you get a phone wet, you're supposed to bury it in dry rice to absorb the moisture."

"Or silica gel," Mark added, wanting to be helpful. "You get packets of it in the box with electrical goods – kettles, toasters, that sort of thing. That's what it's for."

"Exactly!" Emma snapped her fingers, turning to Veronique. "Silica gel, can you remember that?"

Veronique nodded, not sure what was happening but happy to be included.

"Right," Emma continued, "and while she runs to get that, we can stick around and—"

"You won't be staying," Death insisted.

"Great!" cheered Mark. "We'll hitch a ride with Veronique and be out of your hair... I mean, head."

Death stared at them for a moment then pushed himself up out of his chair. He crossed the room to linger on a row of wall ornaments. Scythes, pole arms, halberds, pikes, and long axes of various kinds from all cultures were hung in a horizontal line, all the way up the wall to the highest point of the ceiling. Death ran a hand over one of them.

"You're sand dodgers," he said. "Evaded death on a whim outside prediction. But your sand was set to fall regardless. Even if it is delayed by hours, days, or years, you were meant to die at that moment. An error caused by condensation won't save your life."

"But," Mark said, "you saved us. You stopped us from hitting." He was struggling to make sense of the limited information he had available.

"I did not *save* you," Death said. "I brought you here, same as any other soul, to move on. And your next move is over there." He pointed to the door to the garden, which opened on its own. The only thing in sight was the river.

The River Styx. Like the band.

"So, we're categorically dead..." Emma's lips quirked with the hint of a smile.

"No." Death rubbed at his temples in frustration.

"We're still alive then?" Mark asked as he picked up his hourglass, tapping at the crust of sand stuck to the inside of the top bulb. He shook it for good measure.

"Not exactly. Find Charon," Death said, "and tell him... Tell him whatever you want."

It seemed that Death had simply given up on them and bid them to go away. While it was clear they were unwelcome here, Mark and Emma were no clearer on their current health status. They turned to Veronique, who was looking at her superior in a concerned way. Then she turned to them with sympathy and a silent nod that they should go. Please.

They stepped outside through the open door and looked down the winding pathway to the river.

"So..." Mark whispered, "do you know how to drive a boat?"

CHAPTER FOUR

The thick fog rolling off the River Styx was beyond humid. It was like walking into a cold sauna. It was as grey as the sky in spring, but everywhere in three dimensions. Mark and Emma held hands as they entered it so they wouldn't get lost on their way to the water's edge.

"How wide is this river?" Mark wondered.

"It doesn't look too wide to me," Emma said.

"Let's find out." Mark picked up a smooth pebble from the riverbank, wrapped his finger and thumb around it, and sent it skipping across the water, but it was lost in the fog after the first bounce. "I reckon that was at least a four. Still got it."

Emma scoffed. She picked up a large rock and threw it as far as she could with both hands. It landed with resounding splash somewhere in the fog. "It's pretty wide. Don't think I've swum in a river since primary school."

"I haven't swum outside of a kiddy pool. Ever," Mark admitted.

"That's not right; we went to Ayia Napa the year we met?"

"I went to the beach, but I didn't swim."

"Oh."

"And the ocean isn't like a river," Mark explained. "The movements are all— It's towards the shore, and with a river it's kind of sideways."

"Right." Emma nodded enthusiastically. "It's different ways of swimming."

Mark eyed the water, the formation of a plan building in his head. "Hey, maybe if we drown here, we'll go back?"

Emma stopped and tried to stare at him judgmentally through the fog. "You seem quite keen on dying. Again. Ironic given the effort you went to trying to stop me."

"I want to live. Just need to figure out how to get us back to… Earth," Mark said matter-of-factly, absolutely sure he could apply logic to their predicament. Maybe they needed to kill themselves in limbo so they could live again?

"But I don't want to go back," said Emma. "I chose this. Well, not *this* exactly. But death anyway."

"I didn't. And I don't want to be dead. You aren't going to resent me for trying to stop you, are you?"

She sighed. "You made a right balls-up of your rescue effort. Look, I was very much in my right mind when I planned what I was doing at the time. I thought it through. Even how I might have hurt you. I accepted that."

"And you still did it," he uttered, the pain evident in his voice. "You still went ahead and… tried to do it, without even telling me. What if I never found your letter? Or if I'd waited until after seven? What if I'd just happened to go for a stroll on Pier Head the moment you took your leap and you landed on me?"

"That would be pretty rubbish, and very unlikely."

"Or even worse, if I didn't get there until after and slipped on your brains?"

"What if you just stayed in and didn't bother to find me?" Emma said, becoming quite cross. "Like you were supposed to."

"Then I'd be a crap flat-mate, wouldn't I?"

The creak of wood and a splash of water interrupted their argument. A figure appeared from the fog, first as a silhouetted shadow against the ivory-white air, and then as a man, hunched in rags threaded with an inlay of coins and thin golden braids. His skin was tight across bony old hands and a long, wet beard hung from his face.

"Two souls, going out?" a haunting voice asked.

"Are you Charon?" Emma asked in reply.

"That I am," he said, gesturing at the wooden craft beside him. "The boatman of the River Styx. Have ye the toll for crossing?"

"Toll?"

"A coin of gold," he said, then he opened his mouth and stuck out his tongue, "perched here, in yer jaw. Have ye brought such a thing?"

Mark took out his wallet and shuffled a few coins around. "I have sixty pence in change. I don't have to put it in my mouth, do I? Can we skip that step?"

"Ugh," Charon groaned. "Where's your horseman?"

"Went for a nap and left us to it."

"We're sand dodgers," Emma said. "Whatever that means. Death claimed us early because his sand timer thingy got all moist."

"Hmm?" Charon grunted. "That hasn't happened in nearly a hundred years! What's he done to make this such a bothersome trade?"

"I don't think it was his fault," Mark said. "He thinks it's the river. Or the fog. Or maybe the 'too good to be true' faux-mahogany hourglass he got from AliExpress really was, er, too good to be true."

Charon gripped his oar with a menacing tightness. "If yer not dead, then ye shan't be stepping foot on me ferry."

"Can this take us back to Earth?" Mark asked. "To the living world? Ideally, we would like not to be dead, so if you could—"

"Speak for yourself." Emma interrupted.

Charon lifted the oar from the water and jabbed it at Mark. The oily water splashed on the ground, then quickly slithered back to rejoin the murky depths like it had walked out naked from the bathroom straight into its mother-in-law.

"I said nay!" he exclaimed. "Yer too heavy. It'll sink my boat to carry you with all yer flesh and guts and bits. Souls only, and only those who can pay the toll."

"Well then, what are we supposed to do?" Emma asked. "Can we walk up the river instead?"

"Ye'll find nothing thataway," Charon warned. "Naught but the impassable Limbo, where the poor souls without payment wander forever, to drown in the river or sulk on its shores, eternally wistful of the lands they could have reached."

"What happens if they drown?" Mark asked, hopefully.

"You ever breathe water?" Charon asked. "Forever? In yer lungs meant only for air?"

"Oh."

Charon laughed cruelly. "You poor things. Pilfered from yer own deaths in honest error. The poor bony bastard must be kicking himself over you at this moment." He chuckled. "He's an angry reaper when he does mess things up. Very angry."

"He seemed more morose than grim over it," Emma offered, "if that helps."

"I'll wager he is." Charon hitched his cloak and stepped back onto his boat.

"WHAT GOES ON?"

Death's bellow parted the fog all the way across the river, and a wave of oily water pushed the boat away. He looked furious – as furious as one could while sporting a tweed jacket and diamond-patterned golf slacks, holding a Tesco *bag for life* full of basmati rice in one hand and a four-pint bottle of semi-skimmed milk in the other. The copy of *Heat* Veronique had asked for was rolled up in his jacket pocket.

"Why are you two still here?" he asked. "Get in the boat."

"They're not getting in my boat!" Charon insisted.

"Yes, they are," Death commanded.

"They aren't."

"They are."

"They're not!"

"They *will*."

"They won't!"

Death sighed, relenting. "Okay. I'll front their toll."

"Your credit's no good here anymore," Charon said. He pushed the boat further away from the riverbank with a splash of his oar. "Too much meat. Too fat, too plump."

"Hey!" Emma shouted.

"I think he means me." Mark patted his belly, trying to suck in his gut.

"They're your problem!" Charon called as he faded into the mist. "Your mistake!" He continued shouting further rejections until he was gone from sight in the white fog. Death sighed and turned to leave. Mark and Emma stood by the water's edge, not sure whether to follow or stay put.

"He won't take us, will he?" Emma said.

"No," Death agreed.

"So then," Mark said, more concerned than before, "what should we do?"

Death didn't respond. He just walked away. Like an old man coming home from the corner shop having spent his last pound on a scratch card instead of topping up the electric meter, and now he wouldn't be able to heat up his soup. The whole ordeal had been too much.

He did not forbid them from following, so Mark and Emma lagged behind him. The fog rolled back in around them and clung to them close. Their clothes were damp. Mark shivered in a stray breeze.

"He never gave me a proper answer," Mark said. "About drowning."

"We should assume that we're alive. Ish," Emma said. "We're just lost. We... we've come to another country without a visa. We know we can be here, but officially, we're not the right kind of citizen to stay. Like Tom Hanks in an airport. That's how I'm choosing to see it."

"That's good then. There's still a chance. A convenient quirk. I can work with that."

"It's decidedly inconvenient." Emma dragged her feet like a petulant toddler.

Death stopped at the door and waited for them, just to make sure they were coming, but with the vague hope that they wouldn't. "I'll say it again, don't plan on staying long. If you can, make yourself useful to Veronique while you're here. I won't have you be a burden to me. Or her."

"Yes, sir," Mark agreed.

"Don't *sir* me," Death demanded. "Don't be familiar. Don't expect any rewards or favours. I'll expect you'll cross that river one way or another, mark my words."

"And then we'll be dead?" Emma asked. "Dead and gone?"

"Yes," Death confirmed.

"Fabulous."

The horseman huffed and entered his cottage. Mark and Emma gave each other stern looks. Sure, they'd argued before over what felt like life-or-death decisions – Brexit, vaccinations, whether to watch the first episode of a new series knowing full well that if they start they'll end up bingeing it until five in the morning and feeling dreadfully tired the next day, the age-old discussion over whether to add ham to a carbonara, or whose turn it was to empty the dishwasher with both parties adamant that they had done it last time – but this was different. This really was life and death. They were poles apart and neither side was prepared to compromise one iota. In a way, Mark was glad it had come to this. He regretted blurting out his feelings to Emma at the most inopportune moment, and he regretted her reaction even more. If he could take solace in anything from today, it was the fact that he was still alive or close enough to it.

CHAPTER FIVE

Life in the Death household – which was an irony to consider in itself – was largely dull. Death retired to his den down the main hall. There was no TV, as the medium was not yet dead. Death did have a Marconi radio though, which exclusively played mournful melodies, woeful ballads, and songs about dying from musicians that had long since or recently passed.

Death lay back in his favourite recliner chair and read to pass the time. He either opened up one of his many books on the history of those who'd died, or he would manifest a newspaper with obituaries of both famous and mundane people and the lives they once led.

Veronique tended to the house and the outbuildings. She kept things in order, clean, dustless, and generally maintained a sense of sterility in the place. She made it look like a museum piece rather than a lived-in home – which, in Mark's mind, was fitting. She made the place look and feel like the home of Death. If it were too lively, it would feel like a joke.

Mark tried to ignore his nerves and get comfortable on the stiff sofa in front of the fireplace, which looked like it had never once hosted a fire before. Dead cold, as most things here were. Emma, on the other hand, tried to be slightly more proactive.

"Is there anything we can do?" she asked.

"Hmm?" Mark said.

But Veronique clapped her hands and pointed to the kitchen. "Actually, there is."

Emma followed her back into the linoleum-floored room. It felt a little bigger than it looked. The backdoor led to another wide-open field of flowers mixed with various kinds of wheat in the midst of growth, like a field that had gone to seed after a year of neglect.

"Don't mind that," Veronique said. "The garden, I mean. I can't keep up with it."

"Why does it grow at all?" Emma asked. "I figured, in a land of death, there'd be... nothing?"

"Just rocks and dirt and gravel? How dull. This afterlife is not quite so bad. It does become redundant after a time... a bit boring. The long wait for things to happen is the worst. Occasionally, monsieur will return with stories of some wild death that struck his fancy, which helps remind me of being alive."

"How long ago did you die?" Emma asked. "I'm sorry if that's a touchy subject for the dead, but—"

Veronique turned to her with a coy smile. "You know? It is a hundred and four years now. One hundred and four years since I was alive." She flashed a chipper, dimpled smile.

"Oh," Emma said. "I'm sorry?" She tried to sound happy and apologetic at the same time, so Death's assistant would hear whichever she preferred, but it came off as very confused, which was about right.

"I was a nurse," Veronique explained, "on the frontlines of the War. The trenches were the very embodiment of death. I thought

Hell had come up from the ground and replaced the countryside, turning it black and dead for miles. And the men there... There was so much death, I knew it had to be from another world. That hell of war was all we knew. No way to escape it, nowhere to go. Only to die, or live and then fight until the death again."

"Oh dear," Emma said.

"Sounds like being an Everton fan," Mark quipped as he joined them in the kitchen.

"I was rescued from a triage post and taken through the trenches by a brave man. He carried me off to protect me. Said my life was worth more than his. If he died, one less gun would be firing, but if I died, my hands would heal so many less soldiers. I thought this was wrong; 'You cannot be right!' I said. 'You cannot die for me!' And the yellow cloud descended to choke us. I tried to run, to honour him and prove him right and worthy. But it was not meant to be. I felt myself soaring through the air after choking on searing-hot poisonous air. And then I was here."

"That is harrowing," Emma said.

"Apparently," Veronique concluded, "had I lived, some lives could have been saved. But their lives or deaths would not have ended the war more quickly. I was brought here and given a choice: I could cross the river to my death or remain on this side of the river to fulfil a purpose greater than myself. I decided to stay, with the soldier's message in my heart."

"Do you help or heal many people here?" Emma asked.

"No, no. Not at all." She shook her head. "My help is mostly superficial. From nurse to maid, that is what I have become. But it is not all bad. As I remain, I have come to appreciate so much of life and death – and Death himself, too. However, he is a... how do you say? He is a *curmudgeon* lately. The duty he has is a dire one indeed, and never stops, no matter how he struggles to keep up with it."

"He hasn't gone out to collect more souls since we came here, has he?" Mark said from across the brunch bar. "Has he stopped, er, reaping on our account?"

"People die whether Death is there to shepherd them or not," she said. "Only, without his guidance, they are left to wander and find their way here through the void. The ones Death takes are brought to the river more directly, and all die in ways unobstructed by the other horsemen."

"Horsemen?" Mark replied. "War, Disease, and.... Hunger, is it?"

"Pestilence and Famine," Veronique corrected him. "In fact, you can meet them. Soon!"

"Should we though?" Mark asked nervously. "I think I'd prefer not to meet any horsemen. Other than a police officer, maybe. Or a polo player."

Emma looked at him with deep, confused concern. Then it clicked, and she immediately rescinded her expression.

Mark chuckled. "You thought I meant water polo?"

"I did," she said. "I did think that."

Veronique opened the pantry cupboards, noticing immediately that things weren't quite where she had lovingly placed them before. Emma and Mark looked anywhere but at Veronique; Mark even began to whistle in an attempt to reinforce his innocence. But his eyes betrayed him when they strayed to the Marathon bar he coveted. Veronique picked it up and tossed it over to him.

"Bon appétit."

"Thanks." Mark caught it mid-flight, once again marvelling at the weight of the bar and generosity of Mars Wrigley.

All the standard major food groups were represented in Death's kitchen by defunct brands and food fads that had long since gone out of style – again, mostly from the seventies. Veronique pulled out a selection of pre-prepared kitsch party foods and placed them on the counter: cocktail sausages, a deep baking dish full of quiche, half an orange stuck with toothpicks that held chunks of ham and cheese like a meat-and-dairy sputnik, and one gelatine mould that contained a giant trifle.

"For my anniversaire," she explained. "I have arranged a party. Une surprise... with his comrades invited to celebrate!"

"That sounds lovely," Mark said. "The whole cast of the apocalypse under one roof. Not on Earth for an evening."

"The monsieur needs some revelry," she said. "I would not speak ill of the master, but the work is becoming hard on him. It is not your fault, no. Many faults have come about that he can't find the time to fix. It is the unfortunate nature of this work of his. More people die, and he has less time to find the ones who are worth his reaping."

"A nice party with old friends," Emma said. "That should cheer him up. And if he's in a cheerful mood, he might just be inclined to work a little harder on his *faults*, right?"

Veronique nodded, and Emma realised that she could prove to be a valuable ally in her quest to die properly by crossing the river.

"So," Emma said, feeling cheered, "how can we help, if at all?"

"We must rearrange the living room," Veronique replied, "dress the dining table, and prepare the favours for the guests before they arrive."

Just then, there were three knocks on the door. Light but firm.

Veronique gasped, clapped her hands in excitement, and ran for the entrance. Mark and Emma held their ground in the kitchen and watched as three figures entered, garbed in great regalia from across the ages. These must have been the horsemen: War, Pestilence, and Famine.

War was equipped with gallant plate mail in a roman style, with bulging metallic muscles and robust red paint – or the splatter of blood – rusting against the ironclad cover. Pestilence wore a plague doctor's beaked mask and a robe covered with such filth that it crawled with life. A whole clump of dirt rested on his shoulder, with worms wriggling freely in and out of it. Then Famine, diminutive and bony, with taut skin across his body and a face covered by a gently swaying veil. He appeared the weakest but stood tallest and somewhat noblest of them all.

"Oh?" Pestilence said. "Guests? They seem quite healthy. Come out and let me check you over."

"They are guests of circumstance," Veronique said. "If you do not mind them here..."

"It's no bother," War said, in a woman's voice. She removed her helmet and revealed herself to be an aged but stately and demure woman.

"War is a woman?" Emma said out loud before clasping her hand over her mouth.

"Why wouldn't she be?" War asked. "War is what drives men to battle and to kill, and there's no motivator more present throughout your history that has turned the cogs of hateful battle than the want of a woman."

Emma turned to Mark, who was nodding along.

"Mark! Emma!" Veronique called. "Help me lay the table, if you please. We will be ready soon." She turned to the other horsemen. "Please, be comfortable!" Then Veronique fled with her human companions to arrange the stage for dinner, while the horsemen sat and chatted.

And all the while, Death sat in the dark of his den, alone with his own displeasure, which slowly grew as the shadows deepened and the lights in his room died down...

CHAPTER SIX

I t was dark in the house and eerily silent. Death exited his den in the evening, expecting to hear the exchange of whispered intrigue between Veronique and his unwanted guests. He antici- pated hearing them chatter and gossip about their human trivia, about the celebrity lives they held in such high regard over their own – for the perceived superiority of acting, or 'influencing,' or other meaningless talents – and that he would be the one to stride in and remind them that even those so-called celebrities they fawn over will have deaths of far less consequence than theirs.

But that would have meant reminding them that they were special. So he would stay quiet. They were special because he failed, and he wouldn't again. The only words he had to share were of thanks for Emma's handy rice tip, since it had worked, and their hourglasses were now condensation-free. Surely it would only be a matter of time before the crusty scabs of sand would fully dry out and fall. He could, thereafter, prove their deaths to Charon and send them on their way in a matter of time.

If only he could find them. For some reason, Veronique had

left the sitting room dark along with every other part of the house. He knew there was nowhere for her or the other two to go. Not unless they wanted to try the river again, but without him to negotiate, it would be pointless. They also couldn't have wandered into the void of Limbo – into the infinite expanse of nothingness, where the numbness of non-existence would eventually stop them from thinking thoughts of any kind, forever.

"Kids these days," he mumbled. He strode forward, confident of having memorised the sitting room setup so that he could find his way to the torch on the wall. His deep muttering covered the slight whispering giggles that hid in the dark, "...may as well cut off their heads and be done with it..."

BONK!

"AGH!" Death roared with his hollow voice and hopped back, clutching his injured knee. A panicked voice skirted around the room, rushing to get the torches lit.

"Surprise!"

Everyone was there. Veronique, Mark, Emma, and the horsemen sat around the good dining table with ill-fitting party hats on. Mark and Emma tried their best not to feel silly but were sitting beside War, still in her formal armour, and Famine, still in his relative nothing, who were all the more joyful to be showering Death with a bright surprise. Mark blew on a paper horn and Emma let rip on a party popper.

Death stumbled his last and slowly returned his throbbing leg to the ground. He turned to the entrance where a seventh stray voice groaned, and saw Charon standing in the open doorway. His leg was still chained to his boat; ever the ferryman, unable to cross the river over which he eternally ferried souls. The chain was just long enough for him to get to the door, so they had to have the party in the sitting room. All the furniture had been pushed aside to make room for the fully extended table. And a little side stand had been pushed up to the door for Charon to linger near and rest his Babycham and pineapple on.

Death couldn't help but smile – sort of. Death smiling was always suspected or assumed, as he had no face to smile with. The huff he let out wasn't dismissive but accepting and just a little appeased.

Which meant the surprise was a success.

———

Veronique had her time as the centre of the party, but after that, it was left to the horsemen. They went through an array of drinks, constructed by Veronique and served by Emma, and plucked away at the party food plated by Mark. The humans and human-ish faction eventually retired to the guest room, which Veronique stealthily prepared for the duo to stay in, while Death, War, Famine, and Pestilence caught up.

"It has been a while, hasn't it?" War said, as she put her sword up against the table leg. Pestilence took off his bow and Famine played with his scales on the table by tilting them one way or the other.

"All of us together? We're usually so singular. Or, at best, always seeing each other in passing," Famine noted.

"Hmm," Death affirmed.

He was the sole scavenger of the cheese and ham hedgehog. He slipped the toothpicks into his mouth and the food on them simply disappeared.

"These are delicious." Famine reached for a fourth sweet treat from one of the plates. "What are they?"

"Top Hats." Death nodded in agreement. "Wonderful. Marshmallow covered with a peppermint placed on top of melted chocolate, which is then left to set. Veronique's idea. Says they should only be eaten after eight."

Charon glanced at the Death-themed clock on the wall: a dark horseman with two scythes as hands. It had stopped.

"How can you know?" he asked.

"It's always after eight somewhere." Death reached over and popped a top hat into his open jaw, and it disappeared. "Sublime."

"How's work? Busy?" Pestilence asked War as he scratched his chin.

"Some of us are busier than others," War responded pointedly.

All eyes turned to Famine.

"I'm not happy about that," Famine said. "It's the ages."

"Age has wrought us unwell," Pestilence agreed. "This age of medicine, technology, longevity – people surviving all my finely crafted illnesses for years upon years. They're lucky I like my work so much, else I might've given up and retired some time back."

"It's all uphill from here," Famine said, helping himself to a large portion of the trifle. "Especially for me. People get paid to drill wells and provide food now. Even victims of war get to eat."

"Oh, do they?" War asked with a posh arrogance. Famine rolled his head at her.

"I've taken pride," Pestilence said, "in the littlest things. Leprosy was my personal favourite and look where it's gone. All but vanished. The last leper colonies have been emptied, sterilised, and turned into fancy hotels. But malaria – that's the gift that keeps on giving. Each mosquito gets infected by me, personally. Millions of the little pricks, all flying around stagnant bodies of water. And the cure still hasn't caught up to the disease. It's just like the good old days, a bit. Makes me teary-eyed for the past."

"Every single one?" War asked incredulously.

"By hand, yeah," he confirmed. "Nice way to pass a rainy Sunday."

"When does it ever rain?" Charon asked.

Thunder rumbled in the sky. A few drops plopped against his coat.

"Cheap parlour tricks," he grumbled as he tried to fight against his ankle chain to avoid the downpour.

"But very effective." War smiled. "Be thankful it wasn't hail stones the size of tennis balls."

Charon downed his Babycham and held out his glass, hoping someone would top him up. Reluctantly War scraped back her chair and did the honours.

"Well, I'm doing fantastic," War boasted as she charged Charon's vessel. "Border disputes, an oil obsession, and once that's all gone... roll on the Water Wars. Oh, I'm looking forward to all that. Population growth is out of control. Countries with populations in the *billions* throwing armed men across territorial lines for decades at a time, just to gain an inch of land they value for some new, subjective reason. And the intrigue is just *ooh!* Give two men peace and quiet, and they'll fight over who has the loudest farts!"

"I wish these generations would value traditions," Charon complained. "I haven't seen a coin under a tongue in aeons. Men come buried in worthless things, unfit for bribes. It's a disgrace. Even the millionaires brag of the lives they led and still come coinless, no better than peasants. And I refuse their crossing, so then they come back with *lawyers* to complain. It's a madness."

"Hmm," Death said, and their eyes turned to him, their host, to carry on. "It's all a bit much, isn't it? All this work, for nothing."

The horsemen sensed that the mood had dropped quite severely. In the end they couldn't raise their voices against him, not quite so confidently, being that all their effort and all their accomplishments still had to pass through *him*.

"So, when are we going to meet the new arrivals?" Famine asked, trying to lighten the mood.

"You've met them already." Death tried to throw some Bombay mix into his open jaw but most of it missed and skittered across the carpet.

"We saw them," War interjected, "but I wouldn't say we *met* them. Don't know the first thing about them. Be interesting to get their opinion on our little discussion tonight. A sort of 'voice of the customer' focus group."

"They're indisposed," Death said as he quaffed his mead. "Their opinion matters not. They will be in Charon's charge soon enough."

"Not unless they've discovered some coin in their undergarments, they won't," Charon replied, picking at some dirt under a fingernail. "You know the rules."

Pestilence took up his glass and directed it at each of his fellow horsemen.

"Who," he challenged, "do you think has done the *most* work out of all of us, hmm?"

"Me," said War immediately said.

Pestilence scoffed.

"What, you? Certainly not *him*." She pointed to Famine.

"You will find," Famine said, matter-of-factly, "that starvation was the key component in propelling man's fearful ascent into civilisation. In their historical ancestry, from their primal roots, man has only ever contested nature in pursuit of food – and often failed. The Ice Age alone sets my record at, oh, I don't know, some few thousands of years of human history unwritten – a bit higher than yours, I think."

"Wars are fought," War said, "over food. Any death in pursuit of taking the food of another land or tribe counts as mine."

"But farming ruined you both," Pestilence said. "And thus,

when I ruin farming, it leads to so much worse. A sick farmer can't feed anybody, and who's left to fight then? The bugs? The air? This malaria here is a slow burn but I promise you, it's a winner."

"At least you always have Alzheimer's," War said. "Makes a strong man weak enough to forget he was ever a soldier."

"And to forget to eat all day," Famine said.

They all toasted to the ill humours of mankind, while Death quietly smouldered in his chair.

"And all of that," he said eventually, "every soul dead in any way, goes through me."

He raised his glass to the open air.

"To us," he toasted. The others returned the gesture stoically. Death was hardly the life of his own party. But he was right.

CHAPTER SEVEN

Night came over the land between life and death. The night of the grim afterlife was darker than the night Mark and Emma knew. There were no stars, but there were lights. Blazing chariots ran across the sky like headlights in the distance. They watched from the guest room window as the horsemen left on their mounts into the air and scattered across the vast domain of the Limbo side of the River Styx. Charon hiccupped and tentatively made his way back to the shore on foot before disappearing into the fog.

"I would've liked to have talked to them all," Mark said. "To maybe... get some answers."

"Answers to what?" Emma asked.

"Like... how most people aren't really dying to them anymore. What do they count for? You're a case in point. Where's the horseman of depression?"

Death knocked and opened the door to their room. They stood at attention from their seats near the door and tried to be pleasant.

"Did you like the party?" Emma enquired.

"Veronique set it all up," Mark said. "She's a wonderful lady. And she did this whole room for us – we helped a bit, of course – and we assumed it would be okay to stay, but, uh..."

"Hmph," Death huffed. "I don't have the time or clarity to think about what to do with you just now. That last Jägerbomb is stuck in my head. You two will stay here for the night, and come morning, I'll think of the next steps."

"Of course," Emma said. "It's not like we can just... run away or anything."

"Quite," Death agreed. He sighed and shuffled off down the landing towards the stairs. He padded down them and entered his room across from his den. His bedroom was dark, but different from the sitting room with the lights out. It was just dreary. A place where light couldn't shine, and everything was black. Peering in was like staring into the shadow of a shadow.

Back in their room, Mark and Emma returned to their chairs and looked at one another. Their situation remained unchanged in its uncertainty.

"Looks like we're sharing," Mark said, patting the woollen blankets. He stood up and began to undress.

"What are you doing?"

"Getting ready for bed. I suspect we'll have an early start." Mark threw his jeans over one of the chairs and started to unbutton his shirt.

"Can't you just sleep in what you've got on?"

"Ewww. No. I'll get too hot... I'll leave my boxers on."

"I should hope so." Emma walked round the bed to the other side. "I don't want to be woken up with something prodding me in the back, be it a hand, elbow, or anything else."

Mark climbed under the covers and lay on his back, looking

up at the ceiling. He bit his bottom lip, not sure whether to speak his mind.

"Can we at least talk about—"

"No," Emma replied as she kicked off her shoes and squirreled under the blankets fully dressed.

"Fine."

"Fine."

———

Veronique visited the two of them in the early morning hours before Death surfaced. He was awake but not in a thinking mood. All his thoughts were bone-cracking screams from his hangover. He spent the better part of the morning smoothing his fingers over his skull, trying to subdue the throbbing. Again, this left Emma and Mark without guidance and Veronique in search of company.

You could cut the tension in their room with a knife. If Veronique noticed, she was too polite to comment or let it stand in the way of a great idea.

"Good morning," Emma greeted her.

Veronique took a seat on the edge of the bed. "Would you humour me for a moment?"

"Of course," Emma said. "We're your guests and Death's. We're willing to humour you however you wish."

Veronique sighed. Something was on her mind, perhaps rooted in the festivities of the night before.

"Do you need help clearing up downstairs?" Mark asked. "Quietly, to not disturb him?"

"No, I did that already," she said. "It was my party, so my duty. I'd never ask him to help. You see, Death— He is... old."

"How old exactly?" Emma asked.

"As old as all of time," Veronique replied.

"And he's still working," Mark said, impressed. "Makes a pensioner look soft."

"But he cannot carry on like this forever," Veronique continued. "Even before I died, I could not help but find pity in him rather than hate or fear. He reminded me so much of me, going through the hell of war to tend to others, bearing the pangs of heat and bloody wounds, all to stop their suffering. Oh, and he was kinder too, back then. But so many died so quickly. And the 'War to End All Wars' continued into the Second World War, and the dozen or so wars after. He's been run ragged ever since the Industrial Revolution. The more humans there are, the more he must work to keep their souls moving to the other side. And when they are stuck to linger with no clear way across, which he cannot help, he is chastised by the souls he reaps as lazy. But he is not, I promise you that. He's just old and tired and... he needs help."

"Well, we can't have Death retire," Emma said earnestly. At least not until he'd found a way to help her pass to the other side. "That'd be... bad."

"It would be bad," Mark agreed. "If our souls were meant to linger in our bodies after death, forever, it'd paint quite an awful picture of eternal existence for most. Especially us."

"Yes," Veronique said. "Without Death, souls would inhabit unmoving bodies and feel the pain of dying forever."

Mark frowned. "Would we still feel, for example, our brains... exploding out of our skulls and all over pedestrians in the street?"

Veronique locked eyes with him and nodded. She touched her throat gently. "I still felt the mustard gas in my throat, decades after I came here. The memory of pain stays with you. And it becomes all you can remember. Forever."

"Yeah, we need Death," Mark decided. "That's not a fate for anyone."

"But how can anyone help him?" Emma asked. "It's kind of a one-man show, from what I can tell. Is what he does even learnable?"

"It could be," Veronique said. "As I have learned much. Death has made it clear to me that there are things he can do that I could do, but which he does not want me to do."

"Why not?" Emma asked. "Even I feel like it's improper to send Death out to the shop to pick up a Double Decker and the latest copy of *Bella*."

"Well," Veronique said, "if you could return to the living world, what would you do first?"

"Live life with a passion. Knowing that every moment should be cherished because it could quite easily be your last," Mark replied, all the while looking at Emma.

"Bravo!" Veronique smiled, patting Mark on the upper arm.

"I don't want to return to the living world..." Emma sighed. "I want to be here. Well, not here here. The other side of the river."

Veronique looked back and forth between them. "You are an odd couple, non? Why wouldn't you choose to live? To be together. Go to see the world? Resume your life as planned?"

"Actually, I should have clarified yesterday. We're not a couple. We're flat-mates," Emma explained.

"Mon Dieu! Excusez-moi, I just assumed—"

"Just flat-mates," Emma repeated.

"Not for want of trying..." Mark whispered under his breath.

"Don't," Emma warned.

"Could we?" Mark asked, thinking that perhaps Veronique's company might actually be preferable. "Live again, I mean?"

"My life, as planned, was sort of meant to end right then," Emma said.

"Mine wasn't," Mark added quickly.

"That's what concerns monsieur the most," Veronique said. "Entrusting the powers of Death to those who were once mortal would distort the viewpoint required to carry out the duties a bit too much. Death was never mortal, never living. He has always been as he is, always the reaper. He knows nothing else. It is natural for him to do this job. And he knows it is not natural for others to learn it."

"Can we go over our alternatives?" Emma asked. "Do you know what it's like on the other side of the river?"

Veronique shook her head. "I never fully died, so I never crossed. No one ever comes back, either. And Charon, le salaud, he gives no answers. Too bitter, too irritable to be helpful. Only complains all the time."

"He did seem the sort," Mark said, "to spit in your eye and tell you it was raining."

"Do you think Charon would change his mind? Maybe treat me as a special case?" Emma wondered. "Maybe he'll waive the whole coin-collecting business and just let my soul pass on, laissez-faire style. Maybe if you asked him, Veronique, he might listen."

"Imagine taking the ferry across the Mersey without paying a fare," Mark said. "The Council would go broke in a week. Can't see him agreeing to that. And there's some untold millions of souls lined up on that riverbank in Limbo waiting to go – none of them have coins either."

Veronique reached into her apron and pulled out a pouch of tobacco and a packet of papers. She deftly rolled a cigarette, licked the gum, and placed it in her mouth. She handed the box of matches to Mark.

"S'il vous plait."

Mark obliged, striking a match and lighting her cigarette.

They both watched as Veronique inhaled deeply and blew a plume of smoke towards the ceiling.

"The way I see it—"

"Ow!" Mark shouted, throwing the still-lit match, which had burned his finger, to the floor.

"The way I see it," Veronique began again, "you are at a crossroads, no? Mademoiselle Emma, you accept your death and wish to pass through to the afterlife?"

"Right." Emma nodded.

"D'accord. However, Monsieur Mark, you wish to return to the world and have a second chance at life. True?"

"Correcto." Mark tried out his best attempt at a French accent.

"That's Spanish, not French, you doofus," Emma scoffed.

"No mind. I think there is a solution that might help you," Veronique mused, "but only for one of you. And the problem is... I cannot tell which one."

Emma's interest was piqued. "What? What's the solution?"

"If you were to help monsieur with his reaping, he may grow to like you and maybe, just maybe, grant you your wish."

Emma and Mark exchanged glances, the realisation dawning that they could potentially work together towards achieving very different outcomes.

"Would you consider it?" Veronique asked. "Being Death's assistants?"

"Well, what would you do then?" Emma asked. "We wouldn't want to step on your toes or crowd up your kitchen."

"I am just a personal assistant of sorts," she said. "House-keeper. Maid. I'm asking if you would become Death, as well."

"Woah. Hang on," Mark said. "I thought you'd been here for a hundred years, and he still hasn't sent you back! That's hardly a sure route back to the living."

"I didn't say it was a quick solution. Only that it was a possible solution. And I am happy here. I neither wish to pass over nor pass back."

"...Would he actually let us?" Mark said then, hopeful that this scheme might, at worst, enable him to return to life and, at best, spare them the existential dread of the unknown eternity beyond the river's shores.

CHAPTER EIGHT

"No," Death said in a commanding tone. "It is a loathsome idea, at best."

Veronique sat with Death in his den. He had Emma's scandalous hourglass on the stand at his side. It was half-full of rice, some of which was now stuck in the narrow funnel, and –worse – the scab of sand was still adhered fast to the inner wall. At least, he thought, the mist of condensation was gone. He knocked on the top once more just to check if the grains would fall or not, but no. They didn't.

Behind Death, one of the bookshelves was at a right angle to the others – an open doorway to the Hall of Time – through which were rows and rows of shelves, and on each of them was an hourglass, as far as the eye could see. Some were expired, lives that had gone by with great anticipation. Others were still running, duties he had yet to fulfil at a specified time, yet to be reached. Some were brand new. And others had yet to start falling, the sand suspended in the top bulb – lives unborn and awaiting the first step on the grim march towards their inevitable end.

With the door open, the low hum of the constant fall of sand filtered through glass carried into Death's den, a white noise of sifting that replaced the stagnance of the air. The chairs were few. After all, it was his private room, his study upon the doom of the human race and the ending of all their grand designs. He had one non-hourglass ornament which hung high on the north-facing wall, a scythe of ancient, almost prototypical design with a short and shallow blade and a gnarled handle made from a fallen branch.

"Monsieur, please listen to the reason," she pleaded. "This event is somewhat unique, no? An opportunity, one might say."

"It's an opportune mess," he asserted. "Every moment that it isn't solved is a pain of my own unmaking."

"So surely it would be prudent to make lemonade from these lemons, yes? I believe that is the phrase they say. Take a bad opportunity, and twist and grind it until it yields fresh... juice."

"The juices of life and death are never fresh. And far more bitter than any lemon." Death held his fist up to his mouth and muffled a cough from deep below his sternum. "I'd be a laughing stock to the other horsemen, to the other restless deities and forgotten idols of the old eras. None of them have assistants – not in earnest. All their assistance lies in the whims and wills of humans to make a mess of their own existence, which they're quite frankly expert at."

"I hate to say it, but you are tired, Monsieur. You must feel it. You cannot deny that you have become... fragile as of late."

"Fragile?" he snarled. He hit his hand against the arm of his chair and there was a slight *CRICK* sound. They both looked down. His little finger was broken, hanging on by a knuckle. He sighed and reset it back in place. "I am Death. My strength lies in the stroke of my will and the speed of my horse, which *you* need to brush today. I am too busy."

"Staring at unfailing sand?" she asked. "Or because the last time you brushed him, you could not sit straight for a whole day because your spine was knocked out of place? If you hadn't fallen on your posterior, it never would have set back to the way it was."

"I fell on purpose that time," Death insisted. "And no. There is another reason even you cannot deny, same as the truth you claim to spit in my face. They are human. They are prone to errors made in emotion. They might judge as they reap and deny death to those who it claims. They would see a suffering child about to take her last breath and decide to let her live in agony, rather than claim her soul, young as it is, for eternal purgatory. They do not understand the necessity of death. Least of all the woman, who squandered her own life to meet it quicker."

Emma, who had been listening from the other side of the door with Mark, entered the room at this remark.

"Oh, come off it," she insisted. "You'd rather keep us here waiting, biting our nails off and grinding our teeth down, just in case we happen to die again?"

"Yes," Death said. "And I expect you to be as quiet as lice about it."

"Not mice?" Mark asked, squeezing his way in.

"Mice are not quiet," Death said. "They squeak and scurry in the walls. Lice are so silent you can't even hear them. And they're just as *bothersome* as you."

"You don't even have hair," Emma said. "A bald man bemoaning problems with lice sounds very much like Death talking about the value of life to a suicidal woman."

Death coughed out a dry chuckle. "Woman is a bit of a misnomer for you, *girl*."

"Or is it, perhaps," Emma began, "that you feel intimidated by War? To see a strong woman take power with the same level of grandeur as you? You think a woman can't be Death as well?"

"The fact that you saw War as a woman is very telling of you,"

Death said. "All I see is a mountain of corpses, and in Pestilence a mountain of bugs, and in Famine a mountain of sand. These eyes" – he poked a finger into one hollow eyehole – "see a world which you cannot, an absolutely *objective* world of ideas, not things. That is what you are lacking. Death cannot be painted in the shades of the many colours of your morality and ethics. It is utterly black. And never shines, even under the sun!"

Death, in his rant, took too many breaths and summoned up a coughing fit. A bad one. A retching, heaving kind of cough, where the air fought against his non-existent throat. Veronique immediately got up to tend to him and pat his shoulder blades, since they were the most solid part of his back. His jaw fell off, and still he coughed with long wheezes.

Emma and Mark held back for a moment. Their mood shifted. They were willing to fight for their lives, but not at the expense of another being, unliving or not.

"Sir," Mark started, after he'd scooped Death's lower mandible from the floor, "with all due respect – I think you need us. However temporarily we might stay. At the very least, we won't be as much of a burden if we're picking up your slack."

"Slack," Death muttered. He grabbed the bone from Mark, snapped his jaw back in place, and controlled his breathing once more. "You think Death can slack off? The very notion defeats my purpose. I do not slack."

"Maybe that's why you're in this state," Emma said. "An eternity of duty would wear on anyone, even you. Especially now with the world as complex as it is. People dying – like me – without a war, famine, or plague sending them over the edge. Or dying in accidents while trying to preserve the life of another." She turned to Mark with a thankful grin.

"Sentimentality is unbecoming of Death," Death said. "Would you take the soul of a child whose time had come?"

"Yes," Emma said confidently.

"A good man who was slain in cold blood?"

"...Yes," Mark affirmed.

"A... family of six who careened off a cliff?"

"Yes."

"A... a mother killed by her own son?"

"Yes," they both agreed.

"A son killed by his mother?"

"Yes." Emma clenched her fist with a passion.

Death looked at Veronique, who tried to give him a reassuring look. "Would you take her soul?"

"What?!" Veronique exclaimed. She released him to fall back into his chair.

"Would we have to?" Mark asked. "I thought you and her had a deal."

"If her time has truly come," Emma said, "and she has accepted it..." She looked at Veronique, and the housekeeper gave her an approving look.

"Hmm..." Death coughed again. "What about each other? Would you, if you could, end one another's life in that fated moment where you were meant to perish together?"

Mark held Emma's hand. They both nodded and answered together, "Yes."

"Wow, that's some cold-ass shit right there," Death said. "I thought humans were supposed to be empathetic and— and piteous. You're ready to smoke just about anyone."

"Well," Mark spoke up, "in the present circumstances..."

"I guess it makes sense," Death said. "You did try to kill your-self. You can't be quite right in the head."

Emma opened her mouth to protest but shut herself up and accepted his slight.

"Why you're so eager to help though, I'm still to deduce," Death pondered.

Mark and Veronique exchanged glances.

"Very well." Death leaned forward and rose to his feet. "I shall assess you for this duty. But know that it shall be hard. Harder even than what I have relayed to you now. To become Death, you must be ready to cast aside your very humanity and paint your whole world black."

They both nodded. Veronique clapped her hands together with a cheerful smile. She was glad to see everyone working together – Mark and Emma with a growing terror as the weight of their reality sank into their shoulders, and Death with the confident, smouldering glare of a billion lives lost in his very presence.

It had been a productive morning.

CHAPTER NINE

A gold stater flipped in the void, a diminutive mark from an ancient era that was pressed and minted before most coins were counted. On one side was the bust of Alexander the Conqueror, king of the whole middle world in his lifetime, taken early by a bout of pestilence most unexpected. In his wake, he'd left an empire splintered into wars, and unchecked famines across the desert plains came with his absence of control. And through it all, as the young king conquered, he left Death behind him in great mounds of corpses. Given this insatiable thirst for bloodshed and domination, he was still regarded by all four horsemen as a bit of a lad. In fact, many centuries later, Pestilence admitted to having something of a man crush on Alexander but strongly denied it the next day, blaming his regrettable actions and words from the night before on some particularly potent Jin Dynasty rice wine.

Charon rolled the coin over his fingers. He only ever moved with so much grace and conviction when money was in his hand. His hunch shrank, and his posture rose when he played with his gold. His crooked grin went rigid as he flipped the coin in the air. It landed, and he stared Alexander back in the eyes – a man he'd met and ferried long ago. One who had the good conscience to die and whose death was preceded by the imitators meant to take his place. All of them were Alexander – even in their souls, they believed it to be true. But all of them died, and all their souls met the ferryman; their grand scheming could not trick the eyes of Death.

Charon sighed. All around him was water, and his brevity on land was only ever greeted by dissent or passive entertainment at his expense. He was the accessory to the horsemen, despite being as instrumental to existence as they were.

"It's not fair," he declared. He clutched the coin hard and sat back in his boat. The wood creaked and racked against the placid surface of the slow-moving river. The oily water rippled with colour, then the circles of light retracted and balanced back to a pure, lifeless white. "They never heard of a hippo before? 'Oh, but it's not a boat, Charon,'" he said, mockingly in the tune of any one of his dissenters. "'You can't ferry souls on the back of a beast, Charon.' Never mind elephants and horses with long backs or camels... All things man has ridden over water. And none for me... Whales, even. A whale might live nicely here."

He turned and looked at the water. It was his only mainstay. Its ripples were like a voice in his ear, which both comforted and mocked him. He looked at his coin, one that he'd plucked off his finery under his dingy, fog-soaked outer robe. "Not worth it anymore..."

With no souls waiting to be ferried, Charon would let a coin toss decide which shore he would moor on. The south shore was the shore of the unliving, the place where souls met the boat to cross to the other side. It was Limbo, purgatory, all manner of void without purpose, a desert of the unreal. The north shore was the side of long waiting, where the souls that crossed over would linger to see who else might come to cross before making their final journey into the world long after death.

Great leaders seeking companions, apprentices, and followers to remember the feeling of being alive. Lovers torn apart by ages who sought reunion with their loved ones. Parents seeking children or their own parents from the fog. Great teachers of the past who sought knowledge of their future. Wise men whose words once twisted Charon's oar to row them across without payment. And the debt-stricken souls, with sly mouths, who promised a payment they never could procure nor render. There were more of them than Charon cared to acknowledge.

Heads for north, Tails for south. He flipped the coin with extra, angry vigour, and it careened to the side, into the murky depths.

"Damn," he muttered.

———

The home of War was a home many times updated into what could only be described as a sprawling complex. First built like a longhouse of Viking tradition, the original building had since become an artistic foyer for the rest of the rooms. Lodgings of war from all eras came together to forge a monstrous campus, dedicated to the learning and remembrance of wars in the past. Cultural artefacts from every age adorned her walls, all of them lethal or, at least, were lethal once.

She had broadswords, chipped and broken, hung on display mountings. Beside them, spears and swords of warriors long past, each with a history of whom the weapons killed and when. The remains of the legendary blade Durandal, mere chipped fragments of rusted iron, were in a commemorative case on top of a bookshelf. Next to them was the bullet casing of the headshot that killed JFK.

War sat deep within her complex, in a Colonial-style extension modelled in honour of the genocidal takeover of the New World – one of her fondest time periods. War sat in a casual rose-red pantsuit in an office chair and beheld a wall of screens. Television, other news media, and then live streaming were the battleground avenues of modern war. She had a stock ticker to track the relevant corporations tied to arms trades and private military enforcement. Behind her were pictures of various world leaders, some alive or recently dead, whose war efforts continued – even past their own rule – keeping War very much in business.

One screen captured her attention. She grabbed one of about twenty remote controls and upped the volume to the loudest it could be. A news report in English – the language she adored the most – described a most unusual occurrence.

"The withdrawal is going to schedule, as international and domestic military bases clear their troops out. Authorities have informed the Russian Federation that Ukrainian forces will be dispatched to handle domestic issues within their own cities. The Russian Federation has confirmed that this withdrawal is under a joint operation with the Ukrainian government."

"What?" War muttered.

Another screen came up: two men shaking hands in suits inside of a building in Panmunjom, a simple structure that sat astride the border between North and South Korea.

"Ambassadors met for the first time in years to negotiate the establishment of the first connecting highway between the two countries. Though plans are still in the early stages of develop-ment, North Korea put forward this bid as a means of beginning talks of peace through mutual trade."

"Bugger off," War snapped.

One last time, another screen demanded all her attention. A conference between two men – one in an Arab headdress and one in a suit with a Star of David pin prominently displayed on his jacket lapel.

"The Israeli minister has concluded the first of what he hopes to be many discussions with the Palestinian representative over this ceasefire. It's too early to call, but it seems that peace may be within reach in the Gaza region for the first time. The US President had this to say on these talks…"

The screen cut away, and War hunched over with a groan. She clutched at her side and stood up on a limping leg. She rolled the leg of her pantsuit up and patted at the skin of her left shin.

There was a spot of blood on her hand when she pulled it away. She looked down and saw an old wound, one long forgotten about, that had been newly pried open. Her body was all scars under her armour, but all healed and hardened. No wounds should have been left to reopen. Not after such a long, long time…

Following their conversation-cum-job-application, Veronique had filled the large brass tub with steaming hot water and ushered Emma away for a chance to relax and rejuvenate, telling the men in the house, in no uncertain terms, that they were to steer very clear of the bathroom for a while.

Mark waited in the dining room for his turn, devouring the breakfast Veronique had laid on for him. As much as he yearned to be back in his flat, alive, and away from this place, he was already very fond of Death's housekeeper, especially her baking. As Emma entered, he picked the last of the croissant crumbs from his plate with a licked finger.

"What on earth are you wearing?" Mark laughed.

Emma self-consciously rubbed her hands down the fabric of her borrowed attire: a navy-blue smock and baggy brown trousers.

"Veronique took my clothes to wash when I was in the bath. These were left at the door."

"They bring out your eyes."

"Laugh it up, tiger," Emma smirked, "there's a change of clothes for you, too."

Death coughed. He did so freely and almost arrogantly, in Mark's direction.

Emma grinned at Mark, thinking she had got the better end of the deal compared to the enormous tartan trousers and yellow diamond-patterned jumper he'd been gifted. The group had adjourned to the sitting room, which Veronique arranged to better support their interview. She put the fire on, which somehow made the room colder. It stole all the heat for itself and left Mark and Emma in a shivering state while Death sat comfy in his thick robes with a paper in his hand.

"Can you ride a horse?" he asked.

"I rode a horse when I was a little girl," Emma said. "Not for very long, but I still remember the basics."

Death turned to Mark.

"Willing to learn," he said, flashing a thumb up.

Death grunted, bemused. "Can you read an hourglass?"

"Y-yes?" Mark answered. "You just... look at it, right?"

"You'd think so," Death muttered. "Can you reap?"

"Is that a metaphor?" Emma asked. "Or a business term?"

"With a scythe."

"I can," Mark affirmed. "I did, once. When I was a lad, we

stayed in a cottage near Abersoch for the summer. A neighbour had me cut his lawn, but he liked things quiet, so he taught me to use a sickle on the grass."

"I cut my own hair once," Emma said. "And never played with sharp objects again. But, if it's a matter of practice..."

"Can you judge a man's life," Death asked, "well-lived or no, with but a glance in his eyes? And hear the story of all his sins from naught but the final sigh that passes his lips?"

The two paused to consider their answers, and how to best say no.

"I saw a YouTube video once of a famous criminal interview," Mark said, "and how they could tell he was lying by like... how he blinked and looked up to the ceiling when he was bending the truth. So, I reckon I could learn the rest of that."

"No, you can't," Death said. "Not unless you pry out your own eyes and view the world through the objective lens of absolution."

"Is that an elective surgery?" Mark asked.

Death put his paper down on the stand nearby. "This is hopeless, pointless, and even in jest, it is not at all entertaining. *But* it is novel and unique. You already defy the status quo to an unsettling degree. Therefore, I am willing to see you try. But do understand, this is a great inconvenience to me. Especially as I'm the only horseman so overworked that he needs to take on apprentices. If you succeed, you will succeed in my name exclusively. Your success will be my success, and your failures will be *your* failures. Is that understood?"

Emma sighed. "Yes, I'm familiar with that kind of work."

And she was. Emma made others look good at the office. Creating a presentation at the drop of a hat for the sales team because 'you're so much better than me with PowerPoint.' The late-night email to suppliers to ensure everything was on track for the event tomorrow that she wasn't even invited to attend. She bought the milk out of her own pocket so the leadership team could offer guests a coffee. No word of thanks, no acknowledgement.

"But there's no short way out," Death said. "Until your final grain of sand falls from your glass, you will be indentured to my service. And then, it's across the river with both of you."

Mark winked at Veronique, his fellow conspirator, but she didn't return his smile this time. Something in Death's tone told her, categorically, that the chances of Mark returning to Earth in any capacity other than to harvest the souls of the dead were slim to none. But Mark didn't notice. He was all in.

"What about the toll?" Emma asked.

Death stomped on the ground. "My foot in Charon's mouth will be the toll if he defies me." Then he went weak in the throat and coughed again. He tapped his hand against his chest to clear his breathing. "But first, you will need training..."

CHAPTER TEN

The realm of the dead, the land between lives, the waiting room of eternity was vast and uncoordinated. But like any vast land in which no order exists and opportunity is scarce, humankind found a way to achieve order, even in death. Those who failed to take a ferry across the river either did so with some great intention in mind – pious or not – or lingered out of some fated connection with the undead. The lost souls of purgatory refused to stay lost and thus collected into communities, which then built up over time, out of the void and into the wilds.

Veronique attached a cart to the back of the pale horse and hopped in with Mark and Emma as Death rode astride his horse, pulling them into the great land of Limbo to act as their guide. She was only 104 years young as a spectre wandering eternity, but she had come to know those who took to their aimless punishment of the doldrums and their many proclivities.

The first group the two apprentices-in-training had to visit were unexpectedly welcoming. A group of Shaolin monks awaited them at a temple built up, brick by brick, over millennia from the mud of the ground and the heat of their own ever-burning disciples as forge fires. Their devout determination persisted even in death and even in the face of conflict with their own beliefs.

Death dropped the others off and waited for them to leave the carriage. Veronique unhitched it and let him loose.

"I will return," he said. "I still have my duties to fulfil. I cannot lecture you forever."

"I feel like a kid again," Mark said. "Getting dropped off at school. Do you think he'll help with our homework after he finishes work?"

The pale horse whinnied and interrupted them with its death shriek.

"Your education here will be in scythemanship," Death shouted down to them. "Though all lives are equal in death, accomplishments in life still hold to the soul in this form. And these stubborn ones refuse to accept that they're dead."

A monk approached with great respect in his posture. He was older, perhaps mid-sixties, and exceptionally well built. "We are awaiting our path to enlightenment to be opened and will wait an eternity for our opportunity to be reborn."

"I already told you that's not how it works!" Death exclaimed, before cracking the reins and flying into the sky as the monk bowed to him. Veronique held her position near the carriage while the monk took in Mark and Emma.

They walked the grounds with their guide and beheld the structures man was capable of in the otherwise featureless plains of uncreation. Everything was made of baked earth. Great bells were polished and pressed together with such force that the hardy clay came to mimic the metal it should have been. Their food, also made of mud, was made with such distinct care and detail that each dish moved and smelled like it was real.

"How does all this work, exactly?" Emma asked.

"Shaolin," the monk explained, "is a way of discipline, to hone one's body as a temple unto the Buddha, and accept enlightenment not in this lifetime, but in a thousand—"

"I mean about the clay and stuff," Mark corrected him. "Sorry to interrupt."

"It is alright," the monk said. "There is always an opportunity for me to finish. As to how things are made here, simple human desire has shaped our creations."

"Aren't you lot all about ridding yourselves of desire?" Mark asked.

The monk turned and faced him with a smile, then flicked Mark's forehead. "Don't get snippy."

"Aren't you lot all about peace and tranquillity?" Emma asked.

He turned to face her. She held her hand over her forehead to protect herself, but he flicked her nose instead. The two were left reeling in surprised pain.

"Yes," the monk answered, "but we're not about being made asses of by others. That is why, in life, we train our bodies. The way of Shaolin was a way of warriors, not dulled by the teachings of enlightenment but honed. The sects separated sometime after I died into the one you know – of peaceful segregation and deep meditation – and the warrior class who defended the Buddha at each crossing of history's conflict. Those who would kill were not seen as lesser in the Buddha's eyes, for there was too a saint of Buddhism who gained the presence of divinity during war. They followed him into battle, while the rest claimed defence over their home and never ventured out."

"I see," Mark said. "You've got fighty monks and peaceful monks."

"And monks on fire," Emma pointed out.

"They are the truly committed," the monk explained. "Those who repel their new reality and await transcendence in the flames.

They burn forever, never changing, always in pain, yet it does not bother them. They can die a million times, but on the million and first, if they ascend, then all was worth it."

"Not everyone can do that," Mark said. "Obviously."

"It is not easy," he said. "Not in life, nor in death, to endure the pains of an unchanging world. But we persevere. Others are not as patient. We have maintained our own status quo in death, unchanging, unified by the pilgrims who venture into the void to find more believing souls that seek the Buddha's grace in this unheralded land. Through faith, we are unified. We are strong."

"And those without faith?" Mark said. "Or of different faiths – how do you all cooperate?"

"We don't," he said. He kicked up a staff and caught it with a twirl. "That is why we train."

"A-ha." Mark nodded. "Do you have the cool one with a sharp blade on the end and the little tassels?"

"Your presence has been described to me as quite unique," the monk explained. "You are still living, yes?"

"Yes," Mark said, without a convincing amount of confidence.

The monk thrust the pole into Mark's chest and knocked him back, along with all the air from his body. Emma immediately advanced to defend herself, believing that the trial had already begun and that her new instructor was testing her fighting prowess to see which of them would be fastest to teach. He hit her on the head, then swept out her legs. She landed hard on the ground. Despite the pain in her hip, she was quickly back on her feet. She reasoned that the faster she could master the art of Death, the faster she could earn the right to pass over to the other side.

"And you?" The monk beckoned for Mark to advance.

He was a little slower to get back to his feet, still feeling winded. He was, however, just as determined to master the art of Death as Emma – in a bid to curry favour. He was naturally a people pleaser, so it wasn't a huge shift, and he'd always been a big fan of martial arts movies, even if he lacked the skills and coordination to ever be a practitioner. This, he thought, would be tough, but it would be fun.

Mark advanced again, this time with his staff raised like a jousting pole.

Whack, whack.

And he landed on the ground with a thud.

"Ow."

"If this had a blade on one end," the monk announced, "would you have survived that?"

"I barely survived it without!" Mark groaned.

The monk tapped the blunt end of the staff to the ground. "We have not forgotten the fragility of being human. We will train you, as such, until you have unwavering confidence with a staff in your hands. The blade upon it shall be so ingrained into your hearts that you will not hesitate to swing it when the true article is in your grasp."

"I cut grass as a lad with a sickle once," Mark said. "Can I skip this bit?"

He got tapped on the head again. Hard.

"Stand," the monk commanded. "And we shall begin."

The fact that their introductory beat-down wasn't the beginning gave them both pause.

Veronique watched from the cart with a few chunks of Terry's Chocolate Orange pressed in her bony hands as the two apprentices got beaten back and forth by a crowd of monks for a full day and a half before moving onto more formal training. By the end of it, she either expected the last of their sand to fall or for them to become true masters of the bladed staff...

And she'd brought plenty of tea and snacks to watch it all.

CHAPTER ELEVEN

Time passed in the realm beyond life... ish. The concept of time passing was difficult to gauge. Most of the purgatorial residents had no sun or moon, day or night, and ebb or flow of events. Even the monks, who were hard at work training Mark and Emma, could only guess at the passage of time – though one of them routinely meditated by striking a bell with his fist every second.

So, a hundreds of thousands of seconds later, Mark and Emma's training was marked as "good enough" to be complete. Therefore, they were each given a scythe and were set to square off against their training master. Mark's scythe was more of a very long crook, with a metal hook at the end, which was bladed on the inside. Emma's scythe was a bit shorter, a little less than her height, and the blade was narrower but it had a solid grip at the butt.

"Do not fret over injury," the monk said. "There is nothing you can do to stop me."

"That's encouraging," Mark said. "Even if we chop you into bits, you'll somehow keep on going?"

In answer, the monk spun a bladed staff of his own in a darting movement, cutting through his own neck. His head slumped off, and he caught it with his still-moving hand.

"We probably can't do that," Emma said. She looked at Mark. He shrugged. Maybe they could, but it wasn't worth the risk for a party trick. The monk reattached his head.

"We are already dead," he said. "We have accepted this. Though this is not our ideal place to rest for eternity, it is still a restful one. The only death that accepts us now lies beyond the uncrossable river."

"Can't you just go all *Enter the Dragon* on Charon, nick his ferry, and steer it across the river yourself?" Mark asked. "Hypothetically? As far as I can tell, he's not a terribly bad man, but... surely, someone must have thought of it?"

"It has been sternly warned against," the monk explained. "One who cannot pay to cross the river will be dumped into it. And there is no way out, no path to walk across – only an endless drop of sheer agony, into a forgotten void that lies beneath the still water."

"And I suppose swimmers have all tried and never come up?" Emma asked.

The monk came at them. The time for talking was over. They had some proving to do. He swiped at Mark, who blocked his blade and rocked himself back defensively. Mark countered; he tried to catch the monk's staff with the blade of his scythe – a quick manoeuvre but a miss.

Then Emma. The monk swung at her. She rolled backwards and flailed her scythe out far. The monk leaped over it. She swung again, stopped halfway, and yanked it back towards her. The monk backflipped to avoid the snaring swipe at his ankles.

"Good," the monk said. "Reach, and yank. This is the motion of the scythe. To close the distance that death creates in all mortals, you must pull them in by force. This is the philosophy of the scythe, and by internalising it, you shall achieve greater heights of skill."

"Do we get a belt or something? Always wanted to say I was a black belt."

"A belt is for keeping your trousers up," replied the monk.

"So that's a no then." Mark's face dropped. He looked crestfallen.

The old monk took pity on his new protégé. "If it means so much to you." The monk untied a length of material from his waist and handed it to Mark. "Here."

Mark beamed as he accepted the gift, wise enough not to snigger as the monk's baggy pants fell around his ankles. He clutched the belt in his hands, his most treasured recent possession.

The two of them bowed ceremoniously to the monk. Their training was complete. Not that they were masters, but they were competent enough. Out of its own body, no mortal soul would have the good conscience to resist them. Nor would they be armed, presumably. Really, their intensive training seemed like overkill.

Regardless, they left the monks' sprawling complex and returned to Veronique.

"How did it go?" she asked.

Mark tapped his scythe on the ground. "We have achieved a warrior god's level of enlightenment and ancient fighting skills."

"We've achieved an understanding of which end of the very sharp, pointy things to hold, and which to swing at someone," Emma clarified.

"Oh, splendid," Veronique said. "Monsieur should be back soon. You could, perhaps, cross blades like noble fighters, to prove your first step has been taken, no?"

"That might be a bit cheeky," Mark politely insisted. "I mean, he's very well conditioned, seasoned even, at this. It'd come off as a bit *rude* to say, 'oh, alright then granddad, let's see what you've still got.' 'I just learned to tie my shoelaces all by myself; let's have a race,' right? That's— that's presumptuous of us to do that, right?"

Emma, who sensed that Mark was desperate to get out of such a challenge, felt slightly more confident. "Does he actually use his scythe, do you know?"

"He always has one with him," she said. "And he changes them as the seasons come and pass. I'm sure some of them just needed to be resharpened. But no, he won't. Replaces the whole thing. Le infant discarded with the bath water. The other horsemen have their tools of the trade, and they always seem proud to show them off. Perhaps it is more for the aesthetic than for combat. But I went with him willingly when I died. And I was quite glad of it. So, perhaps I have simply not seen what use he has for his scythe in his day-to-day activities, other than keeping the garden trim."

"Rebellious souls," Mark said. "Ones who won't go easily. That sort?"

"Hooligans," Emma added.

Then, a sudden, thunderous sound came from above. The hooves of an ancient dread filled the air like foreign heartbeats invading the chests of the living and those less fortunate. A mortal pulse sowed a hideous sensation through the air and into the ground, fostering the growth of some shadowy filaments on the surface as if the earth itself quaked in fear. Death came on his pale horse, a flowing shadow of a robe trailing behind him, with a glinting scythe held over his shoulder.

He dismounted, and all was still. The hoof-falls of his pale horse silenced the trembles of the ground. He hadn't seen the two tag-alongs in a decent amount of time, and it seemed to sit well with him. His posture had returned, though his health still seemed lacking. Even for a skeleton, he seemed pale and thin.

"You're not dead," Death declared.

"Our training was a success," Emma said proudly.

Death groaned. "That's... not *great* news."

"Can we even die down here?" Mark asked.

Death unshouldered his scythe, resting on it like a crutch. "That's a fascinating question I hoped would be answered in my absence. But it appears not, at least not in the weeks you've been here."

"Weeks?" Emma asked.

"Yes, from an earthly perspective," Death clarified. "Time is but a fleeting shadow and reminder of mortality that those herein no longer require. Millennia, decades, mere moments all intermingle and intersect. The last moment of one eternity could coincide with the start of another. But time marches on regardless – its measurements are all convenient falsehoods, but its results are all the same." He patted his hand on his chest. "Time is a great ally of mine. Though unruly, it always brings men closer to me."

"So, we're being properly missed then," Mark said. "At least by our landlord."

Death squinted, suddenly curious. "What are those you're holding?"

"The monks gave them to us," Mark said. "We practiced with all manner of scythes, but these feel the most right for us."

"No offence to yours, of course," Emma said. "It's just too... impractical?"

"It's great for threshing," Mark said, "but a bit unwieldy for shepherding humans."

"Hmm," Death looked at his scythe and then to the nearest monastery pillar. Veronique was busy hitching his horse up to the carriage so they could all fly back home. "It's not an easy thing to do, but impractical is not an apt word."

"I suppose," Mark began, "the more we talk about the practicality of weaponry and its usage, the closer we'd get to War's expertise."

"Though we're new and accept that everyone must start somewhere," Emma said, "would you mind showing us what skills you have with your scythe?"

"Emma!" Mark exclaimed in a hushed voice. "You're not asking our *host* to prove himself, are you?

"I just want to see," she insisted. "For comparison, how we might—"

Death swung his scythe. Not in any practical way. It was a ceremonious swing, flat and swift, out and to the side. The great pillar marking the monk's border was chopped like a reed split by an axe. Then a great wind followed and pushed the clay structure down, where it returned to a slump of formless grey mud in the featureless void.

"After thousands of years," Death said, "you figure it out. For you, just swing the sharp part at anyone who causes you trouble. That alone is sufficient."

Death walked to his horse, using his scythe like a cane, and mounted it once more. Mark and Emma looked back apologetically at the monks who gathered around their lost structure, either to rebuild it or kick the remains around. The two of them couldn't stick around to help, it seemed. They had something more important to do...

CHAPTER TWELVE

The group returned to Death's homely cottage. Mark couldn't help but notice the condition of the front garden outside the home, the once overgrown and weedy field of brush, brambles, and all kinds of fallow wheaty things. It had all been cut very short, and no traces of it remained. It was like Death had spent a great deal of time and labour mowing his lawn. Though it probably only took a few swipes, one per direction all the way to the front door.

The house, however, was slightly less orderly. Veronique's absence showed. Tables and chairs were unadjusted, a collection of dirty pots lay piled up in the sink. Used cups were strewn about. The curtains were unevenly drawn. A scythe had fallen blade-first into the floor and had just been left there, embedded into the decorative parquet, too deep to pull out.

"You two," Death called to them. He snapped his fingers. At his behest, his robes transformed, first into a blocking mist of inky darkness, then into a beautifully tailored single-breasted suit, which fit his phantom proportions like a second skin – but in

Death's case was actually the first skin. "Your next lesson in Death's duty lies at the end of your life."

Mark and Emma looked at each other with some concern. They left their new scythes at the door, next to the unused coat-rack and collection of umbrellas, while Veronique cursed in French as she moved into the sitting room to undo the damage of the few weeks of bachelor-pad living Death had left in his wake.

Death led them through his den and the hidden library-shelf door into the Hall of Time, which was lined with hourglasses on all sides in every available space for what Mark and Emma could only guess to be miles and miles. He eased himself into his favourite battered old chair and indicated they should take a seat too. Two hourglasses lay on their sides on the gilt-edged coffee table. Mark and Emma recognised them as belonging to their own lifespans, the symbolic and mystical (but very real) lifelines that held them off from a true death for now.

On a stand opposite them was another hourglass and a shallow dish filled with twice-bleached basmati rice. Death twisted open the top bulb of the hourglass and pinched a few grains of rice onto the top of the sand, which trickled down one tiny grain at a time. He fastened the lid back on and held it up to them.

"Tell me what you see," he said.

"Sound advice being followed," Emma said smugly.

Death groaned at her.

"Uh, an hourglass?" she said this time.

He groaned again, bordering on an impatient growl.

"Life?" Mark asked.

Death sighed. "This is, indeed, that which measures life. The time one has left to live filters down as grains of sand. Each grain is a moment, some significance, and the flow is different for them all. Some flow quickly with much greatness; some are merely half-full, or even less when they come into existence. Each a tragedy of a different length, but each inevitable. If you took all the sand that lies in every desert of your world, that much sand would only account for one day under Death's duty."

"That's a lot of sand," Mark said.

"That's a lot of duty..." Emma said. "I mean, how many people die every day? Of anything? It's got to be a couple of thousand at least?"

"The sand lost," Death said, "is not only lost in death. There are myriad ways to make the sand flow quicker... and some mysterious ways that may make it *stop*." He threw a glare at their stuck glasses. The top bulbs were empty, save for the scabs of sand hardened to the sides. Each had a handful of rice piled into it, which made them look doubly full.

"You must learn how to measure and correct each hourglass," Death said, "and what timing is needed to precisely gather the associated soul as the final moments flow down. And you must do this about one thousand seven hundred times per day and venture out that many times to reap the souls and bring them to the river. For that is on average how many die, each day, across the territory you now call the United Kingdom."

"How many houses does Santa visit each year?" Mark asked. "If he had to do that every day, he'd be worn to a skeleton too."

"Are these all ready for collection soon?" Emma asked as she motioned around the room. "Or are these... here for another good reason?"

Death picked up an empty hourglass from a shelf, one with no name, no decor, something pure and simple. He opened the top and rubbed the tips of his finger bones together. Sand was produced and filled the hourglass's top bulb. He continued rubbing until no more came out, then he fastened the top back on. With the assembly of the hourglass complete, he held it up and wiped a distal phalanx along the brass panel. As they looked on, letters appeared, etched into the plaque at the base of the hour-glass – Noah Archibald Simmonds.

"This is a life," he said, "taking form. Its end has been deter-mined. Though fate is not certain, this life within it can never be replaced, and once it starts flowing" – he shook the hourglass and the sand shifted to start a slow trickle through the pinched neck – "it persists until the end."

"So that's Noah actually being born?" Emma asked.

"Hmm, yes," Death said. "All death starts at life."

"I thought there'd be someone else doing that," Mark said.

"If any other had the responsibility to manage and maintain life," Death replied, "why would they then deliver this life to Death? If there were such a horseman as Life, then doling out life would be their job, yes?"

"Like a stork," Mark said.

"Or a cabbage patch farmer," Emma offered.

"And letting that life they'd made fall into death would be a failure, wouldn't it?" Death continued.

"I mean," Emma began, "in an economic sense, providing life for you to reap would be mutually beneficial if you could provide something to Life too. Like, stability? Keep the population from getting too high?"

"That milestone was passed years ago," Death said. "Your blasted Industrial Revolution has made it impossible to manage your troublesome growth rates. And so few countries have the audacity to slip back into the negatives."

"You're welcome?" Mark said.

"Life is a matter of death," Death declared. "Its importance cannot be trusted to any other. And if you become Death, or at least operating as my proxy, it will be a matter for you not to mismanage."

Death reached down for the lever on his chair to turn it into a recliner. He pulled it, and the room started to drop. Mark and Emma fell as the walls rose around them. The floor zoomed downwards. And on all sides of them were the shelves and the hourglasses, an infinite amount, reaching down into a depth they could not measure. They lost sight of the ceiling and then continued descending for minutes.

Then, finally, they stopped. The fireplace, the one part of the room that wasn't a shelf covered in hourglasses, was extinguished and filled with sand that spilled out as if it were rain coming in through the chimney.

"There is a finesse to this," Death said. "One you will have to learn. To find the proper amount to fill each hourglass." He got up from his chair, which immediately sprung the reclining bottom out. He grunted and pushed it back in, then proceeded to pick up two simple, empty hourglasses. He handed them over.

"Feel their weight," he instructed. "Their lightness. Life without death has no meaning, no purpose. No measure. But life lived for too long becomes a heavy burden. There is a rightness you must discover. A 'just enough' touch to fill it to. Then, that life can begin and begin to end."

Mark and Emma held the hourglasses, weighing them in their hands. They did feel light, much lighter than expected. The glass was cheap acrylic and the wood was nothing more than a laminate. He brought over their own hourglasses as well. He handed Emma's to Mark and vice versa.

"Feel these," he said.

The two took their own lives into their hands and compared the weight, like scales.

"Wow," Mark said. He turned to Emma. "It's... surprisingly heavy."

"Is it?" she asked.

It wasn't the first time he'd grabbed her life in his own hands.

Remembering what had happened last time, he gripped it a bit tighter and focused on the empty one instead. He compared the weights of a life lived, well or otherwise, and one yet to start.

"Fill them," Death said, "until they feel settled as yours do. It will take a different amount of sand each time. Some may fall faster than others."

With that, Death pulled his hood up over his head and vanished.

Mark and Emma made their way over to the fireplace and started filling the hourglasses up as they were shown. They experimented with the weight until it felt just right. One was a little shallower than their own – a life destined to end even before theirs did. The other was much denser, although the sand flowed faster, a life filled with events already taking place.

"Happy birthday to both of you," Mark said.

"Sorry we killed you," Emma added. "By... letting you be born."

Mark made a sour expression. "Yeah, that's what we should say to our firstborn, isn't it? Just apologise straight out of your womb."

"Our firstborn?" she asked incredulously.

"I just mean—"

"Let's just gloss over the fact that we're flat-mates, not in a relationship beyond sharing bills, and we're dead. Well, dead-ish. Knowing what you know now, you'd still want to bring a child into the world?" She held up her hourglass to reinforce her point.

"Nothing beyond sharing bills?" Mark spat. "It's fine if you don't see me the way I see you. I get it. I really do. But our relationship, to you, is really that simple? That transactional?"

"I'm sorry. That came out all wrong." Emma softened, reaching over and placing a hand on Mark's arm. "I didn't mean that. You were... you *are* the best friend I ever had."

"Good save."

"Thanks."

"And you still owe me twenty quid for last month's electricity."

Emma laughed. "As soon as we get to a cashpoint."

Mark picked up the nearest empty hourglasses and passed one to Emma. They worked in silence, learning to appreciate the value of life, no more than a handful of sand at a time.

CHAPTER THIRTEEN

Over another long, ill-defined period of time, they became fairly adept at sifting sand. Emma tended to add fistfuls at a time and then pour any excess back out. Mark, however, was much more cautious, sometimes just adding a pinch at a time, as though he was seasoning meat.

"Loving the TV chef flourish." Emma said, bemused. "Just missing a sprig of parsley."

"Whatever works," Mark responded, not taking his eyes off the sand.

They both weighed their hourglasses in their hands, pleased with the results. Emma's top bulb was almost full to the brim. Mark's wasn't even halfway up.

"Moment of truth?" Emma said.

"Sure."

They exchanged hourglasses, checking the weight.

"Spot on." Mark nodded appreciatively and snapped the top of Emma's hourglass into place. As he did, the etching appeared on the name plate and the sand began to fall in a blink of an eye. "Happy Birthday, Nadia."

He smiled and slid the hourglass across the floor before immediately picking up an empty one, about to start the process all over again.

"It's like *One Born Every Minute*." Emma funnelled the sand from her cupped hand. "On steroids. Without all the screaming and bodily fluids."

After a bit of a slow start, they'd found something of a rhythm and had filled well in excess of two hundred now fully flowing hourglasses that lay around them on the floor. Nadia was placed on top of Harry – Emma's fourth that morning – to begin a second tier.

"It's a bit mad we're basically creating lives," said Emma.

Mark thought about it for a second, then shook his head. "We're not though, are we? The creation bit's happening in beds, on floors, in stationary cupboards all around the world. We're just starting the timer."

Emma laughed. "You're comparing this to throwing a couple of fish fingers in the oven for twelve minutes at two hundred degrees?"

"Two ten, if you want crispy breadcrumbs. But yeah. It's still amazing and a privilege."

It was all about feeling, and that feeling came with a sense of awe and dread over their power. Swinging a scythe around – a dangerous object meant to brutally take a life – was one thing. But feeling the weight and judging the time that remained in a human life was another thing entirely. Their morals felt stretched. They were doing only what was necessary for life to begin, but in the end, all that life would terminate somehow.

They continued to work their way through the empty hourglasses, but there were always more waiting to be filled and infinitely more that were already running. It felt like they had achieved very little in far too much time. When they took a break and stood up from the floor, their legs were locked up, and their backs felt crooked.

"I could see," Mark said, "how this could get compromising after some time."

"It's like working in a mine," Emma said. "Eventually, the whole body gets compacted just to deal with the conditions."

"Do your knuckles hurt?" Mark asked. "From scooping the sand?"

"A little. But my nails have never looked shinier."

Death appeared suddenly in the space, and Emma spilt a handful of sand on the floor.

"Sorry, baby," she whispered and scooped the sand back up into the hourglass.

"Lesson over," Death announced, and stomped his foot.

The walls zoomed down into the floor with the same elevating blur they'd experienced before. Mark and Emma braced their collections of filled hourglasses nearby before they were pinned to the floor by the increasing g-force.

"You've learned the feeling of a proper life," Death said. They reached the top floor. The den-cum-elevator juddered to a stop. The hourglasses teetered, but none fell over. "The rest is mere regulation. You cannot tamper with the sands of an hourglass already present. You can't add more or take any out. The addition of rice for moisture reduction purposes though, seems fine."

"Luckily," Emma said.

"Further," Death continued as he stood, "when one is nearly empty, you must make the judgement on when and how to collect the corresponding soul. Some moments are more obviously lethal than others. In your case, your final moments were meant to come without any consternation. But this predicament has rendered you unable to die. That is an essential measure you must always take: if even one grain of sand remains, a single moment not yet fulfilled, the life cannot be taken. It must be waited out completely until that last moment is gone."

"So if a very boring person," Mark said, "intentionally locks themselves away to prevent any life experiences from coming their way, they might live longer?"

"Eventually," Death said, "all things die. Again, though, the measurement of moments and significance differs greatly. Some men live through wars yet sieve through moments of their own with more lethality than the soldier who sits gripping his gun behind a barricade. Boredom is relative. Those monks are prime examples. Some live into their hundreds because they measure their moments quite differently."

"So, monotony can save time," Emma said, thinking of the endless pile of insurance applications that greeted her every morning at work and how, eventually, it had been a critical factor in her decision to end her life. "If I'd known that, I would have kept my head down at work and just let the days pass me by."

"Isn't every job repetitive in a way, whatever your profession?" Mark wondered aloud. He had been content at work. The job itself, creating online ads for food and drink brands, could be a bit samey. He had made it interesting by coming up with witty puns and plays on words to – in his opinion – improve the copy and the effectiveness of the advertising. More often than not, this ended with Mark receiving a call from an apoplectic brand manager, who would prefer the 'hired help not to fuck with an award-winning copywriter's genius.' And Mark was okay with that. He was a firm believer that it was better to try than stay quiet in the corner. But occasionally, his off-the-wall copy ideas worked. The brand allowed the agency to go off brief and let the data be the judge. And it worked. He'd helped them smash their quarterly target for broccoli florets sold or helped successfully launch a new energy drink and, on both occasions, the agency had reaped the credit and Mark was slipped a £50 M&S voucher. Win–win.

"Boring lives are simple to judge," Death said. "You can time them evenly. Their sand flows slowly. Some lives, born sick or poor, end early and yet are eventful. Their sand flows fast. Pick up one of the hourglasses you filled. You will judge, for yourselves, the life you have condemned."

Mark and Emma each picked one random hourglass from the group which they'd filled and held them up. Mark's was very full, to the top, and trickled slowly. Emma's was about three-quarters filled and flowed a little faster.

"Give them years," Death instructed. "Go with your first assumption."

"Right," Emma said. "This bloke, Jack, is going to live into his nineties and do a whole lot of nothing about it. Nearly a third of life spent living on his pension."

"This one, Maisy," Mark said. "Um... middle-aged? Maybe fifties? Quite exciting."

"A number," Death said. "Whole and complete."

"Ninety-one," Emma assessed.

"Uh," Mark stuttered. "Um, forty-five – no, fifty-five. Fifty-three? Fifties, but fifty-eight? Maybe fifty-seven?"

Death snatched the hourglass from Mark's hand. "How long is long enough? If it were up to you, you would give them every chance to save themselves and avoid their inevitable end. Yet, speaking practically, you are the opposite of their salvation. Even if you could double the sand in this glass, it would still mean they have to meet an end by your hand. This one ends at forty-nine. You were too generous with your assessment. Even if you think it's wrong, you must be cruel and acknowledge only what you see, what you know to be true."

"Was I right?" Emma asked.

"Ninety-two," Death said. "Not bad."

Emma nodded confidently, while Mark sulked a bit. He wasn't upset that he'd gotten his guess wrong, but the way he was wrong and the strict lecture about it struck him a bit raw. He was too hopeful and proud of humanity to be the grim judge he needed to be beyond the border of life, which wasn't a terrible thing. He wasn't so cynical and dour as to have confident faith in his ability to doom others.

But Death was. And Emma was... good at maths, so that made sense.

"When an hourglass is empty," Death instructed, "it is placed among the collection. A life that passes on over the river is stored, never to be recalled. This is to remind me which souls have fully passed and which ones are still waiting."

"And ideally," Mark said, "we want them all to pass. Eventually."

"There is only one boatman," Death said. He walked up to the window which faced the river and its fog. "One who is chained by his own convictions and tradition. Life has changed, culture has changed, yet none of those reflect their true end."

"I'm pretty sure we've fought a lot of wars over whose version of the afterlife is right," Mark said. "It's a hot topic."

Death brought over an hourglass that was still running, with most of its sand on the bottom. "How much time does this person have left?"

Mark squinted at the sand – the way it fell, the shape it took – and then glanced at the name on the plate. "Georgie!? George Banbridge? No shit!"

"What?" Emma asked.

"It's my mate from school," he said. "Primary. He's still kicking, going along! What a small world."

"And how long does he have to keep *kicking*?" Emma asked. "You get to know that before he does. Think of it. You could show up at the next reunion and tell him to his face when he's gonna die."

"I wouldn't do that," Mark said. "George was a good lad. He bought a packet of cigs for all of us after school once. We didn't smoke any of them, just traded them around for fun."

Death groaned impatiently.

Mark reaffirmed himself and took another hard look at the contents. "Uh, thirty-odd years left?"

"Fair," Death said. "So then, in thirty-something years, you will descend to the mortal realm and follow him, to wait for the fateful moment of his death to collect his soul – yes? Just wander around and watch him live until something happens to make him die?"

"Uh..."

"While thousands of others," Death continued, "die around you, out of your sight and without your knowledge, you'll dedicate your only power to this one soul and no others for a time, until thirty-odd years pass?"

"Well, I shouldn't have to do that," Mark said. He turned to Emma, uncertain. "Should I?"

She shrugged.

"Precision," Death said, "is important. It keeps you from wasting your time on someone who *could* reach their final moment and leads you more easily to someone who *will*. Learn how to measure the falling of the sand in years. Then months. Then weeks, days, hours, and minutes – down to the moment when the soul is ripe for reaping."

"Is there one with less sand that we can do as a practice run?" Mark asked,

Death groaned and tossed an hourglass at him. Mark panicked to catch it.

The hourglasses were invulnerable to any harm from the outside. But seeing Mark fumble over his own anxiety was a brief reprieve for the impatient Death.

CHAPTER FOURTEEN

Death was out and about, reaping the eternal souls of humanity to place them without ceremony in the all-consuming void of purgatory. If they thought their day wasn't going as well as planned when Death made an appearance, it was only going to get worse when their souls found themselves mocked for their poor foresight by the unfeeling hand of the boatman, Charon.

At Veronique's request, she, Mark, and Emma went outside to wander the grounds.

She took them to the back meadow, a run-down stable over the hill. "This," she said, "is where monsieur and his comrades keep their backup horses."

"Backups?" Mark asked.

"Yes," Veronique explained. "Any horse in a storm, or so the saying goes. They have their favourites, of course, as would anyone. Horses are good friends and company if they are trained well. And these horses are the kind which can transcend the

95

boundary between life and death, to carry those of this unliving space back to the earthly world."

"Why horses?" Emma asked.

Veronique shrugged. "I suppose they are too old to learn to drive?"

"I think horses have great significance to them in terms of a larger aspect of human culture and history," Mark said. "Else why would War not ride a lion, or Famine not choose to ride some kind of giant locust out of the sky?"

"Do not be silly," Veronique said. "There are no lions here. Horses die and come here too. They're tamed and put to work."

"Horses have souls?" Emma asked.

"All living things do," she said. "But wild animals cannot be herded so easily. Horses can. So they tend to gather up and find their way to this pasture to graze and await a calm, guiding hand."

"But if all animals come here," Mark said, "and if we are to supplement Death's duties, why can't we ride something like a lion?"

"I think," Emma said, "it's more a question of whether you think you can train a lion more easily than you can train an already domesticated horse?"

Mark listened and gathered up her words to make sense of the situation in his head. But he still had more pressing questions as he looked around the vast prairie. "Where are the dogs? Why aren't there any dogs here?"

"They get lost," Veronique said. "And monsieur does not like dogs. He says they always bark at him when he comes for their owners. They rip at his robe when they catch him. He does not bring them if he can help it."

"So, there are ghost dogs on Earth?" Mark said. "Just... everywhere?"

Veronique undid the latch on one of the stable doors and gentle clapped her hands together. A small herd of different kinds of horses trotted out into the field. Some broke into runs and fled from the strangers, while others were placid and timidly ate at the grass.

"Have either of you ridden horses before?" Veronique asked.

"I have," Emma said. "When I was eight. Admittedly, all they did was put me on the saddle and had it walk around on a little path attached to a tether. So as far as riding, yes, but... piloting, no."

"Just no for me," Mark said.

"Mark has a thing with horses," Emma told Veronique. "He doesn't trust them."

"I am not going to justify this again!" he complained. "It's not a trauma, I assure you. It's perfectly reasonable."

"He heard that they can bite a man's head off, and he's been scared of them ever since."

"It wasn't just a rumour, it was a legitimate historical tale. The Greeks had wild horses that learned to bite from fighting with mountain lions, and horses are very strong, so it stands that they'd have strong enough jaws to clamp through muscle. That and they're heavy and they have hooves. If they step on you, you die. And they're so tall. If you fall off one, it's like falling from the top of a parade float. You die. Everything about horses is just a risk of death. Can't even stand near them, or they'll turn and kick you and kill you. They're like emus."

Emma waved her hand at him before turning to Veronique. "So, do you have any lions he can ride instead?"

"No," Veronique said. "But I think I have something that will work."

Emma was given a stallion to break. She had to do all the work of mounting it with a blanket and a saddle herself, to befriend the horse and teach it to love the act of low-scale bondage, which would give her control. Veronique led her on and taught her the ways of bridling. Meanwhile, Mark was given a Shetland pony – a full-grown horse the size of a very large dog. His job was much easier, but he still dreaded actually riding the thing. Not because it was any more dangerous than a full-sized horse, but because he couldn't help but think he looked stupid for trying.

"Okay," Mark sighed eventually. He sat on the back of the Shetland and it grunted at his added weight. They stood still for a moment in the void. "Um... giddy-up?"

Mark's uncertainty didn't help the horse. He tried leaning forward to make it go, tried to shake it with his hips. He tried to not feel like a complete knob, as a full-grown man perched on a child's toy of a horse, but it wasn't working.

"C'mon!" Mark insisted. "We've got to go... reap souls and whatnot. You and me, horse. A blaze in the sky of dark fate and ill-destined ending." He looked out to the field and saw that Emma had finally got her horse laced up and moving. All she had to do was mount it, but the stallion was a free-spirited rebel with a heart of gold and wouldn't be tied down by any human it couldn't trust.

"Look over there," Mark said to his pony, his only friend within earshot. "She's just going for it, isn't she? I sometimes wish I could do that. Not mount a horse – I've done that, it seems. But just... she's even brave enough to take her own life. Not brave, but certain. Certain she can do something, and then she does it. A lifetime of people telling her she couldn't do stuff, and she just got on and did it anyway. She doesn't stand for 'no', not even from a horse."

Emma ran alongside the horse as it galloped and caught the saddle. She lifted herself up with a jump, stuck a foot in the stirrup, swung her leg over and mounted it. It made a short bucking jump as she settled onto the saddle. Veronique rode up alongside her.

"Chest back," she instructed, "hips forward. Ride on your derrière, not your crotch."

"How do I make it slow down?" Emma shouted.

"Pull," Veronique said. She tugged on her own reins, and her horse slowed to a trot. Emma tried to do the same, but her hand slipped, and she turned the horse's head. It naturally moved in the direction it was looking, back towards the stable and into the path of Mark and his immobile, fluffy donkey.

Mark kicked his feet against the pony's sides. "Okay, we're both in danger now. C'mon, get along. Giddy up, rawhide! Move 'em on. Come on! Do you want to be turned to glue? Standing in the way of a train is what makes that happen!"

The pony grunted and whinnied pathetically before finally kicking itself off and trundling forward. It took a few steps, then went into a short hopping gallop, instantly lifting off the ground and into the air. Like it was climbing up an invisible hill.

"NO!" Mark shouted. "You're not supposed to do this!"

"Mark!" Emma shouted as she rode past. She managed to get the reins and heeled her horse to a stop. "How'd you do that?"

"I'd rather be on an emu!" he shouted. "Then this would make sense!"

"Emus can't fly," Emma corrected him.

"They've got feathers!" he shouted. He was getting even higher and wasn't liking it one bit. Veronique reared her stud up into the air and ran ahead of the pony to make it steer back. Emma sat on her horse and let it trot on its own as she watched Mark being corralled in the sky by a jet-black steed. It was like a cloud chasing a child's birthday balloon.

"A lion wouldn't fly either," Emma said. Eventually, Mark

returned to the ground, no less afraid than before. A pony was fine fun, not too high to fall off, but when it flew, it took that advantage away and made it even more dangerous than a standard horse.

The two continued to practice until Veronique took them to their next training area along the banks of the River Styx...

CHAPTER FIFTEEN

Mark and Emma waded into the fog. The clopping of hooves carried them into the depths of the murky mire. Emma, astride her white horse with dark spots over its chest, sat comfortably in control of her stallion. Mark rode beside her on his pony, which seemed to gather up wicks of humidity against the thick weave of its coat.

"What's yours called?" Mark asked.

"Do we name them?" she asked. "I assumed it had a name already."

"I can't decide on mine," he said. "Nothing seems to match the dignity he represents."

"Dignity?"

"Mostly the lack thereof. I toyed with Napoleon, but he wasn't even much shorter than me, at five-seven. The whole short thing was mostly propaganda in the first place, to remain disrespectful even while he ran rampant and conquered every European kingdom of the time."

"He was a spreader of death then," Emma said. "Although, mostly through War."

"Which does bring us back to that question," Mark pointed out. "We're mostly in charge, I think, of either accidental or age-related death, yes? Pestilence would be illnesses, and Famine is sort of not exactly a huge priority in the world right now. In most of the world, I mean. Yes, some parts, but mostly no, and not for long."

"True."

"So, we shouldn't name our horses after some kind of hideous catastrophe or conquering victor of a thousand battles. But naming them after, I don't know, natural causes seem a bit..."

"Well, what about the weather?" Emma asked. "Is there no horseman of floods and fires? Are those part of Pestilence's domain?"

"No, that's probably Death too," Mark said. "Oh, and murder. Not all murder is an act of war."

"But it could be," she said. "If war must be something organised and fronted by leaders, it could get complicated."

"So," Mark said, trying to summarise where they'd got to, "we aren't responsible for sickness deaths..."

"We are," she said. "Death in general."

"But sickness is pestilence."

"Veronique was taken by Death in the war," she said. "So actually—"

"This is all very complicated," Mark complained. "I'm shocked there aren't more horsemen. Or at least, more Deaths."

"I suppose that's the problem. He's been doing it all himself and it's getting a bit much."

As instructed, they reached the water's edge and waited for the ferryman to approach.

"Oh, oh, oh! I know what I'll call him," Mark announced, very pleased with himself. "Stormrider. How cool is that?"

"I like it." Emma nodded. "Okay. You know most of the horses in the Grand National? They tend to have witty pun names. So, how about Princess Die?"

Mark bit his bottom lip, glancing at Emma's mount. "You do realise," he said softly, "that your Princess Die has an enormous knob?"

"It's the pun. Princess Die. D. I. E. As in, to die. Death."

"I get it. It's just not really very fair. You'll confuse the poor lad. Give him a complex."

"He likes it," Emma purred, rubbing her face into the stallion's mane and showering him with kisses. "Don't you, Princess?"

The stallion whinnied in agreement.

Charon rowed into view as a blurry shape among the grey field in the air, then tapped the boat against the shore. The coins sewn into his robes jangled lightly from the impact.

"Bollocks," he muttered.

"Afternoon," Mark said. "We still don't have any gold coins, but we were wondering if you could teach us about, uh..." He turned to Emma.

"*Anatmanship*," she said, pronouncing it carefully. "The study of... anats."

"I think we just call it anatomy up top," Mark pointed out. "Sort of the same thing?"

"No, no," Charon muttered. He pushed his oar against the shore and freed himself from the sand. "This damned, blasted river is lower than it was yesterday. There are no tides about on the river. 'Tis an omen."

"Is that part of our training?" Mark asked. "We have to fill up the river?"

"It doesn't seem to rain down here unless it's at Death's command," Emma said. "And it's not sunny or hot."

"Aye," Charon confirmed. "Then it's an omen. But never you mind that. That'll be a work for some other time, for some greater being. I've been told that you will be the new sires to escort the souls of the living to this damned riverbank?"

"Yes, we are," Mark replied. He tried to puff out his chest to appear more manly, but he was still on the back of a Shetland pony.

Charon scoffed. "Poor Old Bones must have mould growing inside of his skull to agree to that."

"It's not like we have anything better to do," Emma told him. "We're still not *dead*, but we can't progress from here."

"Lucky you." Charon turned to them and looked them over. "What was your cause of *almost* death?"

"Uh, suicide," Emma admitted. She glanced hotly at Mark. "From falling."

"I tried to stop her. But didn't do a great job of it."

"Ah," Charon said. "A good splattering and shattering. Bones, blood, and guts all spilled out in many directions, and not much you'd be left to come here with. Here is a wicked truth you humans haven't learned. The way you are brought to a final rest is the way you end up here. Hence, when a burial ritual is complete, gold coins should be affixed to the eyes, under the tongue, in the pockets or jacket or even clutched firmly in hand. In your final memory, how you exit life is how you enter Death."

"I don't think anyone does that anymore," Mark said. "Except maybe billionaires? The really weird ones who build temples and monuments and such?"

"Oh no," Emma said. "What if they were right all along, and you *can* take it all with you."

"Ugh." Mark grunted with disgust. "I can accept a lot, but that's not what I want to die knowing."

"Yes," Charon said, "your human ignorance is sickening. It is an honour-driven deed to bring the value of life into death – for value is what drives so many men to live, and dying without it is to die without that purpose fulfilled. A man not worth even a single coin to hold in his passing is no man worth letting live."

"What about cash?" Mark asked. "Notes? Paper money?"

Charon sternly swiped his hand. "No. Coin. Gold. Gold alloy is acceptable so long as it's more gold than not. It has value beyond what even you entertain of it in your waking hours."

"What do you spend it on?" Emma asked. "Is there some sort of shopping centre on the other side of the river we can't see? A massive casino? Do dead franchises also find their way down here?"

"Would you want them?" Mark asked. "They died for a reason."

"What about that place we ate at back in uni?" she asked. "The little place on the corner that sold all kinds of pies?"

"Oooh, right," he said. "With the cheeseburger pie."

"I'd die for that right now," Emma said.

"No," Charon grunted. "There is no pie shop on the other shore. And you needn't know what's there until you've the coin to see it."

"If no one dies with coins anymore, how does anyone get across?" Mark asked.

"Not my problem," Charon said. "But if a person does have that foresight to be buried with value on them, the value will become part of their soul. But so too will any scars or damage. So too will their souls reflect the state of their bodies and the mind they had when they died. You both, had you come to die as you should, would have the same broken bones and burst organs as when you hit the ground, and you would not stand before me but merely be a slumped mess of pain and anguish wrapped in a sack of skin."

Mark tried to look sorry, but not for saving her. A sympathetic kind of sorry, for the state she would have been in had he not stepped in at all.

Emma looked over at Mark with some judgemental disdain. She recognised he'd had her best interests at heart when he'd tried to intervene. At least, what he *thought* her best interests were. But not only had he intervened, making what should have been her last moments all the more difficult, but he'd decided to tell her that he loved her. This, she hadn't expected and didn't have an answer for. Whilst she rejected his statement with every ounce of her being, it had given her pause for thought. Just a brief moment, a niggling 'what if' that had further complicated matters when what she'd really needed, and prepared for, was absolute clarity of purpose. To compound matters, he hadn't stopped her. He'd accidentally sent her careening over the edge along with himself.

"I will not," Charon said with a tap of his oar in his boat, "load in someone bleeding or leaking or otherwise broken, for it is not my duty to carry them off to the shore beyond. It is your task to correct the bodies which come to you broken. As a soul, they can no longer be hurt, and the pain they feel is only the memory of the pain which they incurred in death. When a soul is brought here, it must be whole. You must rebuild them back to what they were before death so that they're be presentable enough to me that I may entertain their passage across."

"What about pharaohs?" Mark asked.

"Eh?"

"The Egyptian kings who were buried with riches and surrounded by wealth, but they also had their organs removed and placed in jars for... some holy reason."

"Ah, yes," Charon said. "They were always light. Just a bit lighter than the rest. A missing brain means missing language. And their tongues were missing too. Very quiet rides, they were. Those were the good old days."

"So as long as they look okay and can afford it," Emma summarised, "that's good enough? Even if they're filled with sawdust or lit on fire?"

"Yes, yes," Charon said. "The bones, mostly. Put them back together right before you bring them here. Doing so will also help them accept their death, when they are less broken than before. Leave a man with all his injuries, and he will become loathful, wicked, and destructive. And I will quicker let him fall into the deep abyss than put up with the rantings of a madman on my journey across."

"It's good to know you have standards," Mark said sarcastically.

Charon did not mind his snippiness and rowed away.

He had nothing to teach them but what demands he made of Death, and it left Mark and Emma wondering which of the two cantankerous old avatars was the true end of life: the one who left souls to drift aimlessly as shells of their former selves, or the one who left them stranded in exchange for money he couldn't even spend?

The world of death was a tricky, senseless thing. But it was a world they were both willing, and now trained, to navigate.

CHAPTER SIXTEEN

Mark and Emma were on track to becoming grim apprentices. They learned to swing their scythes, manage sand, ride horses, and set bones and organs into bodies after excruciating and violent horrific deaths. That job was not one of hands-on practice, but a barrage of text and visuals through Death's collection of encyclopaedias. They spent days grimacing at the horrors and fragility of the human body and how to make it right again while Veronique worked on the last touch of their deathly ascension: their robes.

"You know what?" Mark said, looking up from his book on human disembowelment, hoping that reading it backwards would somehow provide instruction on turning an inside-out man back to normal. "I have total respect for doctors. How is it possible to memorise all of this?"

"Monsieur Mark!" Veronique called. "Could you please come here? I need to take your measurements."

Mark put his book down with a sigh. Then he turned to Emma. "I never got fitted for a suit before."

"Just put your hands up, stare ahead, and think of England."

"I'll shield my eyes just in case she bends over and shows a little ankle."

Mark left the sitting room and returned sometime later in a flowing, floor-length dark robe and matching hood that covered his face like a tattered shadow. All it revealed was his grimacing mouth, which had been touched up very slightly with some foundation to give him a pale complexion – not skeletal white, just more sallow and shadier around the cheeks, like a goth coming home from all-night bender. He tapped his scythe on the ground and tried to puff out his chest, but no matter how he moved his body, the whole thing fell down and drooped over him to make him look a bit chubby.

"I am become Death, destroyer of worlds..." he growled. "No, wait... I'm Batman."

"You're in a night dress," Emma said.

Mark pulled the hood back. Then another hood. "More of a burkini actually."

The whole robe was layered, two robes in one. The outer layer was much wider and intentionally tattered, like pre-torn jeans. The layer underneath was solid and fitted to his body, a full robe with a tightly cinched seam that ran from his left shoulder to his hip.

"I'm sure it looks better in motion – watch." He took a swift couple of steps across the room, hoping that the fabric would flow after him. It kind of did. He made another short dash back to the same place and tried to see if it looked as good as he thought.

"Do I flow?" Mark asked as he sashayed towards Emma. "I want it to look like I'm gliding towards them."

"You look like the Scottish Widows bird thought she was coming into a big inheritance but then found out Hamish spanked their life savings on whores and lines just before his untimely death," Emma said, then changing her voice to a husky rasp added, "Now she will have her vengeance!"

"I'll take that," Mark insisted. "That'll work as long as I look imposing flying through the sky. Hopefully, there's enough excess material to cover up the pony so no one can see it."

"Madame!" Veronique called. "It is your turn."

Emma got up and passed Mark as she walked into the hall.

"Now this I can't wait to see," Mark said with a nod.

Emma scoffed and went with Veronique.

Mark lingered in the doorway, practising his walk. He had half a mind to try and peek but shook the notion off. Given how much was still left unsaid between them, adding "peeping Tom" to his rap sheet wasn't going to make those future conversations any easier. Also, they were in the land of the dead. There was nothing that killed the mood quite like a suicide attempt turning into a double suicide that only sort of ended up working.

Mark soon went back to reading his book, not for pleasure but because he wanted to remain practical. While wearing Death's old, retired robes, stitched back together by Veronique, he wanted to remain composed and well informed of his future duties – to be deathly.

He opened a book on the sexualisation of ritual death in different cultures. The ties between sex and death in religion. Da Vinci's unabashed horniness when designing all manner of Christian artworks. The ties which bound man's crotch with the crosses he bore across the ages. Female anatomy and how everything was put together...

He put the book down and sat, hands over his lap, very calmly and tried not to think. He was in danger. His robe was just tight enough that if he stood up, it might show that he was more excited than he should be. He thought of England – of debt and painful cycles of mind-numbing, soul-killing work and the ill reward of paying so much in tax and rent he couldn't save for a deposit to buy a house.

He went from being super excited to just the right amount of sad. When Veronique had given them a possible way out, he'd leapt at the chance. He was certain that if they pulled this off and got into Death's good books, there was a chance of reward. But nothing Death had said indicated that the reward would be the opportunity to live again. Far more likely it would be Emma's interpretation that proved true, that Death would use his sway to expedite their crossing of the river with the boatman. He brushed his hands over his face to ease the growing grief across his brow. Then he heard two sets of feet coming up the hall along with a strange creaking sound.

"Monsieur," Veronique declared, "your flat-mate is—"

"Please don't get his hopes up," Emma said.

Mark looked over. Emma was in a leather catsuit with a tight-ness that contoured to her movements without wrinkling. It didn't just hug her figure; it damn near suffocated her figure, like a second layer of skin that was dark and foreboding but totally revealing. The only part of her ensemble which wasn't black and shiny was her face, which was dolled up in lively makeup that couldn't hide her own natural blush.

He loved it.

Mark clapped his hands together. "Veronique, you are a miracle with a needle."

"It is nothing like suturing open wounds," she said, "but great fun! Monsieur Death has nothing like this. I brought it all in on my own."

"Please tell me you can't see my nipples in this," Emma said.

Mark leaned in close to inspect her. "Oh, yeah, there they are."

Emma covered her chest up. The rubber squeaked against itself.

"That was the suit," she said quickly. "This— this isn't me at all, I think. Maybe the second one would be better? Sorry."

"It is okay," Veronique said. "I would be happy to oblige. You have my thanks for letting me experiment so much."

"Oh, yes, have fun," Emma said. She walked away with a quick, squeaking stride. "That was the *trousers*," she insisted.

Mark looked at his own suit and wished it could have been a little cooler for a moment. Long flowing tatters of scrappy, distressed – and distressing – robes weren't really his look.

Eventually, Emma returned. Her new outfit was somewhat similar. No longer a thing of latex and rubber, it was an outfit in parts, with a dark-undertoned blouse and skinny jeans - black, of course. She had leather horse-riding boots, also black. She wore a wide-brimmed derby hat that flopped down just enough to hide her eyes and accent the blood-red lipstick which stood out against the pale makeup on her face. Instead of a robe, she had a very long coat – functionally a robe – but with buttons to tie it together and an ornamental belt to complete the ensemble.

"Very nice," Mark said. "Off to a day at the races."

"Yes," Emma said. "And at the end of every race, all the horses die."

CHAPTER SEVENTEEN

Death was proudly presented with his two apprentices, wearing their robes and wielding their scythes, at the stable out back. And he sighed.

"This was a waste of time," he muttered.

"You can't be certain of that," Mark said.

"Oh, yes, I can," he retorted. "You've no idea the folly you are capable of, representing me in those preposterous costumes or on those pathetic mounts."

"Well, I'll give you mine's a bit fancy dress on a budget," Mark said, "but what's wrong with hers?"

Death huffed the question away, unwilling to answer.

They both mounted up and followed him and his pale horse into the meadow. The trio rode together until they picked up enough speed to ascend. Mark got the hang of it, sort of. He veered a bit, but his pony managed to keep the same speed as the stallion and Death's old grey mare.

"You must practice opening tears between worlds," Death

said, "so you can move effortlessly from this place to the other. I will not be your doorman."

"How do we do it?" Emma asked.

Death leaned back and held his scythe over his shoulder. He gripped it tight and swung it forward, like he was about to throw a javelin, then stopped, pointing the tip ahead in the sky. A fissure of crackling purple lightning opened. He dove under it, and the hole sealed.

"You must cut ahead of where you are," he explained. "And focus your will on the space which you have opened."

"And this is possible because of magic?" Mark asked.

"It is possible because I am Death," he corrected. "And if you are, too, then it should be possible for you."

"I believe in me," Mark said quietly to himself. "Be the best reaper I can be."

"Believe harder than that," Death said. He galloped ahead through the air and gave them some space to practise while circling above like a hoofed vulture. Emma tried first. She swung her scythe down and held it forward. A few stray sparks flickered in the air ahead of her, and she ran into them. It was like getting too close to a sparkler. She shied away and dipped her hat to cover her face.

Mark tried as well. He held his scythe out ahead of him and felt it sort of snag on something that wasn't there. He figured that had to be the right feeling and tried again. He managed it that second time and tried to will whatever he'd caught into tearing. Purple sparks started up far ahead of him until they formed a seam. It wasn't quite wide or tall enough to enter, but he'd opened something, right in line with his head.

He wondered, for a second, what would happen if a portal wasn't big enough to fit a whole body and closed around it. To avoid finding out, he managed to duck to the side, spinning Stormrider in the air in a barrel roll just in time.

"Nice flying," Emma said. "How'd you do that?"

"Right," Mark began, "so you know how – when you have a piece of paper, and you tug on it in two opposite directions, it doesn't tear? Like you're just testing the strength of the paper in your hands. But then you twist just a little to make a little tear, and you pull again, and suddenly it's torn the whole way through?"

"I guess," Emma said.

"Like your *Clubcard* coupons," he said. "You know the way you pull on them to separate them from the letter, and they don't budge? But you tear it a little on the edge and then they pop right off the rest of the sheet?"

"So am I cutting, pulling, or tugging?"

"All of the above," he said. "It's tense at first, but you just kind of *want* to tear it and then you do. And then you must keep tearing and ripping, but one good tug gets it started."

"Okay."

Emma tried again. She swung her scythe and aimed. She felt that same tension as though she'd caught the hook of her blade on an invisible something and wanted to pull it apart. Instead of yanking forwards or pushing down, she gently nudged the blade's tip forwards to poke a small tear. The purple lightning crackled deeper, mimicking the feeling she'd torn a small piece of whatever it was. Then she pulled just slightly, like putting a car into first gear gently enough to hear the transmission crank itself over. The hole she'd opened grew slowly, too slowly for it to be large enough when she approached it.

Her stallion leaped and jumped over the whole thing, which burst apart behind her as the portal collapsed. She gasped in astonishment.

"Are we magic?" Mark asked. "Or are the scythes magic?"

"Or the suits?" Emma added.

"What I'm really wondering is, if we did all this when we were alive, would it have worked?"

"No," Death boomed. "Do not prattle. Practise."

His presence killed the joy they were feeling with their sense of power, but they stayed on task long enough to figure out the nuances of the technique. In the end, they both managed to open a decent-sized hole in the air, and each time they evaded it for fear that it might actually work, rather than it being too small or covered in lightning.

They returned to the ground to give the horses a break from all the running around in the open air. Their hooves weren't tired, but their lungs were. Mark walked his pony around like a dog, while Emma let hers roam on its own. Death came down and dismounted with a stifled cough and groan.

"These portals are the only manner," he explained, "of getting you there and back again. And the souls you carry with you must cross through as well. Once they do, you deliver them to the river and ride off to reap again. This, a thousand times a day or more, is what you must do."

"Is there enough time in the day for a thousand?" Mark questioned. "Let's say it takes us ten minutes on a good, fast job to get someone's soul and bring it back. And we just rock up, pick them up on the end of our scythe, swing them into the hole, and drop them at the river. That's how it's done. Ten minutes. Six an hour. Six times twenty-four... That's a hundred and forty-four. Not even two hundred."

Death groaned. "Your obsession with time and the human perception thereof is getting annoying. When you enter the living world, normally, time ceases. You are amidst the chaos of death, at the end of a life when there are no more moments that can come to pass. No more moments means...?" He waited for Mark to catch up, but only had the patience to wait for about a second. "No time! It doesn't pass the way you think it does anymore."

"So when you say months have passed for us," Emma said, "really, on Earth, are we still falling from the roof?"

"No," Death said. "Your circumstances were unique enough that your real bodies had to come with you."

"Which means our real bodies would be going back," Mark said, "but not ageing anymore, due to no time passing. Even after thousands of 'years' doing this?"

Death sighed, and his ragged breath caught something in his non-existent throat, eliciting a short bout of light coughs. "You won't be doing this for the same degree of time. You are still mortal. Your sand will fall, *eventually*, and by then, I will have seen my fill of your tawdry work. Until then, you can work so that you do not disappoint me, but do not assume you will be replacing me – you *won't*. I'll make it easy for you."

He held his finger up. A storm cloud gathered directly over his head to bring in a shield of darkness, which made his robe even darker and the skeletal white of his face much whiter.

"One hundred. Your trial period shall end after one hundred reapings. I shall assign you the first few, and from there, you must use your sandmanship to know what souls require attention, your scythemanship to open the way which leads them to you in the shortest time, your horsemanship to locate them in the complexity of human society, and your anatmanship shall be tested when they are returned here and prepared for the ferryman." His finger turned to point to Mark and Emma, and the cloud spread over them. "And if you fail, I will *choose* to fail you and cast you into the river itself, where you will not be recovered."

Suddenly gripped by a crippling fear, Mark unconsciously reached out to hold Emma's hand. Rather than take it, she reached across for a hug. Mark and Emma held each other. In Death's complexion on his featureless face, they saw the presence of a fearful authority that they could not deny. After so long being guests – and dare they say, friends – in his home, they returned to their natural human condition and feared Death all over again.

The sincerity of his promise struck Emma hardest. She was used to threats from management that were supposed to transform an underperforming workforce into superstars. She was also used to being the one on the team who was doing her job and doing it well. She didn't need the carrot or the stick, she was naturally diligent and conscientious. Emma's problem had always been not being noticed and not taking the credit. Less able colleagues were often carried along on her coat-tails but had learned the art of singing their own praises, and the net result was always the same – they were the ones that got the promotions, the salary bumps, and the recognition.

But not this time. Emma had wanted death, and had even been prepared to leap willingly into its final embrace. Now, finding herself in Limbo, she needed to prove herself a worthy reaper to avoid an eternity of torment and, with Death's help, pass to the other side. She silently vowed to not just deliver what was asked for – but to give Death himself a run for his money. She would reap like her afterlife depended on it. Because it did.

The impromptu hug he received from Emma did more for Mark's soul than he could have imagined. Not a word spoken and yet he knew in that moment that he had been right to try to save her. He was right to tell her how he felt about her, although the reaction hadn't been what he'd wanted. He saw a strength in Emma that most ignored, and whatever trepidation he felt about the monumental task ahead of them, he knew he wouldn't want to have anyone else but Emma at his side right now. As much as he felt underprepared, undertrained, and overdressed, he really wanted to avoid being cast into the river for all eternity. And so he gripped the long handle of his scythe and saluted Death.

"Let's hunt some souls!" Mark announced with gusto from his diminutive mount. He gently tapped his heels and his pony walked on.

CHAPTER EIGHTEEN

Charon noticed a bright flash in the sky, closer to the river's shore than normal. He scoffed at it as he rowed along on his lonely ferryboat, ever the porter of nothing but his own disappointment and sorrowful loneliness. Death's apprentices, those two mouthy upstarts, were starting on their way back to the human world.

They had more power and freedom than he. His only companions were his coins, which he couldn't even enjoy anymore for fear of losing more to the water. He rolled one around on his fingers, but a shiver sent it falling, and it lodged hard between two of the planks forming the ferry's deck.

"Damn your eyes, man," Charon chastised himself. He bent down and used his fingers to try and pry the coin back out, but it kept slipping out of his grip. He tried to use his sleeve instead but to no avail. Then he thought it might be a good idea to roll it out, or apply pressure on just one point to flick it out like a lever. He pushed it down until it scraped out and catapulted away. The coin flipped, almost over the side of the boat, but Charon caught it before it spiralled too far. He sighed with relief and reclined back in his seat.

Then he felt water around his foot. When he lifted it from the planks, he discovered the coin pried out exactly enough tar to turn the shallow hole into a tiny leak. Even his coins betrayed him now. He clutched the coin in his fist and threatened to throw it off into the distance but relented. The gold was his only companion on the boat. He had to keep as much of it around as he could...

The skies over Liverpool were uncommonly sunny – a brief stint of summery weather to break up what had become the droning monotony of seemingly endless spring. The streets were only slightly wet from the rain that had fallen hours before. The day seemed calm and joyful all around. It was hardly a day anyone imagined being their last.

Yet Mark and Emma were there to ensure that day would be the last day someone ever got to see. They hovered high above the city with Death over them, a looming shadow of order.

"This," he declared, "is the city whence you came. Therefore, I must imagine you are quite accustomed to its topography and geography."

"Yeah," Mark agreed, "from street level."

"You will start from here," Death said. "Assess the hourglass. Hold it and observe the shifting of the sands within. It will direct you to where the doomed soul is. Even held at an angle, the sands will only fall and pile in that one direction. Follow it and find your first duty."

"Then bring them back in one whole piece, and let Charon call them poor and worthless?" Emma confirmed.

"Yes," Death said. "If they are not dead with coin, you will inter them into purgatory eternally, or until the ferryman finds some other source of value in human life to hoard. But don't be too hopeful about that. Do not tarry or dawdle. Do not speak to the dead if you don't have to, and do not answer too many of their questions."

"Is there a chance that we'll need these scythes much to fight off rebellious spirits?" Mark asked,

"Absolutely," Death said. "And remember, when you cut a soul, you need to put them back together. To that end..." Death pulled a thick-looking hessian sack from his sleeve and threw it down. It fell over Mark's head like a tarp. "If they will not ride on your saddle, they'll ride as luggage."

Death reared his horse and exited through another tear between worlds. He left his apprentices to their duty, high over Liverpool, with nothing but the dread and misery of their new vocation as it sank in fully.

"You know what I worry about?" Mark asked.

"I'm worried about a lot of things," Emma replied. She looked at the hourglass. It was for Richard Baskerton, and the final grains were nearly gone. She could count how much sand was left, and it fell at a regular rate. "Let's worry about them after work."

Mark nodded and stuffed the sack down between his legs where it was probably safest. He followed Emma's stallion as they began a steep dive towards Crosby. It was an affluent area neither of them was accustomed to, nor had ever spent much time visiting.

"You know those places," Mark remarked, "where you'll never be able to afford to live, even if you save up for the rest of your life?"

"Yeah?"

"Well, we're here, and we're dead. So it's true."

She nodded her head a bit and followed the sand. When they

got down to street level, they were surprised that no one was stunned to see them. People seemingly passed by without noticing the two pitch-black deathly figures on flying horses armed with enormous razor-sharp scythes.

"Must be common around here," Mark said. "Rich folk culture. Don't want to stop and point in case it's a new trend they haven't heard of yet, and they accidentally get cancelled."

"It's in here." Emma pointed to the nearest house. "How do we...?"

Mark shrugged. He walked up to the door and tried to knock on it. His hand hit the surface but didn't make any noise. His entire presence was ignored by the world at large, even by the door. Then he looked at his scythe.

"Cover me," he said. He stepped back off the porch steps and tried to wedge the blade of his weapon between the door and the frame. Emma looked around, curious as to what exactly she was supposed to do. In the row of identical homes, there was no space around the terraced house to shuffle into a path or side alley. There was just a front door and the neighbouring homes that sandwiched it together.

Mark, flustered that his scythe blade wouldn't jimmy the door open, prodded the lock with the tip of his scythe handle instead. He heard a stiff metallic unlocking sound. His scythe, which could tear open holes between worlds, no doubt had some power over mere brass lock tumblers that acted as boundaries between the indoors and the out. He gently reached out to open the door and ended up falling through it. *Now* he was intangible.

"Fine," Mark groaned. Emma came in after he picked himself up. "A lot of silly rules to navigate."

Emma held the hourglass. The bulb twitched a little, indicating the direction they should travel. Just two grains of sand were left. One fell. Then, at last, the top bulb was empty. The world went still. Light ceased, and everything turned grey. The moments of the life they were there to collect ended, and so too did time for that life. Their duty bound them strictly to that fate, and so they had to share it until they were through with their task.

"Let's go," Mark said. "I don't know how long we can be here until we've technically failed."

"Lots of silly rules," Emma agreed.

They both ran up the stairs and headed for the master bedroom, where they found their man dead in his bed, with a belt around his neck. Richard Baskerton was a mild-mannered local councillor whose stint in office came at the cost of a great deal of corruption. Emma and Mark knew him. At least, they knew of him. He'd accepted bribes from all sorts of interest groups, which trickled down into tax breaks, planning permission manipulation, and good old-fashioned brown envelopes that directly hurt the poor of his ward, all in an effort to drive them to either leave or starve to death in cold, unheated homes.

And, it turned out, he was a bit of a kinky perv. Nothing unsavoury that involved others, but the man had a penchant for auto-erotic asphyxiation. He referenced gallows and hangings quite a lot in retaliatory comments to public condemnations of his behaviour. Never decapitation, just hanging. It was plain to see it was usually on his mind.

His body lay dead, aghast, blue, and foaming from the mouth, while his spirit lingered morosely at the side of his bed in his underwear. "Who— who are you people?" he asked.

"Uh..." Mark began. The situation was beyond awkward. No introduction he could think of seemed to suffice. He'd just walked in on a man who'd tried to get too happy and died from it. An awful man at that.

"We," Emma declared, "are the horsemen of Death, the

reapers of souls, the grim phantoms of fate come to bring you to your destiny."

"That's very good." Mark tapped his scythe's handle on the floor in applause. "Clear purpose, concise call to action. You would have made a fine copywriter."

"Thanks, partner." Emma grinned, glowing in the praise.

"What?" said Richard. "No. I'm dreaming. Ain't no way I'm dead. I've done this dozens of times before. Ain't no way I keeled over like this!"

"But you did!" Mark said, just as bombastically as Emma had started. "You, who choked the life out of your own constituents and district dwellers, you who have noosed the very people you swore to serve, have now fallen to the knot of your own making. The bindings of your own demented pleasures have brought you to the ultimate suffering!"

"You, sir," Emma riffed, enjoying their impromptu back and forth, "choked out choking the chicken."

"No!" Richard cried, then he fell to his spectral knees and wailed into his hands.

"Oh, this is fun," Mark whispered.

"Let's not enjoy it too much," Emma said, hiding a giggling smile. "Work is work."

"Yeah, but this sort of work can be rewarding. Very rewarding indeed," Mark added.

The two of them lorded it over the cowering spirit, enjoying the power now that it was in their hands.

CHAPTER NINETEEN

Mark and Emma returned to the other world. It was just like tearing a stocking. It seems nice and strong until it's pinched just right, and then the tearing never stops. The portal opened, and they delivered their quarry – the disgraced and dishevelled politician – to the River Styx to meet with Charon, where he was dismissed for his failed offering, and then they left him in the discomforting void of resting spirits. His fault for not meeting a proper end.

With a swipe, they returned to Earth – though not together. Emma emerged over Liverpool, where they left. Mark, meanwhile, was somewhere else.

"Oh, cool. Brighton!" he exclaimed.

The pier over the sea was in sight and just as majestically understaffed as usual. There was hardly anyone out on the streets. A few brave water sports enthusiasts were on the beach, though the surf wasn't quite up, and the shops all seemed to be waiting for customers to start their retail therapy.

He took the hourglass out from inside his sleeve, which he

found surprisingly spacious, a great place to hold things, and tried to get his bearings. The hourglass was leaning to the east, so he turned Stormrider, searching for the soul.

He steered his horse downwards and started to tour over the town on his own private expressway. "Now, this is special. The kind of view people would pay a couple of grand for. And would be able to afford it, too." There was just a tinge of jealousy in his thoughts. The Insta-perfect life he imagined he might lead living somewhere like Brighton was always just out of reach for him. Even a visit felt expensive. Now it would never be realised.

The sand changed. It shifted slightly to the left, westward. He was hot on his own trail. And he now realised, potentially, why. They'd each taken an hourglass to double-up on the work. The hourglass, or the life the hourglass represented, determined where the portal on Earth opened. He inspected the hourglass once more, squinting to make out the name on the brass plaque. Henrietta Bower. Her time was due quite soon. He continued to follow the path the sand drew until he wound up at a sheltered accommodation complex.

It was inevitable that he'd find his way to a pensioner one way or another. Most of the dead died of natural causes. There was no war in the UK, apart from maybe a class war, nor any vast network of serious crime. Crime, yes, but not quite as organised as the politicians would lead the people to believe. So, naturally, most of the dead would just be part of the course of nature.

He rode down and landed just as everything went grey, and a bit indigo. All the colours in the world went "dead". Anything lively, bright, and happy turned to grey, and everything else went morose and blue. The startling change sent him reeling with a bit of confusion before he adjusted to it. He had a job to do.

He tapped on the door's lock with the handle of his scythe and walked through it. That part he'd gotten down. He was a home intrusion expert, and he'd come equipped. The home was a simple little apartment on the eastern end of a retirement village, a campus of low-rise brick buildings connected to a clinic dedicated to geriatric care. The worst cases, or ones without decent pensions and a house to sell to pay for it all, had mere rooms and units in the complex, while the rich and respected got their own bungalows to die in. Apparently, Henrietta was one of those lucky few. But not lucky enough to live.

The first thing that struck Mark about the interior of bungalow number seven was how bare it seemed. Even through the grey filter of time standing still, it was clear that every room had been painted the same depressing shade of magnolia. Whilst there were some items of furniture, nothing seemed to match, and nothing seemed to fit in the space the way it should. It all felt and looked very temporary. It had all been dumped in the room in a way that suggested it wasn't placed for comfort or convenience, but rather, the removal men had done themselves a solid by making it easy to extract again... when the time inevitably came.

Mark's eyes were drawn to a framed photo on the wall. There was nothing particularly striking about the image of Henrietta, who sat sandwiched between two grinning middle-aged men he assumed to be her sons. It was more that it was the only personal decoration in any of the rooms. Mostly it upset Mark that the screw used to hang it was off centre. Someone had clearly put the photo up to "make the place a bit more like home" and hadn't wanted to take the time to hammer a nail into the wall. Why bother when a perfectly good screw is going to waste on the wall already?

Mark peeked in at the old woman's spirit as she stood over her body, which lay still in an adjustable bed.

"Oh dear." She sighed. "What'll the manager think?"

"Henrietta?" Mark said. She turned, a stiff-faced old woman

with a tucked-in lip that was held back from anything but a frown. She saw the spectre of death and his spectral paunch that stuck out from his artful robe tatters as he moved in with his scythe in hand. "I've come to take you away from here."

"Yes," she said. She moved over to a nearby armchair in a small sitting room arrangement— a luxury she obviously hadn't enjoyed in many days, or maybe weeks, and wished to experience one last time. Mark invited himself to sit across from her. As he did, Henrietta sighed, and she seemed to somehow de-age. Many of her wrinkles left, her wispy hair thickened into a bouquet of curls, her skin went from a sickly pallor to a more robust tan, and her eyes glistened once more – cataract-free and with purpose. She reached an ideal state – the last time she felt alive was how her spirit chose to die.

"Tell me," she said. "Do we play chess now?"

"Afraid not."

"What is it like? This next step I am about to take?"

Mark adjusted himself a bit better in his seat and tried to be less menacing with his large scythe, which towered over them like the harbinger of death it was. He wasn't willing to lay it on the floor, just in case Henrietta was only playing at being a frail old lady, and he needed to lop off her noggin at a moment's notice. Instead, he laid it across the armrests like a safety bar and rolled it around so it stayed balanced, which meant the blade was right next to his wrist when he rested his arm. There was no way for him to be proper with her, despite her best efforts to be as ladylike in death as she surely was in life.

"I'm not supposed to tell you that," he said. "Or much else."

"Why leave it a mystery?" she asked. "Who can I tell to spoil the surprise? I'm clearly gone from this life. I'd like to know how to prepare myself for the next."

"Yeah, I would like to know too," Mark admitted.

"Are you not Death?" she asked.

He tilted his head back and forth, uncertain of his own answer. "Effectively, yes. Death is expanding its service provision now to include a wider range of... talents involved in undertaking the... uh... undertaking. As it were."

"Is this a position afforded to just anyone?" she asked.

"No," he said. "But that's part of a list of things I can't tell you."

"Hmph," she huffed. "I married into a noble family and outlasted my first husband long enough to inherit a substantial fortune. Then I was courted by some gainful younger man who saw my wealth as a means to improve his own personal future. That man was arrested for embezzlement and having allegiances to foreign governments. I'm not a stranger to the better-kept secrets among the elite. It is always telling of a new body of leadership to ask a simple question and not receive a simple answer. Simplicity, I learned too late in life, is a fine reprieve from living itself. Life is complicated. People are complex. But simplicity is always so fleeting. I wish I'd cherished it sooner – but that's the queer twist of fate, isn't it? That those born into fine things only appreciate simplicity later; after all that lustres loses its lust. But those born too far to even admire what others are given will never appreciate their own simplicity the way it is coveted."

"Hmm." Mark nodded. He wondered just what to do. He felt comfortable talking with her and letting her talk. There was certainly no one else around, and with time stopped, he wasn't exactly waiting for anyone, but he felt as if something was off. He wondered what might happen if he just left her there, stranded in her final moment. If he left, right then, would time resume? Would she be left to wander as a ghost and watch what happened to her body, legacy, and wealth in the days after her death was reported?

Would that be any crueller a fate than bringing her to purgatory and letting her wander on the riverside forever?

"I'll tell you this," Mark said, after he'd decided what he should share. "The place you are going is simple. But it is a degree of simplicity you may not find enjoyable."

She arched her eyebrows. For her, that was a mark of great shock. But she nodded and took in a last, deep breath of acceptance. She held out her hand for him to take like a gentleman. Mark took up his scythe and took her hand to help her up. The old woman died with grace, accepted her fate with dignity, and endured the ride on the back of the pony with quiet respect.

Mark accompanied her in silence, but during the trip, he promised himself that if he was ever afforded the chance to live again, he'd visit his nan more often. Every day, in fact.

CHAPTER TWENTY

Mark returned to the void of death to drop Henrietta off. He looked down along the riverbank bordering the infinite's featureless plains, and saw a speck of black which stood out from its surroundings, like a single peppercorn in a pile of salt. He flew down to join it, and met Emma on the ground.

Mark helped Henrietta off the horse. She gave him a polite tap on the hand as if to say, "job well done" and saw herself off to her infinite waiting room. Mark watched her leave for a moment, then went to Emma.

"How was it? Where's your soul?"

She pointed at the water. Or rather, under it. "He died from an overdose. Sobered up as soon as he met me. I brought him here and told him to wait for the ferryman. He asked what would happen if he swam for it. I told him he'd sink and never come back up and he just..." She dropped her arm down.

"Poor sod," Mark said. "Well, no problems though, right? No issues?"

"None."

"Didn't have to cut him down and patch him back together?"

"No. He just hung on. Cried slightly. I think the drugs were holding back much of his own inner pain from years and years. Couldn't cope with himself without them."

"Well, that's sad," Mark said. "Mine was just a nice old lady. I didn't have the heart to tell her that there was nothing waiting for her here at all. Nothing but a vast, open, endless sprawl of nothingness and—"

The two heard the jingle of metal nearby. They turned and saw Henrietta step gingerly aboard Charon's boat. Mark ran over to inspect the scene.

"What's this?" he asked.

Charon grinned and unclenched his hand. He held two thick, beautiful gold earrings, solid plates with hooked latches, and a golden wedding ring – a parting gift Henrietta willingly gave up. She died with some of her jewellery on.

"'Tis just enough to match a fare," Charon said. "The ring itself, which so many bring, is hardly worth enough, but you, my dear, are an honoured soul and cherished too."

"I thought you only accepted coins," Mark said.

"Gold is gold," Charon replied. He slapped the oar into the water and splashed a bit onto Mark's robe. "It'll be coin when it's blessed my pocket long enough. Careful now, my dear. The boat is safe to sit in but stand not, else ye'll find no bottom to this lake."

"Can you tell me what is on the other side?" Henrietta asked.

Charon chuckled and spoke in a low tone, and they grew distant enough into the mist over the river that his churlish voice no longer reached the shore that Mark was stuck on.

"Huh," Mark huffed. "Well." He put his hands on his hips, and Emma joined him with her horse and his in tow. "So, women are more likely to get to the other side than men are..."

"How do you figure?"

He pinched an ear between thumb and forefinger and wiggled it.

"Sounds like?" Emma questioned.

"It's not charades. I mean men aren't usually buried with gold earrings."

"Ah," she realised.

"Or necklaces or anklets or loads of rings."

"Some are," Emma corrected him. "Mob bosses. Rappers. Instagram influencers."

"True. And Manchester United supporters."

"But generally, yes, you're right."

"If we get back to life," Mark said, "we need to make sure we're always carrying gold on us. At least a few ounces. I'd rather risk whatever is over there than stick around here forever."

"What about the poor?" Emma asked. "Who die clutching nothing, with nothing?"

"Last in life, last in the afterlife..." Mark nodded. "It's a bum deal all round. Been voting Labour all my life. Please don't tell me the bloody Tories were right all along and it's all about the wonga."

"Don't worry." Emma rubbed Mark's shoulder. "They're never right. Even if they are, they aren't." She puckered her lips curiously, then reached for her saddlebag and took out an hourglass. "Let's both hurry to the next one. Take our minds off all these questions, so we don't go mad."

"Are we really at the point already," Mark said, "where our lives have got so complicated that we must distract ourselves with work? Last time we did this to ourselves, you tried to kill yourself."

Emma sighed. "Last time, it was because I was in an economic chokehold that was treating me like a second-class citizen in my own country for daring to want more options to plan for my future. This is slightly different."

"It's still about the future," Mark said. "And ironically, we still need a substantial amount of personal wealth to progress."

Emma didn't argue further. She mounted up and expected Mark to follow. And she had the hourglass, so the portal was hers to make and close at will. Mark hitched up and lifted off the ground just as Emma took off. He caught up to her just in time as she swung her sickle forwards and opened the portal to...

Nowhere. Nothing. No cities in sight. Nothing but rolling green hills and fog. Despite their spectral bodies, they could still feel a chill in the air and a muggy, mossy scent.

"Is this Scotland?" Mark asked.

"Is it?" Emma asked. She looked around through the clouds across the ground and spotted a castle in the distance, old but venerated, with its own parking lot that overlooked a shallow lake. "Yes, I think it is."

Mark dove down and into the fog. Emma followed. They spent some time over the narrow country roads and through the dales and rolling hills, taking in the scenery. Practically their own backyard, a few hundred miles away at most, and yet it was a place that felt so unconditionally distant and unfamiliar to them.

Emma followed the sand the long way around, taking high flights over forests, streams, and perfect little hills. They took in all the sights and none of the smells of the perpetually wet woodlands.

Then everything went grey. All the greens faded in a flash. The sky went dark, the fog became thin, and the water was an opalescent kind of foreboding black. Emma didn't need to look to confirm it; the last of the sand had passed through. The fun was over, not that it was ever meant to be fun in the first place. They had to find their destined denizen of the new realm immediately. Or else...

They continued following the sand that nudged against the

rim of the glass for minutes. Or minutes relative to their senses and relative to their speed, which was very fast. They went further and further into the wilderness, passing no towns or villages, only deeper into where more errant castles seemed to rise out of the hillsides.

"I hope they aren't left waiting long," Mark said.

"They'll be glad to see us," Emma said. "I'm sure of it."

Finally, the sand shifted towards a place – a small gatehouse on the other side of a decrepit moat with a rotted drawbridge beside a perfectly functional iron-braced walkway. It was a historic castle which connected to a country road, a tourist trap of sorts. And the sole castellan was in for the weekend and had died at the dinner table, clutching his chest with an untouched haggis dinner sitting on his plate.

The spirit of the man was a gruff, teeth-gritting, strong-looking old Scot with thick arms and a thick beard. "Who're you?" he demanded. "Comin' in my house in the middle of the day without even an appointment. You know the sheer amount o' work I've got to do afore the next sunup?"

"Sir—" Mark began.

"Lookit you!" the man shot back. "Dressed like bloody ghosts on a child's parade float. And you, lass, with yer big hat - didja no hear of an umbrella? You're not supposed to wear yer roof when there's a ceiling above you!"

"Oh, he'll love Charon," Mark said.

"We are Death," Emma said. "And you have died. We've come to take—"

"You think I have time to lay down and be dead?" the man said. He crouched down next to his choking face and screamed at it. "WAKE UP!" The eye twitched. "WAKE UP, YOU LAZY BASTARD! YOU AREN'T PAID TO SLEEP ON THE FLOOR!"

"Sir, you're dead," Mark said. "There's nothing you can do."

The man stood up and took a swing at him. Mark stepped back on instinct, unsure if the blow would connect, but not testy enough to prove it.

"Don't you tell me how to talk to my own body," he said. "If that's me down there, then who am I up here?"

"Your soul," Emma said, "which we have to take—"

"Like hell, you will!" he said. He put up his arms and jabbed his fists. "You'll not drag me into your hell pit, you devil-fiends! Go take a crap in Satan's mouth and tell him it's from me!"

"We don't work for Satan," Mark said. "We've never even met him."

"Aw," the man mocked, "so low on the devil's rung, ye never even spoke to yer boss? Petrol station attendants of the afterlife, that's what youse are. Shelf stackers, who one day dream of being trained on the fish counter, eh? Am I not wrong?"

"Sir," Emma said sternly, "we are permitted to bring you back *in pieces* if need be." She held out the sack, the brown hessian bag barely big enough to serve as a proper saddle bag. The threat carried in the room as real, but the man laughed on regardless.

"Then you damn well better!" he said. He charged, fists up, screaming.

Emma and Mark had trained for weeks under the expert tutelage of the determined warrior monk. They'd reinforced those learnings by poring over the many anatomical tomes in Death's extensive library, committing to memory the name and precise location of every major bone and muscle group. They realised, pretty much at the same moment, that there's a tremendous difference between *knowing* how to reap a soul with a two-handed bladed weapon and *actually using* it to slice at the phantom of another human being with the sole intention of lopping bits off.

This sudden requirement to turn theoretical knowledge into practical application would stump many.

But not Emma and Mark. No, these two were slice happy, ready, willing and able to apply their lessons from the classroom in a live environment without a moment's hesitation.

The man stepped in, swung his empty shoulder socket at Emma, and looked back in confusion. Mark had artfully clipped the man's arm off. It flopped down on the floor and continued to grip on its own. The Scotsman laughed. "Bet you won't do that again!"

Emma swung and sliced off his head. His body stood confused and aimless, like he'd gone blind and deaf at once, while his ghostly head rolled onto the floor.

"Oh, that's just fucking fine and dandy," he continued mockingly from around their feet. "You think I need a body to beat you into a bloody pulp? I've got words so heinous your devil will shield his ears and wet his pants to hear them. I know swear words that Christ himself wouldn't think to ban from his holy scriptures, too profane for Hell, and too unique for Heaven. I—"

Mark picked the head up by the beard and put it, with the arm, into the sack. He looked at Emma, and they both looked at the body, which was still roving around the room blindly swinging at whatever was nearby.

CHAPTER TWENTY-ONE

W ithin just a few souls of starting their proper, true apprenticeship, Mark and Emma were enjoying it. Really enjoying it. Emma's job in life had been dull and repetitive with little chance of progression or reward, and she had yearned for something that felt fulfilling and rewarding – or, failing that, just a bit of appreciation and recognition.

Although Mark got some satisfaction from his job as a graphic designer, it always played second fiddle to his true passion: writing sitcoms. He was prolific; his writing was good, and he had even won a few competitions, but he couldn't find a production company to take on his projects for love nor money. Instead, he kept his head above water with graphic design for an advertising firm, and spent his evenings and weekends crafting new scenarios for his characters to inhabit.

The nature of agency work was plugging through assignments and moving quickly on to the next. It was all about finding a solution fast, with little time to get to know the client or their customers, which meant it was little more than assembly line delivery masquerading as creative freedom.

They were only a couple of souls in, but so far, so good. Despite the stakes being high – literally life and death – there was a beautiful simplicity to their task. Arrive at the appointed time, reap, and shepherd the soul to the riverbank. Clear, defined and binary, with little opportunity for interpretation. Much like jet-washing a patio, there was instant gratification from a job well done and, it seemed, enough variety to keep things interesting and fresh.

Whilst they were happy, it was clear that there was no such thing as a happy death. The closest they could get was someone wanting to die, only to realise nothing was waiting for them on the other side – and that kind of ending was merely the final light of a life that was already drenched in a darkness best left unconsidered.

It was exhausting emotionally, but physically they didn't feel all that tired yet. Their arms were the worst, and the shoulders from which they swung their scythes. Mark's back was a little sore from leaning over to cling to his pony as it rode on, but he was adjusting to it. Much of the toll on them was the unanswered fears, questions, and feelings over what they were doing and seeing – and whether Death would ultimately approve of their labour.

This particular trip had taken them to London, and they made their way past Big Ben along the Thames and across to Waterloo until they reached a hospital. Of course, it was a natural place to find many dead, a place people went to spend their final, futile moments battling disease or injuries.

Their target, Thomas Berringer, was a young man with wild hair and good looks. A tragic youth lost to some hideous violence which required multiple police officers to be at his bedside as he died, and to keep him handcuffed to the bed where he slept. It was a harrowing scene. Mark and Emma felt conflicted over going in and hung out in the off-mauve corridor while time still ticked away.

Despite being repeatedly proven spectacularly wrong, Emma still believed that people were ultimately good but sometimes did bad things – rather than accepting that the world was choc-full of arseholes who took extreme pleasure in the misery of others. Clutching desperately to this hypothesis is how she justified, at least to herself, why school 'friends' had stolen her bus fares, forcing her to walk home every day, and she'd never told her teachers or her parents. It's how she convinced herself that others taking credit for her hard work at the office was her fault for not speaking up, rather than theirs for taking advantage. Most significantly, it was how and why she'd taken out loans she could ill afford to feed the gambling habit of her older sister, Claire, who had promised – time and again – that she would pay the money back, with interest, if Emma could just see her way to lending her enough to stake her next sure-fire bet... It wasn't until Emma's losses amounted to an eye-watering sixty thousand pounds and she simply couldn't access more credit that realisation dawned she would never see a penny back.

And yet, assessing the scene in front of her, and despite all the evidence to the contrary, she saw a possible injustice.

"What do you think happened?" Emma asked in a low voice, even though they were invisible and intangible and not at all physically perceivable by others.

"I mean," Mark began, "he obviously did... something."

"Why don't we get cards or cheat sheets? Little breakdowns of who these people are?"

"I think that's a bit counter-intuitive to us just finding them and shovelling them off the mortal coil."

"It's shoving," she corrected him.

Mark squinted. "Is it?"

"Shove off, as in push."

Mark squinted again. "What even is a mortal coil?"

"I don't— Each time we've arrived, there's been some story behind it, hasn't there? However little of one, all we get to see is how these people die. What if he was helping somebody?"

"Helping who?" Mark asked. "A cartel? Bank robbers? I don't suspect there are police standing at his side with handcuffs on his wrist because *he* was wronged."

"But what if he was, though?" Emma asked. "Some kind of vengeance tale, where he gave up everything, his freedom and his future and now his life, to avenge another?"

"What's it matter?" Mark asked. "The whole reason— Look, if Death were here right now, you know he'd lecture us about precisely this." He assumed a deep, demonic voice, not quite like how Death sounded, but in the spirit of the horseman's foreboding mannerisms. "Knowing people makes you closer to them and makes it harder to take their life. It's your duty, do not think anything of it."

"Oh, I know all that," she said, "but still—"

"'I know all that' is basically the ending of that statement," he said. "If you know all of it, then there's nothing left to say."

"But there is still something to say," she said, "because what if—"

"I don't think I want to hear this," he said.

"What if we had the choice," she started, and Mark closed his ears and started humming, "to let him live a little longer to do what must be done?"

"What would that be?"

"Well, perhaps he's innocent?"

Mark squinted at her again. "It's because he looks like a boy-band member, isn't it?"

"OR..." she said defensively. "Or, perhaps he is guilty, and death is no way out for him. Give him enough sand to get him through the trial or longer. Or maybe he can explain himself better – I don't know. I just don't want to be waiting around wondering why this one and not the tens of others on this floor who are sick and just waiting for their turn next."

"Well, if you want to risk that," Mark said. "But you're risking not only intruding into Death's abode but also stealing a resource of his we were not given lightly, to pervert a very important part of the cycle of life on a whim because we can. Look, I'm all for taking some office supplies for myself. I've done it. All those sticky notes and reams of printer paper that just appeared in the flat? I didn't buy them. My chair? No one was using it. That's harmless. That's okay. That we can do. If we really hate someone, we can chop them up and tell them it's procedure. Easy, simple. But now consider this – that's still us doing our jobs, as expected, without a hitch. It's just us doing the job. If we don't do the job, then what?"

"...Right," she said. She gave it an extra second of thought and waited for Mark to catch up to her. "Exactly. Then what? We do it Death's way or... what?"

"Well, he'll chuck us in the river."

"But that's breaking the rules," she said.

"He's the boss," Mark said. "He can break the rules. That's how power works."

Emma scoffed and walked through the nurse's station desk in a huff.

"I don't like it either, but that's *how* it *goes*."

It was about then that they noticed they were out of time. The colours in the hospital faded, which didn't look too different from normal. It had been mostly whites and greys to begin with, but a few signs changed, and all the scrubs on the nurses and orderlies running by went greyscale.

The man in the room emerged from his own body and looked around. He patted himself down and rolled his wrist around in his palm before he caught sight of the first reaper out in the hall: Mark. He and Mark locked eyes. The man was fearful for a second, then softened up and walked forward.

"Hey, my man," Thomas said, very suave and friendly. Emma immediately hid in the neighbouring room to watch. Thomas extended his hand, then retracted it. "Uh, well, I guess it's a bit late for that, right?"

"A bit," Mark said. He shook hands anyway.

"Ah, still flesh and blood," Thomas remarked. "I thought I'd be touching a skeleton."

"Not this time," Mark said. "Thomas Berringer, I have come to take you to the next world. To your new eternity. Your time has run out, and you—"

"Yeah, but uh," he began, "that's kind of a problem for me, actually."

"Yeah," Mark said. "Death is a problem for most people. The final problem. The last of any they ever have."

"Well, it's not a problem for *me* exactly," he admitted. "given what I was about to go in for. Some trumped up charges to keep a man away from his woman. This plot runs deep, man. I'm telling you – you might even know already. All seeing, all knowing Death that you are. You must know who's really to blame for all this."

"Hmm," Mark hummed. He didn't. His argument with Emma had been exactly about how much they didn't know about those they came to reap, which he was okay with as it streamlined the job. But he wanted to see just how right he was.

"I cannot bring you back to life," Mark said. "It cannot be

done. But if you have anyone you want to see before you go, anything you need to know is happening, then perhaps..."

Thomas bent his head and clapped his hands together. It was good enough for him. Hopefully, it would be good enough for Emma as well...

CHAPTER TWENTY-TWO

Mark rode on his Shetland – a grim and intimidating horse of the afterlife, as he assured his passenger – over the many urban roads and alleys in the stark, grey world of the final faded moment of life. Thomas Berringer had been given a send-off unlike any other, to be pardoned and professed to by the ghost of his Christmas future. But he'd got his gift many months early. Nearly half a year early, in fact.

Emma, meanwhile, caught on to Mark's plan and followed him from below, where a horse should be, suitably far behind the pony so she could see but not be seen. Thomas was too taken in by the sight of London from above to really pay much mind anyway.

"This is amazing, bruv," Thomas said. He held on with a tight grip of his thighs so his arms could spread out and catch the phantom breeze in the unmoving air. "What a way to travel, eh?"

"It gets the job done," Mark said. "Speaking of which, where to?"

"Harlesden," he said. He pointed, roughly, to an area north-west of where they were. Mark veered the pony off from their path out of the hospital. He decided to see just what the end of Thomas's story could have been, to extrapolate from what he could see and find on his own, and then rub it in Emma's face if it turned out to be something really bad. Otherwise, it would serve as a good way to waste time and prove that their efforts would be better spent simply taxiing the spirits they found with as little interaction as possible.

Mark's main fear was about the sand in their own hourglasses, still unseen but ever present like a broken clock one tick away from the midnight of their whole creation. If they were faffing about when their time ticked over, he imagined it would serve to undo a lot of the grace and goodwill they'd gained. The pony was not a living pony; it was one from the afterlife. If they belonged to neither world, what would become of him?

Those last grains of sand, as long as they remained stuck, were the only barrier preventing Mark from becoming a soul himself. As long he remained flesh and bone and performed his deathly duties well, there was a chance – albeit an infinitesimally small one – that he would be returned to Earth.

Mark was keenly aware that he was still in his own body. Thomas wasn't. Their physical interactions were part of a sort of uniqueness to their situation. Thomas was a pure spirit who could probably learn to come and go as he pleased if he were inclined to do so. But lost in a single moment of time, the damage he was capable of would be minimal. One problem spirit would constitute a write-up. Their apprenticeship was on the line.

"Down there." Thomas pointed. "That building, right there."

"The flats?"

"First one on the corner, next to the park."

Mark flew down and landed just outside a block of flats. They were brutalist, former council-owned, and now worth just shy of a million quid each. "Run-down" was a kindness to give to them.

Some kids were outside – young teens who looked like they'd finished trading punches and now reclined on the curb to take a breather before continuing. Whole wardrobes' worth of clothes were hung on lines and bannisters on the window balconies which were sealed up with iron grates.

It looked like a place a man like Thomas, with his tattoo sleeves and death by police guard, would have come from. But he was human. He had his circumstances. Mark just assumed they were terrible and wanted to prove it. Emma made her assumption and wavered, but stuck to fulfilling her own invasive curiosity. She had the power to learn, so why not?

Thomas walked right into the open front door of the block of flats. He went up to the third floor and approached a door. His hand slipped through the handle. He leaned against the door, semi-defeated until Mark caught up to him.

Mark tapped on the door, which unlocked it. Then he held onto Thomas by the shoulder. "With me," he said.

He wasn't sure it would work. And if not, he planned to save face by swinging his scythe and dispatching Thomas, throwing the bits into the sack and straight off to Limbo for a chance to put the kettle on, crack open the custard creams, and flop on one of Death's recliners.

But it did work, and they were both inside the cramped flat where a woman leaned over the back of a chair with a cigarette in her mouth, watching the television.

The flat had seen better times. The crevices where the floor met the wall were all dirty, and most of the skirting board was missing. Cobwebs hung in blind corners, the lampshades were all a shade of nicotine yellow but had probably originally been baby blue. The carpet was torn and threadbare and exposed a whole row of floorboards where the landlord just didn't bother to replace it, and had turned it into a feature walkway instead. The kitchen sink was stacked with dishes, and shards of glass had been shoved under the stove, which had only one working burner left as the rest were all broken.

"She cleaned the place up," Thomas said. "Heh. Had a hell of a row in here."

Mark remained neutral and quiet, but the scene was slowly developing. He caught sight of Emma outside the window. She parked her horse in the air and sort of climbed down the side to get an angle through the window without being seen.

Thomas, as a spirit, circled around behind the woman. "Vetti," he whispered. "Can you hear me?"

"She can't," Mark interrupted. "Your presence can no longer affect this world."

Thomas backed away and nodded. Then he glanced Mark's way. "But yours can." Mark squinted at him. "You opened the lock, yeah? That thing you got... It must come in handy." He walked towards Mark, with a bit of a bounce in his step. Like they were besties and he just wanted to ask a cheeky little favour. "I bet you can open all sorts of things with that."

"I can," Mark said, unconsciously moving the scythe further away. "But only I."

"Is that right?" Thomas said with a sarcastic sort of nod. "Aren't you a lucky one, then? None for anyone else. All that power just for you."

"...Yes," Mark agreed. "I brought you here so you could see her, one last time. That is the only solace I can give you until sometime in the future, when you may yet manage to see her again."

Thomas nodded. He put his hands in his pockets and gave a pained, stiff smile. He feigned acceptance. Then dove for the scythe. Mark backed up into the breakfast counter. Thomas grappled with him and the tattered parts of his robe slipped off. Mark retreated until his back hit the wall next to the stove. Thomas held him by the throat and tried to punch him. The blows weren't harmful; he didn't suffer or feel a thing, except for a sharp, cold breeze which faded into his skin. It was like a refrigerator was coughing on him.

When Thomas realised his blows were futile, he went directly for the scythe itself. He gripped it with both hands. To Mark's surprise, the ghost's grip was solid. It was a spiritual entity, a ghostly implement from the other world. Mark's body was immune to spirits, as it had ever been, but the scythe and his robes were not. And his pony probably wasn't either! The ghost managed to twist the scythe out of Mark's hands and yanked it away.

"No!" Mark screamed. How had he been so stupid? Not listening to advice from others was one thing. Not listening to your own advice was unforgivable. To prove a point to Emma, to earn some points in an imaginary tally, he had risked everything and come up short. There was no explaining this away as an accidental mistake to Death. There was no "I'm just finding my feet, I won't make the same mistake twice" get-out clause... What Mark had done contravened pretty much the entire list of absolute no-nos in one single reaping.

Thomas pointed the blade right at him.

"Can't use it, eh?" he said. A sudden madness took over him – or rather, the veneer of a pleasant, cheeky chappy was finally cast aside, revealing the mad lad he'd always been. "Just like that copper said before I took his telescopic baton and shoved it down his throat! Just like my partner told me – "That shiv's not for you, Tommy! That girl's not yours, Tommy! She belongs to someone else!" Well, it's MINE now! It's in MY hands! That means it belongs to me! It does, it did, she is, and she WILL!"

Thomas held the scythe up, triumphant, ready to swing.

Mark steadied himself against the wall, fists clenched, leg muscles tensed. Mark was not only cross with himself, but he was furious that this horrible scrote had the audacity to take advantage of his goodwill. In any other scenario, he'd be paralysed with fear, well aware of the damage the scythe would do to him. But anger – the absolute rage Mark felt – overrode any wish to cower or squirm. Instead, Mark launched himself forward, ready to tear his adversary's limbs off with his bare hands—

Thomas's head popped off and fell behind him. His body stuck and stiffened with fear, as he stared up from the floor at the carefully placed boot on his forehead. Emma had entered through the balcony window and denied Mark the opportunity to get medieval on his ass.

Mark retrieved his scythe and tipped the body over. Emma stepped back and let Thomas's back bury his face against the floor.

"I guess this," Emma said, "is why we shouldn't get involved in the prior lives of the deceased."

"I don't think they'll all be murderers," Mark said. His hands were still shaking with adrenalin.

Emma nodded. "Maybe the ones handcuffed to beds though..."

"If they've been judged already, let's agree to just go on with that judgement? If we're wrong—"

"We don't judge anybody," Emma said. "For all we know, that's what gets handled over the river."

"Right," Mark said. "That's exactly what it is – and we shouldn't ask again about it."

"I'm not the one who brought him out here," Emma reminded him.

"Right. Leave it a mystery," Mark said. They both nodded and sighed. Then Mark gave the body a tap with his foot. "We need to ask for a bigger sack."

CHAPTER TWENTY-THREE

F ive down, ninety-five to go.

Mark and Emma returned to the plains of purgatory, reassembled Thomas, and left him with nothing but the outline of the river in the distance to guide him to his fate with Charon. He remained silent while they worked. Apparently, the loss of his final revenge, and about 75% of his previous body mass, was enough to quiet him down.

They'd agreed that it was easier to keep their heads down and mouths shut and go to work. To live in death the way they lived in life.

But that thought lasted from their take-off until they returned through the portal. It soured and went rotten in a record short time. The prospect of an eternity of inconvenient servitude just wasn't appealing. So, they agreed on some concessions as they made their way to their next quarry.

"One," Emma said. "We should always take the scenic routes. See what we can of the parts of the UK we've never been to while we have the chance."

"Two," Mark added. "Don't get involved in ghost drama, no matter how compelling. Death is death. It's time to move on."

"Three," Emma continued. "Judge not. There is no right or wrong. Death is the end. Punishment is not in our control."

"Four," Mark said, wagging his finger. "If they really deserve punishment, cut them up and put them in the sack."

"And take a rough ride home," Emma nodded.

"And a scenic one, if possible!".

"Really let them stew in their own body parts to think about what they did."

Mark chuckled. "Okay, five. Uh... No racing the trains."

"Why not?"

"Okay, good point."

"Do we need a fifth addendum?" she asked. "I think we've covered all the important bits already."

"Oh!" Mark exclaimed. He held up his hand to get her attention. "Five: If there is a... compromising situation, involving the presence, or lack, of clothing, we each handle what... matches with us. Agreed?"

Emma nodded solidly. "Good thinking. Because what I'd hate to have to do is walk into the bedroom of some man who stroked out while he was stroking out, possibly also having a stroke, and maybe a yank."

"And I feel the same way," Mark said. "Exactly the same. About walking in on naked women. But I think it's less awkward and less confrontational if we keep to our own sexes."

"Yes, agreed," Emma said. She tapped on the side of the hourglass and examined the name – Shahir bin al Marik. "We've gotten lucky so far with people who speak English, but what if they don't?"

"Are we not speaking some kind of... directly-into-their-mind, universal language sort of thing?"

"I don't know," she admitted. "I'm not sure. We need a system. In fact, maybe it's best if we don't talk at all? Everyone so far has recognised us as Death – at least enough that they don't really question what's going on."

"Just a wave and then point them to the horse," he suggested.

"Yes!"

"Which will work very well for you, because you're not inviting them onto a pony."

"Well, yeah."

"Oh!" Mark exclaimed. "I just thought of number six."

"Six? Really? If we want any more than we may as well work up to thirteen."

"Why thirteen? Anyway, this one, I think, is good. But it's complex so hear me out." He took a breath and organised his thoughts before they all left his mouth in the wrong order. "So, no one is happy about dying, right?"

"No, never."

"Even if it's by choice, we can't assume they will be happy."

Emma nodded slowly.

"So, they might not want to go with us," he said.

"That would be a problem."

"In those cases," he explained, "we need to start being open. So, the way it should go is, we show up, tap scythe on ground" – which he did – "show we mean it, and point them to the steed. I'll be a bit more insistent about it, make it clear that I don't like it any better than them, and then just get on our way. If they need some comfort, like they don't believe it's real or have a breakdown, then we can talk, but we can't tell them everything. We just need to tell them the minimum to get them onto the horse. We only cut people up if they attack us or try to steal our scythes or something. Trust me, if someone is crying, flailing, pounding on your chest, it doesn't hurt. And they probably just need a good cry from... you know, the dying."

"Right."

"And we can talk to them, and hear them out if it's what gets them to come with us."

"So, just in case of an emergency," Emma said, "be empathetic and treat them like a human?"

"Yes. Otherwise... off with their head."

"Daily grind."

"Daily grind," he sighed.

The world went grey, signalling to them that their well-spent time was over, and their duty had to begin immediately.

"Right," Mark said. "Off we go."

Mark and Emma found their target in the street. His neck was crooked in a way that looked terribly wrong at the bottom of some concrete stairs. His spirit was some distance away. Emma's hourglass compass only pointed to the body, highlighting a whole new problem if a soul decided to go on a bit of a wander.

Mark went over first, a dark spectre with a cute pony and absolutely no emotion. Shahir, an Arab man with a thick beard and cap over his head, looked at Mark with fear and disdain before shouting at him. Unfortunately, it was in a language Mark didn't know, which immediately led to Mark doubting his theory about them now speaking some sort of ethereal Esperanto. Shahir shouted again, seeming angry, but there was still nothing Mark could latch on to.

Then Shahir turned and fell to his knees. He went down on his hands and bowed in prayer. Mark stood still, unsure how to manage the situation. He turned to Emma, who waited nearby, behind a tree. She urged him to go forward. He nodded and stepped up to the man, waiting for Shahir to grow quiet until all that transpired between them was his heavy breathing against the pavement.

"You are dead," Mark said. Shahir looked up, tears in his eyes, and Mark nodded.

"No," Shahir said. His mouth moved differently from the words Mark had heard. And he heard it in a monotonal, sort of automated phone-system voice. "This cannot be. This is not what I have practised. You are not the hand to take me."

"I cannot help you," Mark said. "I can only guide you."

Shahir's head sunk in defeat. He got up and paced around, rubbed his eyes, and struggled very visibly with what he faced. He looked Mark in the eyes with extreme intensity and was clearly now shouting again – though Mark only heard a stable robotic monotone. "My life was not spent in vain. It was not. I swear it."

Mark put his hand on Shahir's shoulder. "No life is spent in vain."

Shahir's lip quivered. He leaned in and embraced Mark. Mark had always been partial to a good hug, and willingly leaned in to reciprocate, patting him on the back. It was like slapping the surface of a tub of water, but he endured. He held Shahir over his shoulder the whole way to the pony, which made Shahir laugh. Then he saddled up and the two were away, into the sky. Emma came in from above and managed the portal. From there, the rest was down to process. Shahir wandered off into the void to find those of his faith, convinced that his land was not across the river but somewhere in the desert of dead belief.

"Okay," Mark said. "So, as a test case, that was pretty good. Sort of. We can speak other languages, and if the spirit isn't near the body..."

"That's a good reason to get to them *before* the world goes dark," Emma said. "Probably a point Death would want to stress."

"Which goes against point one, about sightseeing."

"Oof, yeah."

"We really need to grind this out faster."

"That was good though."

"Hmm?"

"'No life is in vain,'" she repeated. "'I can only guide you.' Look at you, wise guardian spirit of the afterworld. So sage." She tugged on his robe playfully. Mark nodded a little at the compliment. His pale makeup turned just a tiny bit pink. "What movie did you hear that from?"

Mark laughed. "I didn't! No! I wouldn't do that!"

"Seven: No quoting movies," Emma said.

"What if they're a big fan? They died wearing a promotional T-shirt and I know who their favourite character is and loads of cool quotable lines?"

"Only for children," she said, "as an extension of point six."

"What about man-children?"

"They get the sack, always."

"That's fair."

Six down. Finally, the apprentices were getting into the swing of things. The game of life and the job of death were well within their grasp.

CHAPTER TWENTY-FOUR

D eath's apprentices were out and about doing his duty unto the mortal plane, which left him with a bit of time to spare and think and waste away. Not liking that feeling of wasting, he decided to entertain some company as he did once every so often. A game of poker, one of the old games passed along in eras past, that led to all sorts of troubles he could enjoy with those who had such similar duties.

War, Pestilence, and Famine joined him. A four-hand game was easier to manage and settle than five. That, and Charon was averse to betting – practically allergic, in fact. Even cashless chips, tendered with faith and good times as the only fiat behind them, were too much for Charon to part with.

At Death's cottage, poker was always a pleasant affair. Partly, it was the collegiate humour, and partly, it was the thrill and possibility of the winner taking all. But mainly, it was because Veronique used it as an excuse to flex her culinary skills – particularly her patisserie knowledge – resulting in a smorgasbord of home-baked delectables.

War appeared in a prim and proper pantsuit, which hung off her nobly sturdy frame. She always had the same smug look of victory, no matter what hand she drew, and had no clear tells but never went all in. Pestilence came with a scarf, which muffled an occasional clearing of his throat. He was all symptoms when he was diseased with a stricken hand, so quiet from him usually meant he was holding something good. Famine was always lacking in royal cards but often raised hard when holding low pairs. And Death drew nothing but dead hands.

They were all conveniently at the mercy of the river and flops to determine the course of their game. Despite a decades-long streak of hapless luck, Death dressed appropriately. He wore dark sunglasses over his empty eye sockets and hid his skeletal face at all times. He sported his Walkman headphones, the threadbare orange ear-cushions incongruous against his inky black cowl. His hollow skull acted as a speaker so that they could all enjoy his well-worn Wham! cassette tape. It took a lot of reading to see whether he was smiling or not without any lips. Overall, it was merely a game of fun and chance. No one walked away a loser unless they felt like one. And none of them did.

Famine cut the cards and began to shuffle the deck – the usual suits had been replaced with Skulls, Swords, Flies, and Blood.

"I tell ya," Pestilence began, "I'm feeling a new epoch coming on."

"How so?" Famine asked.

"There's these stories I'm hearing," he began, reaching for an itch under his scarf, "about clinical trials breaking through with new discoveries, and labs worldwide stepping up genetic research. They're trying to decode and reprogramme bacteria found in wild animals to reverse the effects in humans. Apothcaries are taking off. Might be another industrial-style revolution if it keeps up – a *pharmalution*. I don't know if I can keep up with it without going bottom-up mad."

"What's the harm in it?" War asked.

"Well, it'd be too much," he said matter-of-factly. "Too many dead, not enough suffering. Dead's not my goal, all things considered."

"Indeed," Death said. "A modern plague would lead, mostly, to a harrowing of the elderly and the slow drip of their lives through the sieve of genetic propensity. But target the young, and there'll be none left after to take up a new sickness in full bloom."

Famine dealt each player two cards.

"At least you have something to do," Famine said. "Food production and stockpiles are always going up. So much so that people are now throwing food away. Thank goodness for that; it's the only good news I get from day to day. Can you imagine! Just tonnes and tonnes left to rot and waste – but it's only because people can't eat it fast enough."

They all peeked at their cards.

"There's always someone," War said, "who's not getting enough." She pushed a healthy stack of chips towards the pot. "I'm calling."

"Not before I raise," Famine said.

"Hmph," Death huffed with a call.

Pestilence sniffled and grunted. "Is it getting colder out there, by the way?"

"It's not cold or hot," Death said. "It's nothing. Any perception in Limbo is one carried over."

"Yeah," Pestilence said, "but it feels colder."

"Maybe the river is rising," War said. "That hasn't happened in... ever, but it could be."

"Too many damned souls swimming for it," Famine said.

"Trudging along the bottom, making a dam wall to block the water. A damned dam."

"Unlikely," Death said. "Though Charon is lacking in passengers. I wouldn't be surprised if the waters are rising to claim the whole shore, leaving no trace of the souls left to wander."

"Was it always like that, Limbo?" War asked.

"I've been around longer than all of you," Death said. "By uncountable moments. Before man conspired to war, learned of sickness, or starved themselves on the hunt. Only the rise of society brought us together, but this place has always been the treading ground of the doomed, and back then, the waters were shallow enough for the steel-hearted to go wandering to the other side on their own."

"Poor them," War said. "Kept company now by only those who never had to dirty their feet in so much as a muddy puddle."

"Don't pity the dead that have already crossed over," Death said. "They've escaped that fate."

All eyes turned to Pestilence, who still had an itch he couldn't get rid of. "Oh, uh, I fold."

"Ha!" War scoffed. "What a shame." She laid down her cards. She had a pair of queens to beat out Famine's queen-high.

Eyes turned to Death. He grunted and laid his cards down.

"Well, that's a keeper," Pestilence said.

"Oh," War gasped, when she saw Death's hand.

"No pity for that," Famine remarked.

"A Flush," Death uttered. "All skulls."

"The deck likes you for once," War said. "That's the first winning hand I've seen you draw in aeons."

"This game isn't quite aeons old," Death said matter-of-factly as he picked up the pot. "Though it is nice to see a good hand once in a while." He shuffled the cards and prepared to deal the next hand.

Pestilence coughed. "Sorry. Excuse me, carry on."

"Are you festering some new bug inside yourself?" War asked.

"Uh, maybe," he said. "Truth is, I've been tempting myself with some new projects. I'm up in the air on a couple of them – as in, I'm trying to get them airborne."

"Are you finally planning to go for it?" Famine asked. "Put the whole world out of order?"

"No," Pestilence sighed. "The living ruined all those plans when they glimpsed a prophetic dream in my own conscious mind for an airborne rabies and made all those gory awful zombie movies. Now everyone's got zombie survival paranoia, and they're all prepared to deal with it. Anything that can be cured with a bullet won't work."

"America stands firm," War said proudly, tapping her chest with a clenched fist. She leaned back and winced immediately, rubbing whatever soreness she was feeling in her shoulder.

"Too firm?" Famine asked. He reached for another homemade pastry on the tray between him and Death – one of the many he'd eaten, more than anyone else that evening.

"War's become too static," she said. "All vehicles and drones, cyberwarfare, and such. No one's getting up and running around with swords, spears, and bows like the good old days. Now I'm throwing my back out learning software code to keep up with how people have learned to hurt each other. You used to have to take a sturdy mallet to an ankle to hobble a man... now you just need to block his internet access."

"Such wars without dying," Death said, "have no glory. No meaning."

"But plenty of wealth to be made," War said. "The ideals of the past have been traded off for stocks and shares. The beliefs people held – which some still do – are no longer worth their life in high numbers. There is worth, most certainly, but I've found

the resolve so very lacking lately. The primal needs are all sated."
She turned to Famine. "Which isn't upsetting me quite as much as
it might you."

"Eh." Famine rocked his head back and forth. "A crash will
come. When the humans look at themselves and then back to the
planet and ask where and how they will raise the food they need to
feed so many, the starving will begin. And the planet, too, shall
starve with them." He filled his mouth with pastry, and all the
custard oozed out to fill his cheek. "The deserts are my friends in
this era. You'll see. Resistance is futile. Water will be the next
gold."

"But they will try to resist," Death said. He dealt out the cards,
two for each of them, and then carefully laid the flop, the turn,
and the river cards down the middle of the table. "And more often
than not, they shall succeed."

"That's a shame," War said.

The first card was a five of Skulls. The second was a four of
Bloods. The bets were placed around the table: War raised. Famine
called. Death raised. Pestilence called, keeping himself in the mix.
Death turned over the river – the six of Swords. Another round of
calls and raises. Everyone was still in, and everyone felt confident.
All hands were revealed.

Death won, with a king-high. No one had so much as a pair,
each and every one of them holding out for the straight. It was a
bad hand all around, a dead round. Death took the quite consider-
able pot and if a lipless skull could be said to smile, it was smiling
now. He passed the shuffled deck to Pestilence to cut.

"Don't mark your cards again," Death warned.

"Hey! What? No," Pestilence protested. "That was unin-
tentional."

"Why else would you bring fleas here?" War asked. "And then
conveniently leave them on the card?"

"It worked once for me," Famine said. "Marking the cards with blood."

"Yeah, that's what made the fleas act up," Pestilence said, hands up in innocence. "You're the one who started it – I'm just the one who got caught."

CHAPTER TWENTY-FIVE

The echo of gunfire. There was major panic in the streets. Civilians running in every direction.

Revellers poured out of pubs and restaurants to see if there was anything worth filming on their phones and quickly started running too – unsure what from, and in which direction it was best to head. Mark and Emma arrived just in time to hang out overhead and watch the pandemonium below. In seconds, the street went from busy Friday night to deserted.

They heard the wail of sirens.

"Really?" Mark said. "Are we in the States suddenly?"

"No, look. That's the Arndale," Emma said, pointing to the expansive roof of the shopping mall. "Sad to say we're right where we need to be... Manchester."

"Joy," Mark said. "Gun crime."

"Yes, yes," Emma said. "Well, we're not criminal prosecutors, we're reapers. We just need to find who got shot and take them across."

The two descended to the ground to analyse the situation.

Sirens announced the police were on their way. A man in a black knit cap and jacket stood with a gun in his hand over two bodies huddled down to shield a little girl against the side of a wall. The gunman held a handbag close to his chest – not in and of itself incongruous, thought Mark, as he himself was quite partial to the practicality of a man-bag, but the sparkling diamante clasp was a dead giveaway that it was stolen, and the likely true owner was lying dead at his feet. The man's eyes darted back and forth. He took a position under the stone overhang of a nearby porch and a long-forgotten iron lantern decoration.

Everything stopped right around the moment the police cars screeched around the corner into view. The soul Mark and Emma came to fetch was in fact two souls: the lives of the parents who'd protected their daughter. Fortunately – or not, depending on how they looked at it – it was just them. The girl was unharmed.

"Oh no," the girl's father said. "No. Olivia!"

"Olivia!" the mother shouted. They looked at one another in their spectral forms. They stood over their own bodies, limp and dead, but still huddled together, protective of the girl cowering on the pavement.

Emma and Mark were silently aghast as the dead couple started to cry. They had a very difficult job ahead of them. Mark turned Emma away and pulled her in for a private whisper. "I don't like this one."

"We need to get some lines ready," she said, "because they will be inconsolable the whole trip back if we can't convince them it's for the better."

"It's better that they're dead?"

"No, look," she insisted. "Don't go to their level. Okay? No sympathy. Just work."

"Right, yeah," he agreed, "but still – this is a mess." Mark looked up at the robber. He was hunkered down, protected by the stone doorway, gun up, ready to keep fighting and killing. "And we need to convince them to move on right next to the chav twat that did them in. Will that go well, you think?"

"Oh, yeah," Emma said. "Uh... you ought to block him from sight."

"Just stand here like a wall?" he asked. "Just put my arms out so they can't see past me?"

"Yeah, something like that," she said, and he gave her a look. "No, it'll work. They won't pay attention to you. They'll be too grief-stricken and fearful for their daughter and whatnot to question your presence."

"Right," he said. "Use their daughter's survival against them. That's good."

"I've got this." Emma patted Mark on the shoulder.

They had their plan, and they were sticking to it. Emma turned to the still-grieving parents while Mark stood over the criminal, yet to be apprehended, and cast a spiteful glare down at the man.

The mother and father held one another in their astral forms. When they noticed the hovering figure of Emma with her scythe at the ready, the father immediately put himself before his wife. "Please," he began, "if you must take someone, take me. But if it's at all possible, let my wife live."

"Peter, no," she wept.

"And our daughter," he said. "Our daughter... She— she must live, no matter what."

Emma looked down. The daughter was safe. No bullets were able to penetrate her, and she barely had a speck of her parents' blood on her blouse. She just sat, head tucked into her knees, hands over her ears, in pensive fear, waiting for the bad times to end. Emma looked back up into Peter's eyes. He was resolute and uncompromising. He had it in him to be a sacrifice, no matter what, which made taking him all the easier. But fate had decided on both.

"You both must move on," she said.

Peter huffed up a great breath like he was about to pounce, but his wife held him from behind.

"Peter," she began, "I'm sorry."

"What?" he said, deflated and defeated. "Jen, no. You haven't done anything."

"We're dead because of me," she said. "If I'd... if I'd just given him the bloody bag sooner—"

"No, don't be stupid," he insisted. "It was my fault. I riled him up. I threw the first punch, remember? It made him desperate. I didn't know he had a gun! I thought I'd just solved it, right then."

"But we're only here because of me," she said. "I thought it would be nice to go for a walk as a family. Stupid, really. It's all my fault!"

"No, it can't be," he said.

Jen started to cry into his chest, and he just cradled her there while he looked into the middle distance mournfully. Emma tapped her scythe to the ground. It resonated with a loud clang, like a brassy bell had given its final toll.

"We cannot stay," Emma insisted. She pointed to her horse, which was spacious enough for them both. "There is no time."

Peter's mouth sputtered. He turned to Olivia immediately. "Can she hear us?"

"N—" But Emma couldn't quite bring herself to trample on their obvious hopes. She sucked in a breath and rolled her head back. "Only briefly," she lied. "Make it count."

The couple went on their knees next to their daughter, past their bodies, to take one ear each and whisper things to her. Emma turned around to Mark for a bit of moral support. She was taken aback when he gave her a bit of a judgemental look, just a slight one. He was right, of course. Her own bloody rules. And she'd broken them. It was so much easier to imagine how you'd react to a theoretical situation. Now, faced with a dead couple, who were clearly the victims of circumstance with the perpetrator just yards away, it wasn't so clear cut.

Death had warned them not to get involved. She'd heard the words but not really listened. Deep down, she thought they had been for Mark's benefit rather than her own. She had a job to do and was determined to deliver excellence. The reward for success? Help to cross the river and passage to the afterlife she had yearned for. Just do the job. No drama, no complications. In, out, onto the next one. She should have been hastening the couple, escorting them to the banks of the river. There was no time for idle, point-less chatter.

Emma had been as surprised as Mark when she took a step back to let them give words of encouragement to their daughter.

"Daddy will always love you," Peter whimpered. "Forever. You're the reason I lived, and as long as you live, daddy will be happy."

"Mommy is so sorry, darling," Jen whispered. "Sorry she can't be there to watch you grow up. But she'll always be watching over you. So please, *please* do your best."

"Do your best, love," Peter added. They tried to go in for a hug. Their ghostly tears traced down little Olivia's cheeks. Emma was as uncomfortable as she'd ever been and turned away from the scene, her own eyes beginning to well up.

"What is it?" Mark asked.

"You ever feel so awkward that your insides shift around a bit, and it makes you feel sick?"

"Oh, please don't," he said.

"I can't help it," she said. "I got this way at my grandmother's funeral. People thought I was sobbing. I was choking back *puke*."

"I can't trade jobs now," he said. "I can't fit them both on the pony."

Emma sighed, and her breath caught in her throat. She sighed it out and strode forwards behind the mourning couple. "Now," she said, low and sudden. The parents got up and walked ahead of her towards the horse without another word.

While she mounted up, Mark looked up at the decorative lantern overhead, then down at the criminal directly beneath its spiked bottom. He looked over to the girl who was still within his sights, surrounded by the bodies of her forever silent guardians.

Mark stepped back, took his scythe, and yanked the blade through the lantern chain. A brief crackle of energy surrounded it. Then, something shifted slightly in the suspended moment, and the chain became loose.

When Mark took off after Emma, time resumed as normal. The weight of the lantern snapped what remained of the chain and caved in the head of the gunman before the police had left their vehicles. Mark touched back down on his pony.

Just a moment later, the thief came to and looked up in a greyscale-filtered fog. A grim man in dark robes stood over him with a bladed crook in one hand and a sack in the other.

"Who're you supposed to be?" the robber asked.

"You can ride on the horse," Mark said, "or you can ride in here." He shoved the sack forward.

"I can't fit in that," the robber said.

Mark tapped the handle of his scythe to the floor. "You don't have to," he said.

And so he brought the third, somewhat unexpectedly, dead soul back with him in the sack and took some careful time reassembling him on the river's shore, far from the recently deceased delivered on Emma's steed.

CHAPTER TWENTY-SIX

Things moved slowly in the land of the dead. Without judgment and consequence, the realm between worlds was only as busy as the horsemen could make it look with their intermittent visits to and from the living world. While Death reaped, War employed subterfuge and devilish voices to infect the consciousness of otherwise kindly men to take up arms against their brothers. Pestilence mainly kept his own company, trialling new cultures in a live environment and keeping fastidious notes on their efficacy. And then there was Famine, who mostly stayed at home, but still called upon the infrequent aid of the only other homesteader in Limbo.

Veronique rode over on the back of one of Death's many stable-steeds, eager to see another side of her infrequent house guest. Famine's home was a first-floor apartment above a bespoke all-you-can-eat buffet restaurant. He lived where the food was, and there was always food there. He ate what humans couldn't, and indulged in the rarest things that were effectively no longer able to be eaten on Earth.

Famine answered the door. He was always fit and well fed, an affront to his very aspect to show that all the food which lacked in his wake went somewhere and to someone, leaving those behind to suffer the rage of jealousy on top of the misery of their hunger and know true despair. Yet he looked thinner to Veronique. Possibly due to answering the door in an old vest and threadbare boxer shorts.

"Ah, hello," he said. "Glad you came."

"It is my pleasure," she said. "Monsieur Death has been in his den all day and forbade me to clean it, yet will not clean it himself. He is mulling, I believe, over Mark and Emma's progress."

"Whom and whom?" Famine asked. "Oh! Those two, yes. They're doing well?"

"Apparently so," she said. "They have come and gone without so much as a rest or cup of tea to fulfil their duty."

"That's good," Famine said. "Uh, well, please come in. I'd like your help if you can manage it."

"I shall do my best," she replied. She walked in and looked around. The buffet was in a sad state. A whole head of a Holstein cow acted as a centrepiece with a Taliaferro apple bushel in its mouth. Around it, the exotic, extinct vegetables and rare fruit sections were all soggy and wilted. Fine Persian grapes that had been picked to death during the advent of winemaking were soured in the wrong way. Strange blueish cauliflower framed miniature Cornish hens that were dry with wrinkled skin. Mammoth meat had grown brownish spots from being left uncooked. Dodo's legs were lopsided in the tray.

"Oh, ignore all that, dear," Famine said. "Just some old collections that I haven't gotten around to yet. What I need help with is in the back, if you please."

"Certainly," she said. She walked past the back counter and into the kitchen. The place was filthy. It set off all her home-making instincts at once. She reached for the nearest towel, but found it was already dirty.

"Ignore the mess, please," he said.

"Are you sure?" she asked.

"Oh, it's nothing I can't fix up later. It's just... um..." His stomach growled. He paused. His entire body and mind seemed to lapse for a moment as he fought off a hunger pang. "Right, yes. Uh, have you heard of ortolan bunting?"

Veronique paused. The state of the kitchen overloaded her senses. "I have."

"It's French, I think," he said. "The food is anyway. And you are French."

"Yes," she said, "but it is an aristocratic food, of sorts. A royale dish made for those who... I am sorry, monsieur, but I must comment on the state of your kitchen."

Famine nodded. "I've neglected it a bit, that's true. But all in the effort of seeking new and old ways alike to indulge in the food culture. Bit by bit and bite by bite, these cultures are lost, and when food stops being eaten, it must therefore find its way to me. Any franchise that dies out, their recipes and ingredients come to me, and I can indulge in that which humanity cannot. It's a decent trade, I'd say, to have an infinite supply of whatever cannot be made or found on Earth. And as these practices die out, I am left to preserve them."

"So, the ortolan is fini?"

"Not yet," he said. "I think it's only a matter of time, and I want to be prepared. I want to know how to make it correctly so that when the species and habits do die out, I can preserve them. Now, I have this..." He reached down into a stainless-steel catering cupboard and pulled out a whole, still-living bird. It was a simple, small-looking bird that had been stuffed fat and could hardly fly. "Uh, this is a type of pigeon, not at all the same, but similar enough that I thought we could practice with it."

"A pigeon?" she said, with a sickened curl to her lip. "Are they not diseased birds?"

"Only the ones in cities," he said. "And only the ones that spend time finishing off doner kebabs from the town centre pavement on a Saturday night. This one—"

As if hearing them insult his living brethren, the bird flapped its wings and went berserk, jumping from counter to counter. Feathers went everywhere. Most of them stuck to whatever stain they touched on every surface. Famine ducked away as the bird lurched towards him. It could only be bound up in parabolas from its weight.

Veronique grabbed a thick pot and swung it down over the bird, trapping it underneath, against the counter. It rustled around underneath for a moment, then all went calm.

"Nicely done," Famine said. "Nicely caught. Energetic little beasts."

"Monsieur," she began, "I should like to clean this place up before we start with cooking."

"But why?"

Veronique sighed. "Cooking cannot commence in a place of forgotten manners or etiquette. Cooking is a culmination of the self and one's environment. We do not simply cook food out of whatever hovel or pit we crawl from, or near any mess we have made. There is a human saying: do not eat where you merde, else you mix the two together. And it goes beyond a hygienic rationale. It is the feeling itself of cleanliness that makes food good. You cook where it is clean, and the food will feel clean and will taste clean. If you cook surrounded by filth, you will cook miserable food."

Famine nodded. "I usually just eat and cook as I please. Maybe that's why I've been constantly hungry lately. I'm not eating right because the environment hasn't been right."

"This dish," Veronique continued, "though we do it wrong, it is a feeling. There are better ways to eat a bird than what we are about to do. But the properness is what gives it the je ne sais quoi of passion."

Famine nodded along with a smile. The two of them went to work and cleaned up the kitchen together. Famine wasn't as passive or obsessively busy as Death. In fact, he was strictly under-worked. Veronique was overjoyed to have a partner to clean with. He held her up like a ballerina to dust and scrub the sticky film-coated spots near the ceiling. She mixed a billow of powerful soap suds to cut through the built-up grime and grease that had congealed into stalagmite crystals over the gas hobs.

They swept through the kitchen, corner to corner, until it shimmered back at them with the proud glare of progress. They scrubbed the pots and pans together and traded soap bubbles. The powerful cleaning agent burned Veronique's eyes and throat, but the playfulness made them giggle past the sudsy combat. Then it was finally time to cook.

Step one was already done; the bird was force-fed and fatty. Step two was the preparation. Famine acquired a bottle of distilled grapes from ancient Georgian vines, a wine some degrees finer and more biting than the Armagnac the recipe called for. Then Veronique drowned the bird alive in the liquid until it no longer moved. Step three was roasting. No garnishing necessary. The feathers fell right off as the well-coated skin glistened with a sticky glaze.

When it was done, the whole bird was served. Famine took out a large butcher's knife – recently cleaned and sharpened – and bisected the bird lengthways to share.

"It's not proper," he said, "but I think this bird's a bit big for just one appetite."

"Merci," she said. The very last step was to don a napkin under their chins and eat the bird in shelter from the watching eyes of God, for the act was so sinful it could turn a saintly man into a monster in His eyes.

"Oh right," Veronique said, as she spat a bit out. "The bird should be much younger."

"Right," Famine said with a sharp crunch of bones between his teeth. "That's what practice is for – it makes perfect. You don't always get it right on the first try."

He continued to eat regardless, bones and all, while Veronique gingerly cut and pried her way around the edible meat. Overall, it was still a very savoury dish, well deserving of Famine's dinner table.

CHAPTER TWENTY-SEVEN

Mark flew down to the riverside with a man in tow. A skittish, uncertain man who looked around at everything in sight with wide, seeking eyes. He was lanky and thin, nearly decrepit. He'd died on remand in prison while awaiting trial. Not at all a good man, but a dead one now, not in need of a horseman's judgement.

"The ferryman will be by soon," Mark said. The man nodded his head, and Mark sped off to take his next job. After a brief wait and a roll of fog against the shore, the boatman Charon idled himself at the water's edge.

"Well," he said, "what have ye to offer me in return for passage across this 'ere river of the damned?"

The man opened his mouth and pulled out a golden trinket from under his tongue. It was a timepiece made of solid gold. The internal parts had stopped working, as all time ceased to matter in the afterlife, but the majority of its composition was wrought and shaped gold. And all gold was gold to Charon. He accepted the watch, rubbed it clean with his sleeve, and chuckled to himself over the bounty while the man slowly loaded himself into the boat.

"We're away then!" Charon cheered. "Steady yourself so as not to spill into the waters, else I'll lose ye to the wash!" He rowed away across the river, finally with company and finally with pay. "Yer the first of too many to render me payment for my service. Too long it's been, and too long it stays, that the hands of the living cling too closely to their alms after death. 'Tis supposed to be a nobler act, to give wealth to he who meets you in death. But that practice is long lost. Tell me why you've done this. What great practice do ye honour to bring this gold to me?"

The man shrugged. "I hid it," he said. "I stole it, so I hid it."

"Did ye not know what favour would be given to you here on this river should you produce a token of passage to the boatman?"

He shrugged again. "No idea," he answered glumly.

Charon smiled. "You knew to do it. Could've hidden it anywhere, but under the tongue is a lauded tradition. You sell your tongue to silence in death, never to speak it again 'til the ferryman takes the toll from your mouth. 'Tis reverence."

"Okay." The man nodded.

Charon grew grim and scowled his way through the rest of the trip. The fog broke away and revealed a new shore, covered in reeds and lilting plants.

"Walk on," Charon said, "'til you find the meeting of the paths, and take the one which you must."

The man got out of the boat and walked ahead, wordlessly, aimlessly, through the shroud of mist. His footsteps were so light the reeds barely bent to him. He was already passing on into an airy form without the weight of guilt or conscience remaining. Charon groaned and took to the current to find his way further along the riverbank where his dwelling lay. He looked at the watch again and forced the glass face off. He used his long fingernails to pluck out everything that wasn't gold or valuable and flicked them into the water without a care, like he was discarding lint from his robe. What remained, he pocketed. All in all, it was a fair reward for services rendered.

His boat knocked against a rickety wooden dock and he shuffled out, chain fixed tight around his ankle, up the well-trodden path to his home. It was made of gold, every surface, layered with coins and bars and trinkets – shimmering pieces fashioned together like haphazard bricks. Every piece of gold he'd collected from aeons back and through the millennia, be they ingots from grateful dead nobles and rulers or incidental offerings from commoners – it all went into this one place: a great hoard like a hillside made entirely of loose gold.

He walked past a few unsteady columns and into a lounge where a Viking king's throne sat, one which the king's corpse had arrived, partially singed from his burial at sea. Many more valuables from long-dead civilizations, mostly from Ancient Egypt, rounded out his living space. He hunched over and sat on the throne, swinging his legs together.

The chain yanked back. He was almost at the very limit of his geographic reach – tied metaphorically and physically to his ferryboat – but not quite. He gave the chain a bit of a tug. The iron links clattered as they were released from a snag on a heavy pole made of various golden rods wrapped of gold cords from some unknown deific burial. The force of the metal chain being pulled rocked part of the wall a bit. Charon groaned and waddled over to fix it up.

"Not enough for a patch job," he said, weighing the watch in hand. "But still good for something." He walked around until he found another spot that needed bolstering, more loose rods and hilts and other implements that were bound together into a column that could hold up a ceiling. He inserted the watch face into a gap between two ornamental golden headdresses, like a brickie might repoint the mortar of a dilapidated garage wall. It wasn't quite a perfect fit, but it would do.

"There we are," he said. He patted his hand on the column, proud of its sturdiness. As soon as he did, the nearby wall was compromised. It started to wobble. Charon watched on, unable to stop it. The gold wall tumbled towards him, into the rest of the building, and spilled out as a lovely landslide, pouring down the hill towards the river. Charon breathed a long sigh of relief as he watched his precious gold come to a stop just before hitting the water.

He shrugged and sat down on the newly loosened pile. It shifted slightly beneath him. It was more solid than not, like lying on a rock that was slowly breaking apart but never stopped being rigid and hard. Unyielding, unchanging, forever static, a permanent asset. Gold was the antithesis of death. Thus, the dead brought it to prove their value in life was something that could pervade their ending. It both proved and disproved death, because gold could not die out. It could only be lost.

Charon moved his arms up and down, like a child making a snow angel, and crowded himself with the wealth like a blanket on all sides. It was all his. No other damned soul needed it. The horsemen were left unconvinced that he had such wealth when he bragged and always protested his obsession. What good was it to have so much wealth he could not spend or transform into something else? They did not understand.

"They'll never understand," he muttered. He picked up a coin and flipped it around in the air above his face. He laced it over and under his knuckles, back and forth. Finger to finger. "How could they?"

Charon absentmindedly rolled the coin around until he felt his fingers tense up. The coin fell and hit him on the nose. He didn't even grunt, he just groaned that he'd lost sight of that specific one and looked around for another to pick up. He ran his hand down through the mound of coins and felt them shift away from his hand like hard water. Then he found one and picked it up, an ancient-minted Ottoman coin from a dynasty countless eras old. He looked it over, both heads and tails, and spun it between his fingers faster and faster.

Until he lost it. He pressed too hard, and the coin flew out of his grip, past the wall, and onto the shaly rocks along the river-bank. Charon shot to his feet and followed it. The coins behind him all shifted and sang with a metallic fall as Charon chased the one coin that bounced against the rocks. He nearly caught up to it and bent over to grab and snatch it out of the air.

But then he was pulled back. The chain at his ankle yanked him away. It was stuck on another golden column of his own making. He could only watch as the coin rolled and bounced just out of reach. It was a hair's breadth from the water but too far to retrieve, with the river's waves lapping against it.

Charon turned and frantically kicked his leg to whip his chain free of whatever bound it. He just needed an inch or two of give to reach it. He strained his whole body to reach over. His finger touched the coin – brief elation – but when he tried to pinch it against the rock and drag it over, it tilted up and shot out of his wet hand into the water with a plop, as the river welcomed its prize into the deep.

"Damn," he groaned. He tugged on his leg again and found that inch he was looking for just a bit too late. He looked scorn-fully at his chains before noticing that they were loose. Some of the links had stretched. Not enough to separate them, but more than ever before...

CHAPTER TWENTY-EIGHT

B ack on the grind, Mark and Emma were set on a course that took them to a hospital, and they braced themselves for whatever might be in store.

They'd been to hospitals before, mostly to take out the elderly or unfortunate victims of happenstance, and it had all gone smoothly. The dead embraced their fate and were usually quite glad to be rid of the suffering of their situation. And they were all adults. This time was different. The hourglass pointed them past the paediatric wing doors, and Mark and Emma shared a worried look as they prepared to enter while the world still had some brightness to it.

"Let's hope," Mark said, "it's a very mature young person who has heard a great deal of talk about how brave they were and how unfortunate their situation was, and that they aren't too fantastical about their chances."

The two of them walked through the ward and saw plenty of children who were close to death but fighting hard against it. Their chances looked good. They'd learned fast not only how to read hourglasses, but also how to gauge the remaining life of someone within a fair span from a distance. Most of the kids there had decent futures ahead. Some were teetering on the balance. They were looking for one who had no time left at all.

And they found them in Paediatric Surgical Recovery.

"It could be," Mark said quietly, "that a doctor or nurse has died. Maybe."

Emma held the hourglass up. The bottom bulb, the fullest and nearly complete with just single grains left to fall, was very shallow. Four-ish years at most. She shook her head slowly as the last grains prepared to drop. They rushed in, past the nurses and the doctors in the corridor – unable to physically bump into them but courteous nonetheless – until the sands within shifted and the hourglass pointed them directly into a room where a group of nurses were gathered around a bed.

They heard a long, steady tone, and then the world went grey.

"We're going to hear that sound so many times," Mark said. At the moment time stopped and the final moment of a life ended, the sounds also retreated, except for their voices and the cry of a whining child. Mark and Emma's eyes met. Neither of them wanted to do it. Emma held up a fist and pumped it forwards twice. Mark shook his head and mouthed "No", but Emma nodded.

Mark had transitioned into his new role with aplomb, even relished many aspects of it, but transporting kids always gave him pause. He wasn't particularly clucky and had little experience with children, save for a quarterly visit to see his six-year-old nephew, Jack.

For Mark, it was about fairness – or the lack of it. An adult has had a chance at life. A chance to make a difference. It might have been a hard or easy life, but they had lived and loved, made mistakes, and hopefully had some fun along the way. Kids hadn't.

Despite his reservations, he knew Emma didn't find it any easier, so they needed to decide who got the short straw this time.

They didn't have any straws, so they played rock, paper, scissors to see who would go in. His paper against Emma's rock – she lost. Mark wasn't happy about winning. No one was a winner here, really. Emma checked her costume, adjusted it to be less risqué, and leaned her scythe against the wall outside. She walked in and looked for the source of the cries.

A little boy, Robert, wandered around the room with his hands clasped together and his mouth muttering and blubbering at light speed. Emma could see he was dead on the bed with the doctors and nurses all aghast around him. They were furious at their raw fate, unable to save the poor boy after all their best efforts. Now the only help he had was in Death's waiting hands.

"Robert?" Emma asked. The boy turned to her. She leaned down and tried to smile for him. "Hello there."

"NO!" Robert shouted. He ran behind one of the doctors and hid.

"R-Robert?"

"No," Robert said again. He tried to cling to the trouser leg of the doctor, but his little hands kept slipping through. "No. Go away!"

"Robert, sweetie?" Emma said. "Um..." She stood up, turned away, and mouthed "What the hell do I say?" to herself.

"No more," Robert groaned. "My tummy's not hurting. I don't want to go. Go away!"

"Your pain is gone?" Emma asked. She leaned down and tried to see him. He ducked around the trouser leg and nodded. "That's good! That means it's time... to go somewhere else."

"No," he said. "Mummy is coming."

Emma couldn't hold her smile together. She stood back up and turned to take a silent scream at the window. She wasn't finding transporting the souls of children any easier than Mark did.

"Mummy said when my tummy doesn't hurt, we can go home," Robert continued. "And she would give me ice cream."

"I— I can get you an ice cream, Robert," Emma said.

He shook his head defiantly. "No! Mummy is getting me ice cream. In my own bed!"

"Robert?" Emma said. "Could you stay here, please? I just need to go and find your mummy. Okay?"

Robert slowly unhid himself and nodded. Emma smiled and backed away into the hallway where Mark was waiting.

"Oh god, I can't do this," she whispered desperately. "Not this."

"I know it's hard," he said, "but—"

"Oh, is it?" she said incredulously. "And you'd know how hard this is? How many kids have you had to coach to accept death and explain that they'll never see their mothers again?"

"Six, compared to your two," he responded immediately. "Not that I'm keeping a tally or anything…"

"I just want to cry and give them a hug." Emma clenched and unclenched her fists as she paced.

"Then do that," Mark suggested. "Get down on their level. Give them a cuddle if you need to, hold them tight and tell them it's going to be okay."

"But it's not going to be okay, is it? They're dead."

"And whatever pain, suffering, or horrible accident that just occurred is over. Forever."

He mimed bending down and picking the child up like he was handling a dog. Emma's mouth and eyes slowly widened.

"I mean, it gets him to where he's going," he said.

"That's the last thing we're doing," she said. "Not for this. If you want to put him in the sack, that'll be up to you."

"Right, okay," Mark said. "I'll do it then." He marched straight into the room. Emma waited around the corner, in no rush to stop him.

Robert was standing on tiptoes, trying to look at his body on the bed.

"Want some help up?" Mark asked. Robert looked up at him uncertainly.

"Who are you?" he asked.

Mark crouched down onto his knees to get close to Robert's level. "Well, I'm Death," he answered.

Mark had been in a similar scenario with his nephew Jack hundreds of times. Kids loved to role-play and the trick was to quickly establish the rules and get on with the game. Silly accents helped too. He'd been various cartoon characters, Jack's teacher, an old man they were following in the supermarket, and more recently – as Jack had got older – famous footballers.

This time though, Mark wasn't pretending. He was Death and he needed to explain who he was and his purpose in a way a four-year-old could comprehend.

Emma bit her lip. Mark continued to give Robert his best good guy smile, though the kid didn't seem to understand the word "Death", as simple as it was.

"Is that your name?" Robert asked.

"Yes," Mark said. "And my job. I come to take people who have died to the next world."

Robert looked back up at the bed. Mark bent forwards and scooped Robert up to lift him enough to see himself.

"Who's that?" Robert asked.

"That's you," Mark said. "I'm afraid you didn't survive the operation. You died."

Robert looked back at his own resting face and the doctors

and nurses, frozen in time all around him. It was starting to make sense slowly.

"Why are they all cross?" he asked.

"Because they tried to save you," Mark said. "They did their very best, but they couldn't."

"Why not?" Robert asked.

Mark sat Robert on the end of the bed to spare his shoulders and bent down to see him eye to eye again. He had a thin film of tears over his eyes already. "It wasn't up to them," he replied. "If it were, you'd be alive because you had the very best nurses and doctors looking after you. But no one can predict these things. It simply happens when it happens. I'm sorry, young man. But..." Mark wiped a tear away. Robert reached out and put a hand on Mark's cheek – to comfort him. Mark looked up and saw the same tears welling up in the boy.

Mark reached his arms out, and Robert went into them. The boy cried, quieter than before, as Mark carried him out to his pony in the A&E reception area. Emma led them both back, all the way through the portal to the river, where Mark set Robert down again.

"You may be here a while," Mark said, "but you're a brave boy, aren't you?"

"Will my mummy come here?" he asked.

"Someday," Mark said. "But until then, you should make friends and be happy, okay?"

Robert sniffled and nodded. Mark waved him off and let the little tyke wander down the river path, out of sight and into the void. Mark turned and breathed a long, shaky sigh. He looked over at Emma, who was still a little shaken and tried to break the tension. "I can do first communions and bar mitzvahs too, if you're interested in making a booking."

Emma broke down into both a laugh and an ugly cry at the

same time. Mark followed suit, the tears flowing freely down his cheeks. They took a break until their hearts resettled. Emma threw her hair back and wiped her spent makeup away. "I don't know how you held onto that for so long," she said.

"Cooking with onions," Mark replied. "You just learn to... hold it in."

Emma chuckled at him and leaned against her horse. "You'd make a good dad."

Mark smiled, nodding. "Thanks."

"Don't think I would have had a kid. Probably would have left it on the train by accident or forgotten to feed it. I could barely look after myself."

"Might not have jumped though, with a little one to look after," Mark said.

Emma scoffed. "If it cried that much, I might've jumped sooner."

They both laughed before the weight of what they'd experienced hit them on a long delay. They grew quiet and returned to work, accepting that it would become too grim to joke about in time. Just an unfortunate inevitability of the job...

CHAPTER TWENTY-NINE

Death's cottage had become like a motorway service station, with an adjoining Days Inn for Mark and Emma to rest their weary heads. After so many trips to and from the realm of the living, they came back for a brief break, tea and some biscuits, or a brief nap in the guest room before continuing their endurance run of tending to the infinite dead while Death dealt far more productively, and efficiently, with the dead in the rest of the world. It meant that there was always someone nearby or passing through the cottage while Veronique worked.

It was lively – an unusual condition considering the ages of stagnant undeath that had come before, but she was quite happy about it. She didn't mind the cleaning. She minded the loneliness far more. So, she was grateful for every opportunity to dust up or sweep after some tracked-in dirt from the living world.

She also couldn't remember a time when she took more calls from the other horsemen. It seemed like everyone needed help and was only now ready to reach out and ask. It was like Death had set a new precedent by deploying Emma and Mark, and suddenly the other horseman felt they had permission to request their own assistance. She galloped out across the plains of purgatory to the modest, single-storey home that was the dwelling place of Pestilence. His lawn was usually either dead or abloom with a turgid kind of life speckled with the awful colours of various radiant sicknesses, all experimentations or diseases long since eradicated from the world, that came to fester freely in the otherwise unchanging landscape.

She knocked on the door and immediately felt a clammy film across the surface. Even the door was sick and phlegmy. She wiped her hand on the hem of her apron and heard a wretched cough on the other side as Pestilence came to answer the door. He was never quite as "healthy" as Famine or War, but he never took to being sick despite that. His was a complexion that could take any awful sickness and make it look mild by comparison. Only now, he seemed to be suffering more acutely.

"Ah, hello," he said as he peeked through the door. "Veronique, um, this is a bit embarrassing. Thanks for coming over; I was hoping I could ask you for a favour?"

"Yes, of course," she said. "But if you're expecting me to clean... I am afraid I would not know where to start or end."

"Oh, no," he said, waving her off. "That's not... This place is its own organised mess. Everything's right where it needs to be. Including the germs. Actually, I'm in the midst of working on something and can't go myself right now, but I need a test subject."

Veronique raised her eyebrows at him.

"Not you, dear," he said. "A sheep. It's an ovine illness meant to supplant certain strains of..." He reared back and sneezed in the other direction before continuing. "...sheep and goat that are favoured over..." Another sneeze. "...cattle. More widely spread, through the wool. Be a love and bring me back a lamb, if you could. From wherever, but somewhere industrial – a net exporter. But also organic. The factory sheep are all sterile with how many antibiotics they pump into them."

"A sheep?" she asked. "With thick wool."

"Yes, please," he said. "Any sheep will do, I think. I don't mean to impose too much, I just—"

"No, do not worry. I get it. You're in the middle of something, can't leave. I will do it."

"Thank you." He sighed. "My horse has been feeling down and I don't want to stress him..." He paused as he seemingly choked on and then swallowed something that had built up and overloaded into his throat. "You understand."

"I'll be back tout de suite," she said.

"Thank you." He closed the door and went into another coughing fit. She assumed nothing of it. He worked with diseases all day, every day. Without any reliable subjects, he likely experimented with the efficacy of such things on his own body. But she'd never heard him sound or look so sick before.

Veronique rode her horse high into the air and took out a very small pair of curved fabric scissors, which she swung to open her own portal. She was the first person Death taught how to penetrate the veil between worlds with what she had on her: a field medicine kit. She'd held on to the scissors from that original box and modified them with a finer and longer edge for hemming and trimming curtains and cloth, so she could look after Death's robes and repurpose the ones long since unusable into dapper blackout window dressings.

She appeared somewhere over a wide-open green expanse. Hundreds of acres stretched in all directions dedicated to raising all manner of livestock. She rode around until she spotted something splotchy and white on the ground and soon found herself in the midst of a field of sheep. The sheep were all corralled together, which made plucking one out of the pack a bit tricky. If one suddenly started floating up into the sky, the rest would easily notice and go into a panic. Her presence in the living world had to be minute, minor, and easily explainable through common human forgetfulness.

"Veronique?"

She turned in the direction of the voice and saw, to a shared surprise, Mark leaning against a post outside the fenced area. She waved just as two horses passed between them in a tight race. Emma was riding the losing horse, and a spectral rider spurred the still-living horse on in a dashing lap around the pen. Veronique hurried across and rolled herself over the fence. Mark helped her get the rest of the way and unpicked her dress from where it snagged the wooden slats.

"What are you doing here?" Veronique asked.

Mark motioned to the scene. "We're working."

"You are racing horses?"

He sighed. "The man – Harris Furnell – owns this farm. He got kicked by his horse, but his stubborn spirit refuses to leave until he's bested Emma in a horse race. And that's put us in this predicament because he won't stop unless Emma can stay ahead for a lap. And it's not like we haven't tried to just" – he made a yanking gesture with his hands – "nab him while he goes around, but he's crafty. This is our hardest one yet, and we're both stuck 'til it's done."

"Oh, I see," she said. "That is troublesome."

"I know," Mark said. He rubbed just above his eyes. "Anyway, why are you here?"

"Monsieur Pestilence needs a sheep to test his new plague on," she explained.

"Ugh," Mark groaned. "I know it's all in the work, but I'd rather he wouldn't. What if he succeeds?"

The horses thundered past once more, neck and neck.

"Then it will certainly make work for those still living, won't it?" she answered with a smile. "I had the same thoughts as you – why would War continue after the Great War? It was the final conflict, the war to end all, and then no. World War Deux, Korea and Vietnam, the Middle East, various African nations, civil wars and endless spite, intolerance, and insatiable blood lust – and War was there each time to make it work. And her work was successful, mostly. The same is true with Death. People die, always. It is not such a sad thing when it is everywhere and happens to everyone. They become a part of life, these things."

"What a world," Mark said. "I wonder what it'd be like if they all took a vacation together and left us to just destroy ourselves."

"You may not like the answer," she said. "I once raised the same question. Monsieur Death explained to me that a world without death becomes a world without life. When people know the limit of their life, they will not live it properly. Not live to make each day matter, but only the last few days, or the last few weeks or months, so they will only be remembered by their final time on Earth. Building memories with each day is what makes human life worthwhile – both the good and the bad. Overcoming struggles and finding strength in weak times make life a thing that people love."

"Right, but is this the way to prove it?" Mark asked, and Veronique smiled at his naivety.

The world suddenly stopped and went grey. The horse at the far end of the pen reared up and the spirit fell off onto his back. He'd admitted defeat in some manner and ended the elongated final moment of his demise as the challenge ended.

"Thank God for that," Mark said.

Veronique hopped over the fence and went to the sheep. She selected one that was young but had plenty of thick-looking wool to take with her. She picked it up like a sack of flour and threw it over her head to rest on her shoulders.

"You need any help?" Mark asked.

"No, no," she insisted. "Leave this to me. We have our own duties, non? Focus on yours." Reaching her horse, she planted the sheep down and grabbed a rope to tie it to the side of her saddle. "You are doing fine work, I think, as Death, together."

Mark tipped his scythe to her and trotted his pony over to help collect the rogue soul, who had jumped the fence and gone on the run. Veronique watched how they performed as a team, a natural synchronisation to their riding, culminating with Mark and Emma swinging their scythes simultaneously through the man's neck so they could stop their chase and move on.

She smiled. It was nice having such lively Deaths to tend to, and she looked forward to their next break at the cottage...

CHAPTER THIRTY

The sea. An open invitation to exploration, adventure, and untold perils. The White Cliffs, natural beauty and a landmark so easily visible that the sailors of old could navigate their way to safety from miles out to sea into old Dover. A place of great trade, where the massive ships of the modern day crossed unseen sea lanes to carry freight of various kinds to and from the continent.

Not entirely an ideal place for a swim. Especially not so far out.

Their current task was finding the soul of one lost beneath the English Channel. Fortunately, their horses could float. Unfortunately, the body did not.

"Isn't that wrong?" Mark asked as he stood on top of the frozen waves of the sea.

"What?"

"Shouldn't dead bodies float? For a while?"

"On still water," Emma said.

Mark looked down. "Right, and it wasn't still..."

"You can't swim, right ?" Emma asked.

Mark shrugged his shoulders uncomfortably. "I can. I'm just not particularly good at it, is the thing."

"Oh, right," she said. "Ayia Napa. You just stayed at the beach the whole time while the girls and I all tried to learn to surf. You know there were rumours started about you because of that, yeah?"

"Oh, yeah, I know," Mark said. "My mates clued me in on it. I just kind of..." He huffed. "Uh, it's not important. But the fact of the matter is – how exactly do we get all the way down there to get him?"

"We swim?" Emma suggested. "Princess's hooves are pretty well stuck on the surface here."

Mark tested the water and attempted to slowly, carefully dismount his pony. He managed to stand on the water's surface. He steadied himself and stroked the small horse calm again.

Emma dismounted as well and fought for balance for a moment. "Oh, it's slick."

"Right? It's wet," he said.

They traded a silence – a painfully obvious one.

"We must be able to get down there," she said. She lowered herself and tried to push her hand down through the water. It worked, and her arm slipped in slowly, elbow deep. "Ugh. It's like pushing through jelly."

Mark followed suit and tried to push his foot down. "Oh, you're right. It's gloopy. It's weird."

"How is walking through solid walls easier than this?" Emma asked. She pulled her arm out and reached for her scythe.

"What are you doing?"

"I figure," she said, "if this can tear a hole between worlds in the sky, it could tear a hole through the ocean?"

"Like Moses's staff?" Mark asked.

"We never asked," Emma said, "but the horsemen are from the Bible. They *are* part of the same lore as Jesus and God himself. So those could be real, too."

"Yeah, but Charon is Greek," Mark said. "I think. No rivers were mentioned in Hell. It's all fire, brimstone, and screaming – and even then, that's just apocrypha. The true nature of Hell is the absence of God, as described. What they describe as Hell is attributed to just a place where it's hot and they burned their rubbish, way back in those times."

Emma chose to ignore Mark's unsolicited rant and used her scythe as a spade to dig through the water. She managed to carve a sizeable chunk of water away and worked herself up into a sweat. "This isn't working," she said eventually. "Not as much as I'd like."

"Uh-oh," Mark said. He started to slip down into the jelly and stopped right at his hips. "Okay, I think I've figured this out but don't know how to undo it."

"What is it?"

"I was thinking... about sinking," he said. "Like how you think about going through walls, right? But feet first. And now, if I stop thinking about staying above the water, I can feel myself just going deeper."

"So, just think of flying."

"I have been, but it's not really working." He sank another couple of inches down into the water. "Oh no!"

"Quick, don't breathe."

"What!?" he shouted. "Why not?"

"Maybe if you don't believe in breathing you won't need to do it," she said, with a slight smirk at her own comment.

"Oh, sure, laugh at the drowning man," Mark said.

"I am," she said. She pulled out the hourglass. "According to this, he's directly below us. So just let yourself sink and hold your breath and you should be—" She turned to see Mark's pathetic expression one more time, but he was already under, and the water slowly closed itself up to swallow him. His hand remained, and he raised his finger, giving her an "up yours". She sighed and turned her eyes towards Dover, with an idea in her mind.

Mark, meanwhile, simply sank. He held his breath for as long as he could, then felt like he was about to pass out. He tried to swim up and thought buoyant thoughts, but it was no good. It was a very slow sink. Nothing could make it faster or reverse it. He tried swimming, but his arms and legs were mostly locked into the nature of the water. So, he tried to think of phasing through it. And it worked.

And then he fell faster, with nothing under him that could catch him. He yelled without opening his mouth and plummeted in a steep drop through the water as if it were just air. Then he finally reached the bottom and landed on his stomach. No pain, but a bit of shock. He was on the seabed of the English Channel. It wasn't quite what he expected.

"Woah!" He slapped his hands to his mouth in shock. After thinking airless thoughts, he found that he lacked all need for breathing. He couldn't breathe in – physically. He tried and it was like sucking on a plastic bag. But he didn't *have* to. His voice was just a whisper without breath, but it seemed to fill the space around him, not unlike the phantasmal whisper of a gruesome spectre in the dead of night – a real Grim Reaping kind of voice.

Now satisfied that he could perhaps fulfil his role down here, he looked around him. It was very grey, not unlike the world above when time was still, and fairly flat with some undulating sandy hills. And the seabed was bespeckled with debris. Some was recent and barely had sand enough to dust them up – chunks of boat, lost nets and other refuse pitched overboard by the wandering ships up above. Other things he found were ancient.

"This is a plane," he said as he walked over the wreckage of a long-buried aircraft. He tried to brush some of the sand away. It scraped off like a firmly fitted cardboard sleeve. "Luftwaffe, eh? Good place for you, then." He looked around at the majesty of the polluted sea and spotted the broken mast of a ship in the hazy distance.

It was an old ship of a sailing kind, rotted through and through, but for the thickest lumber and hard polished floors. The bounty on board was also preserved. There were heavy leaden vases and containers, some of which were still fastened shut. "A trade ship? Or a smuggler? Or a military vessel? Sunk this close to shore, it could be any of the above, really..." He toured the deck of the dead ship for a while, and nearly lost track of his duty.

"Any pirate that lasted this long under here is no mere mortal for me to collect, if this is directly down from where I fell. Where was that?" Mark attempted to wander back to where he came from but quickly found himself a bit lost. He traced his steps back to the fuselage of the Messerschmitt and to the body-shaped indent of his landing point, then made a patrol around in a circle. He grew it wider once or twice before throwing his arms up in surrender.

"Where are you?" he whispered as loud as he could. "Hello? Hiss back if you can hear me!" He started to hiss, like a snake clearing its throat, in all directions. He cupped his hands around his mouth and turned like a siren.

Then he locked eyes with Emma, who swam up towards him through the seabed. And then came the man in her grasp, being dragged by his collar and looking dismayed. They seemed to swim up from under the bedrock – from the Channel Tunnel – and were soon skybound again.

"Wait!" Mark hissed after them. "I still can't swim!"

He tried thinking flying thoughts. Eventually, he settled on submarining thoughts and propelled himself up in a spiral to the surface.

200

CHAPTER THIRTY-ONE

Mark and Emma descended on a fairly nice little district of Liverpool, just outside the city centre, into a row of homes that still had backyards. Small yards, just big enough for a table and a couple of chairs, but decent places to live. A place for families. Part of a community. It was a far cry from their own block of cramped, new-build apartments – all glass and cladding, absentee landlords, and buy-to-let mortgages.

"Ah, here we are," Emma said. "Dennis Perth Offdenson. Thy time hath come."

The house was a classic Victorian terrace with minimal external renovations. Signs of roof work were present, but it seemed to mostly stick to pure preservationist standards, as did the rest of the houses on the terrace. Mark went in and Emma stayed outside in reserve, just outside, in case some trouble went down, but it seemed unlikely. Mr Offdenson was quite old judging by the time in his hourglass. He'd lived a full life and the moment of his death ended very quickly after they arrived, a sign that he was already in the transitory state, awaiting the reaper's hand.

Mark kept his time in the house short. It looked lovely, though. Cosy, he thought. A nice upgrade from their previous state of living. Then he thought about it. Their flat was mostly open plan, with no tight halls or sharp corners leading into other rooms. He tried to consider the overall floor space, minus the walls, and whether or not they'd had a better lot than he realised.

He found Mr Offdenson in a library of sorts, a den, where each wall was lined with rows of books clearly dating back many decades, possibly even too many to be read in one lifetime. The collection had clearly outgrown the shelving and piles of books, mainly leather-bound hardcovers, sat in haphazard piles, some forming floor-to-ceiling columns. One solitary low-watt desk lamp illuminated the grey-blue room. A long-haired cat, frozen in sleep, lay on a small cushion next to the brass surround of the fireplace.

Mr Offdenson, a man with a grey beard and full head of white hair, sat on a brown leather chair across from his resting corpse with a pipe in his hand. Spectral smoke floated up through the ceiling. He eyed Mark out of the corner of his oak-rimmed glasses and adjusted them as he turned to greet his guest.

"Ah, hello there," the man said in a posh scouse accent. "You must be my psychopomp, scheduled for just about 12:15." He flipped his arm up and looked at his watch. "You're just on time."

"Yes," Mark said. "Come."

"Hmmm," the man hummed curiously. "Suppose I refuse?"

"Not an option," Mark said.

"Oh, really?" Mr Offdenson said. He seemed oddly entertained by Mark's final notice. He reclined further in his seat and steepled his fingers together. "Well then, I'm afraid I'm going to have to invoke the Tinkerbell theorem and decline you the authority of your existence, my boy. Shame, that, lad." He turned and looked out the window.

"What?" Mark said. "We must get a move on, sir. I have to—"

"Oh, what a bother," Mr Offdenson said as he stood and paced to the window behind his desk. "A bother, indeed. I am a particularly well-educated man, you see. An atheist, through moral decision. I found it to be far more sincere to live without the delusions of a grand scheme quite early on. Rather than succumb to the fear or despair of living a failed life, I observed the world naturally, organically – truthfully! And though I did consider the existence of a soul, I fashioned that no one entity could maintain the power to control all souls together as a God would. That level of centralised power is but a dream of mankind – of rules and despots in history – reflected in the teachings of those who first raised civilisation from the ground."

"Mate, I'm done with school," Mark said. "You're going to have to pay me if you want me listening to this."

"No one," Mr Offdenson triumphantly called, "escapes learning! Nor logic. That is the folly of man's theological empires. They flee from logic and blame the gods for their disasters, but praise different ones in the emperor's control for their great success! They had a hand behind the curtain that blinded them, and they could see through the first delusion, that there is no God. But lacking the faith to govern themselves, they replaced their conjecture with many gods, so they could still feel controlled."

Mark rubbed his eyes. "Mr Offdenson—"

"My boy," he said, "I was not a teacher for *fifty-one years* for nothing. If you are going to address me, I would ask you to do so as 'Professor'."

"Of course, you would," Mark said, tiring quickly of their chat. "I've many other souls to reap, so if you could please, you know... chop-chop."

"I could have taught so many so much," Professor Offdenson

lamented. "My mind was wasted in academia. It is not the thinkers' world anymore, but the world of doers, who are tasked to think less and less each generation. I saw this numbing of minds, this grinding dulling of the wits of my students. They refused to allow me to teach them about the great works of man and the meaning behind them, of the decoding of the God theorems by the great thinkers who infiltrated the church itself to alter mankind's course unto self-reflective enlightenment. No, they just wanted tests and results. They wanted yeses and nos. They wanted faith in the system. Faith without honour! And they held my hands hostage to entrap my mind within their sphere of delusion. Now we are in an age of many who claim to be God, made by man, *ex machina*, and yet no one is willing to reduce themselves to an animist sect of many gods! No, they all want to be the One because they have all the power. Education, healthcare, transportation... bureaucracy is the God delusion of our time, boy! It's what brings us back into the Dark Age!"

Mark looked around the room and to a few frames hanging on the wall – degrees in primary education and various philosophy-based accolades, including a framed certificate from placing first in a regional debate club. The man had a photo of himself with a gathering of children in their uniforms, with "Happy Birthday Mr Perth" painted in big letters.

Mark held back a laugh and turned around.

Professor Offdenson was looking out the window. He sighed and began what felt like another long dissertation. "Tell me, Mr Reaper, who do you serve?"

"Death," Mark said.

"Are you not Death?" he asked.

Mark hesitated. "It's a bit complicated."

He smirked. "Is it a hierarchy? To leave the unreaped souls to a lesser entity who pitches in a degree of work that would otherwise be entitled to a far higher placement in society, but is instead relegated to the whims of a crushing elite?"

"No, that was my other job," Mark said.

"But a job it is," Offdenson said. "A denial of Godhood! A denial of self-importance! Death is a concept above all control, outside of all systematic structure and one even feared by the dogmas of religion. My boy, you *can't* be real, because no Death of any kind would come politely. If it were real, and if you were sincere, then I would not have this chance to speak. This is a calling of a higher kind, beyond even you, which lets me draw breath and think these free thoughts! It is proof that you are nothing more than a hallucination to keep me company while my true mind slows down to its final synapses and flickers off into infinite darkness. And until that darkness comes, I shall remain here" – he sat – "where my mind finds the most comfort among the great thinkers of Earth, to whom we owe all our existence."

Professor Offdenson peeked out of the corner of his eye and – as he expected – Mark was gone. The shadowy figure was no longer in sight. His personal psychopomp, sent to remind him of Death in his dying moments, could not handle the hypocrisy of his own existence. Professor Offdenson sighed and looked over at his desk, to an unfinished manuscript comprised of long unbroken paragraphs written with a typewriter. He gritted his teeth with regret.

Then Emma phased up through the floor, scythe in hand.

"Wha— Again? Another? Did I not disprove you lot indefinitely?" The offended soul shot to his feet and began to march in her direction. "I say, enough! I say—"

Then the infinite darkness came in the form of a sack over his head. Mark and Emma took him back and dumped him head first

– more importantly, mouth first – into the loamy river where he could enjoy his calm cessation from existence and leave the rest of Limbo in peace.

"Too many of them are already roaming around," Mark said.

Emma nodded. "And they're all still pissy they were wrong."

CHAPTER THIRTY-TWO

The land between life and death on the south shore of the River Styx was mostly calm. Death returned from a long reaping haul and noticed quite a few new souls along the bank. Though he only begrudgingly accepted them as such, his apprentices were doing their duties and doing them well. No one had been lost or forgotten. And his own professional hand was able to sort through the rest of the world's dying without having to cast a worried shade over the not-so-United Kingdom.

It was all for the better. He felt tired. The aeons and ages were starting to get to him and piled up against his bony back. In fact, Death let himself consider, just for a moment, that Emma and Mark could grow their responsibilities across continental Europe, further freeing up Death's time. He caught himself hunching and used his scythe to straighten himself out. His back cricked hard. He could feel where the bones in his spine had displaced and reached back to slot them back into alignment. It was a groan-worthy pain that made him lumber back to the cottage with a limp.

He had a moment of free time to himself, judging by the number of hourglasses still on hand, so he undid his heavy cloak and reverted to his gardening garb. He had on jean overalls, a tartan shirt, a straw hat, and thick gloves – he was just missing the ear of wheat dangling from his jawbone to complete the look. His scythe retained its natural shape, for the scythe was originally a tool for cutting grass and remained just as functional to tend the overgrown reeds and wheat of the afterlife.

Death hummed an old, jaunty song as he did his work, a song better suited to the frantic play of a fiddle held by a man desperate to fend off the japing wiles of a deathly phantom. It was one of his favourite kinds of music, second only to the dirge and Mozart's Requiem. Songs all about him, made appropriately dreadful by human hands.

He cut down a swath of grass around the perimeter of the cottage and stepped back to admire his work. The ground had been flattened, with no sharp burs or weedy stalks remaining. It felt good to walk on, like a fine carpet. He turned to continue the work when he saw War riding in on her horse, which dragged behind it a compound tractor. She groaned as she dismounted and had to hold her side as she walked.

"You alright?" he asked.

"Oh, just a strain," she said. "I worked myself out a bit too hard to fight off the fatigue of resting and, well, it's been too long without proper fighting for my sake. I'd much rather see mankind return to close-quarters combat, so I have something more active to do in the off time."

"Indeed," he said. "And the tractor?"

"Oh, it's for you," she said. "I found it among my collection and repurposed it to a field clearer. It was used in the Great War – the one that your girl was part of – when they had to turn any vehicle into one of service. Its original build was equipped with a rotating pin covered in chain whips that smacked the ground to clear mines. But of course, any sword is of service, so the French guardsmen actually used it..." She laughed. "They used it to run down German troops and whip their skulls in when they wandered in too far behind enemy lines."

"It was a hideous time," Death said nostalgically. "The inventiveness of man in finding ways to meet me has always been thrilling to predict and unsatisfying to keep up with."

"In any case," she said, "you may as well have it. It's just a farming tool now. Perfect for your hobby here."

"I happen to like cutting by hand," he said.

"But does your back like it?" she asked.

Death huffed and looked down. He saw bandages slip out from under her pantsuit sleeve that seemed to wrap all the way up her arm.

She caught him looking and tugged her sleeve down. "Just some sores, is all," she said. "You're lucky you don't have flesh to look after. It becomes quite the regime when you get to my age."

"True," he said.

With a strained wave, she went on her way and rode off, leaving the unhitched tractor blocking Death's view of the river. He went down to look it over. The combine blades were all nicely sharpened – reclaimed metal edges from myriad swords broken and left behind from countless wars. Treasures for the horseman that had been repurposed into a kinder new use. Swords into ploughshares.

Death mounted the tractor, fiddled with the controls, and brought it to life. He took it for a lap around the outer field and checked his handiwork. In just a few minutes, he'd completed a whole week's worth of cutting, which would have been outgrown by the time he reached the end of his a circuit with his own tools. He gritted his teeth together to force his version of a grin and continued, resolved to flatten the entire estate before retiring for the day.

Sometime later, Pestilence came by. Death stopped the tractor next to him and leaned over on his metal stool seat. "Hello."

"I see you've upgraded," Pestilence said, pausing to drag in a wheeze of a breath. "You'll reap far more souls with this I'd bet."

"They'd run," he said. "It's not quite fast enough for my liking. Or manoeuvrable enough. But nice for a bit of lawn care."

"That's fair," Pestilence said. "I could've taken care of this field for you, if you'd asked."

"I'd prefer that it grow back," Death said. "Unmutated."

Pestilence chuckled and then descended into a coughing fit, making Death shrink back in his seat. "Ah, yeah. That would be an issue. Where's your lady?"

"My what?"

"The French girl?"

"Veronique is tending to the house," Death said, "and the stable. Now I believe she's exercising the horses."

"Right, well," Pestilence began, "I just wanted to give her a gift for helping me."

"Helping?"

"Yeah."

He produced a set of gloves made of fresh wool, finely knit and cobbled together, just the right size for Veronique. The wool was black and stripey but not dyed. The fibres of the fleece had turned dark from the plague that affected the sheep and rendered them not just colourless but without any pigment at all, and too slick to take on any kind of dye or paint. A plague to turn all sheep into black sheep would soon spread through white-haired herds and crash the market of fresh linens, a plague onto animals and onto wallets.

"Couldn't have made these without her," Pestilence said. "And she seems to like black."

"She claims it is her Visigoth heritage," Death said. "Or some other nonsense."

"Why not have her do some work for you?" Pestilence asked with a cough. "You know, out there? Seems to be going along well with those other two you brought in."

Death huffed. "I remain unconvinced. The work of Death is not for mortal hands to meddle with."

"You think a human would like to see you mowing a field?" Pestilence asked. "Or me... in a hospital? It's been past our time for a while now. More people die of things we can't control than ever. These cyber-thingies are wreaking havoc. A whole raft of viruses and worms and I've never even touched the damn things. We're outdated. And keeping up is—"

Death felt a jerk at his side. He reached into his pocket and pulled out an hourglass that expanded to full size. The last grains had nearly fallen. He jostled it around and saw them fleck off the siding of the glass; just a few more remained to fall, and there was no time to wait. He looked around but his horse was not in sight. The tractor, however, was still under his hips. He turned the ignition, produced his scythe from the air, and whipped the side like a horse. The tractor sputtered forward and made a slow, steady climb into the air. Death made a mighty swing and opened an extra-large portal to fit his tractor through.

Pestilence was left to watch in awe. "Wish I could do that... I don't even have a car."

CHAPTER THIRTY-THREE

The river sloshed with the gentle lap of waves against the shore. Three figures stood in the fog and were revealed slowly as Charon's boat crept close to the shoreside. Two stood with scythes, their sickled blades glinting silver. The other stood in a robe, hands clasped at his waist, eyes closed and face reddened.

The jingle of gold carried in the shifting wind. Charon neared the shore and parted the fog to inspect the spectre brought before him for value – and he did indeed possess some worth eyeing. He was an older man of faith, dressed in fine burial robes and donned with jewelled trinkets, hemmed and rimmed with gold all around. Rings, necklaces, arm braces, and even teeth – which were also gold, as far as Charon could see.

"Well done," Charon said. "It has been too long since you've brought me a worthy soul to cross the water. Time and again ye've failed me in this regard, and I've turned away more than I could count. But now I see we are aligned at last. This one shall—"

The priestly man held up his hand defiantly. "Speak not,

Demon," he began, in a Northern Irish accent. "Let me cast myself before the Lord and receive his judgement at last through my long life in his service. I shall not entertain the dark, enchanting tones of the wicked consorts of the Devil and his ilk, which seek to molest my pure soul before it can be seen untouched, erred, and unfettered in God's eyes."

"Have fun," Mark said, sounding utterly fed up, and walked off.

"Bye," Emma said, clearly also very glad to be rid of the man.

Charon sensed a dreadful shift in the mood as he was left alone with the priest – like he'd only just begun to hear the long dictations those two had gone through to bring a man of God into a godless afterlife.

"Pay the tithe," Charon demanded, "and I shall send ye to the land where God awaits."

The priest turned his nose up to Charon and cast his eyes into the haze-covered sky. "O Lord, for you are the mightiest, and the holiest, thou art my saviour, my creator, and my everlasting light." He went to his knees and put his hands up over his head. "I await thee here at this, the river of despair and torment, that you shall descend and accept me through the gates of Heaven and enter me into your eternal embrace, from now until the end of time."

"The tithe," Charon insisted.

"I shall not listen," the priest shouted, not at Charon but in a projected voice for him to hear, "to these devil-sent fiends who test me and tempt me. I know they are Your doing, a loving stroke to test my final faith. But I am here, and I await thee – God! O Lord! I see and believe you! I hear and obey only you! Grant me wings to your kingdom, show that I am worthy!"

"Wings won't get you across the river," Charon said. "Only I can—"

"OOOO, LORD!" the priest howled. "Thy sanctum and sanctuary calls to me! Even here in this mute abyss, I can feel your pull. I can hear the song of your creation!"

"Pay me!" Charon said. He slapped his oar into the water, getting very frustrated. "I'll take you there, just... just pay..."

The priest removed one of his rings. "These material things," he said, "are not my shackles. They are not my worth!" He turned away and pitched the gold into the water past Charon.

Charon watched it fly with a startled, then downright terrified face.

"I am not bound to this wealth as a man. It is only you, Lord, who shines like gold in this end of all things." He kept taking his gold off and throwing it away. He blathered on about it being easier for a camel to pass through the eye of a needle than a wealthy man to pass to the kingdom of Heaven. Charon started to reach out and catch it. When he did, the priest eyed him and fast-balled it in another direction. He kept going until he was out of gold, then he started to strip down of his robes. By then, Charon didn't care. He'd lost out on the gold before it could be his, and it was gone.

The priest unloaded his laundry onto Charon's boat. He stood with ankle-garter socks and underpants as his only clothing, aside from the cloth skullcap on his head. "See me, Lord! Unhindered! As you made me, unmarred by the sins of temptation. See me as you see all, know all, and let me ascend into your paradise!" He then removed his underpants, went back down to his knees, and began singing hymnal songs while rocking. Charon detested the foolish man's elation and dumped the clothes into the river before paddling away. The man had no money, no gold, no tithe – not even his tighty-whities – and thus, no way to cross.

Charon returned to his golden mansion. He fixed up the

compromised wall that had fallen apart before and rearranged the various thrones to mix things up. He hauled his boat up onto a dry dock and used some golden tools to fix the underside. He scraped off a few clutching, partial hands that clung onto the wood like barnacles, along with fingernails and teeth from the desperate souls who tried to grip the boat without payment and ended up under it before it could reach the other side of the shore.

"Blasted church system," Charon said. "Making loonies stop believing in the value of gold. Why bury him in all of it if it's just going to end up in the ruddy, muddy, bloody water!?" Charon rose his voice to a shout and nearly threw his golden scraper into the river. Instead, he stabbed it into the dock and leaned his head into his hands. Once he'd recovered, he finished treating his boat and went to relax for a moment among his great treasury. He'd used whole ingots as the main bracing walls and stacked coins in octagonal segments that spiralled up halfway and then stayed in straight formations up to a vaulted ceiling where he fitted all his miscellaneous treasures together like a jigsaw.

Everywhere he looked there were items with historic and plainly visible value, yet all of it felt hollow. None of it could get him what he wanted. What he really wanted. His eyes fixed on a golden horse icon, some ancient Phoenician temple fixture that was taken to the grave by a noble priestess many aeons back. His eyes narrowed and his teeth gritted just looking at it. Charon often talked at the icon – poor company, but with the guarantee he would never be contradicted.

"Horses," he mused. "Can't even swim. Can't ford too deep a river. Too good for boats, are they? Who ruled that horses can fly but a boat cannot? So arbitrary. I'm stuck here, gaining insight into the outside world only through those pitiful or pious enough to die clutching gold. And they talk so little of the world and so much of themselves. Mine has been an unchanging lot, shifted only by the sands of the river and built up by this mound of... inequity."

Charon grabbed a coin and tossed it against the far wall. It bounced off and rolled back to him. He continued to bounce it around until it fell flat, and then he picked another out of his slumped seat and bounced it again.

"All they complain about now is money. Status. Wealth. What they left behind. Regrets all tied back to what they couldn't earn or what they earned in vain. Money. Not disease or war or famine. They don't even complain about death. They complain about banks and loans and debts. The horsemen can't see how forgotten they have become. They think they know what rules the world, but do they?"

Charon gave an extra hard toss and missed the wall entirely. The coin flew past his golden shack and clattered against the rocks, continuing to bounce on a certain path for the water.

"Meh," he scoffed. "It doesn't matter."

Ting!

"All this gold is worth no more than dust down here."

Ting!

"I may as well dump it all into the water..."

Ting!

"...and then follow it in myself."

PLOP!

"There's no need for a—"

Clank!

Charon looked for the source of the errant noise, and noticed that a link in the chain of his long, unbreakable shackle had split apart. The links were still connected, but it gave him an few extra inches of movement. He looked out past his gold to the waterfront, still covered with fog, under which lay an unknown trove of gold coins discarded or tossed or otherwise lost in the abyss. Where nature did not intend for them to go.

For if not in Charon's grasp did the river's toll lay, what good was the gold that came all that way?

CHAPTER THIRTY-FOUR

Mark and Emma found their way into London's sewer system, an expansive collection of catacomb-like Victorian tunnels. They were still in great working order, or so claimed countless city administrators, handling effluent runoff and keeping the Thames from being the cesspit it used to be. In most places, they were also a bit too narrow for the horses, so the two had to go on foot through the filthy ankle-deep stagnant water, detritus, and fatbergs.

"Have these always been down here?" Mark asked. Despite the narrow, brick-laden tunnels, his voice did not echo, which threw him off.

"Apparently," Emma said.

"It's not much smaller than what we rented really," he said.

"Better insulated too," she said. "But more water problems."

"Not many."

They navigated by the vagueness of their sand compass until they reached a complex fork of diverging tunnels. The needle pointed dead ahead into the very wall that split the tunnel in two.

"You think they converge again up ahead?" Mark asked.

"This is London infrastructure," Emma said. "They could go up, down, or around at this point."

"We could end up walking back to Death's house," Mark said.

"More like Charon's."

They both exchanged a laugh and then went quiet. They heard a faint, distant humming sound, like someone mumbling a song far down the tunnel. It sounded like it came equally from one side and the other. Mark and Emma decided to split up and ran the lengths of the tunnels. They wound, curved, and split again but eventually came back to the same cistern connected to a more standard blocky platform of relatively modern creation.

Their target, Phillip Coaver, was humming along to an old song by The Who while he worked a trowel against a wall to press the mortar harder into the brickwork, despite already being on the other side of death. Mark noticed he was there first, as Emma rounded a corner further away moments later. He started the formalities.

"Mr Coaver?" he began. "Sorry, could you put that down a moment?"

"No can do, son," Mr Coaver said. He patted the wall flat with the back of his trowel and scraped some of the excess mortar away with a swift sweep. His physical body lay against the wall, hand clutched hard over his chest and eyes shut. Heart condition. The man was in his early sixties but looked a bit younger. He was all wrinkles, with no grey sticking out under his hard hat, and he had thick labouring arms.

"Mr Coaver, do you happen to notice anything strange about yourself?"

"Not much, no," he answered.

"Like your pulse?" Mark said. "And how it might not... be there?"

"No time to check," he said.

"Sir, you're dead," Mark stated curtly. "You died. It's impressive you're able to affect the material plane this much – you shouldn't – but that's that, and this is death. Please put the trowel down and come with me."

"No, sir," Mr Coaver said.

"I'm afraid I have to insist," Mark insisted.

Mr Coaver turned and eyed Mark up and down. He turned back around, clearly unimpressed with what he saw. "This your job?" he asked.

"Happens to be," Mark said.

"You always talk up your work before you do it?"

Mr Coaver stood, trowel gripped in hand, to match the same intimidation factor Mark was supposed to be giving off with his scythe. Emma revealed herself to provide backup. Two blades were better than one. Phillip turned and smirked at them. "Well, look at that. You a couple?"

"Flat-mates," Emma clarified.

Phillip rolled his eyes. "Lucky. A lucky man can work well with a good pal. Doesn't always happen. Be glad it did for you."

"We really must be going," Mark said.

Phillip strode forward confidently and tapped his trowel against Mark's sickle. He was strong. Much stronger than Mark. "Awful big tool you're holding. You using it right, you think?"

"Hey!" Emma shouted. She swung. Mark and Phillip both ducked away. Phillip wove back and recovered while Mark slipped and fell into the pungent water.

Phillip laughed. "Not everyone's cut out to work with their hands, lad. Don't get bruised over it. Save them delicate fingers for payroll." He laughed as Mark got back to his feet.

"What do we do?" Mark whispered to Emma.

"Sneak up on him," she said. "Take off his arms and then his legs."

"Black Knight him?" Mark said. Emma looked at him curiously – then she got it and rolled her eyes. They both turned to confront their mark, but Phillip was already up the access ladder and out of the manhole. They ran to follow. Emma whistled loudly as soon as she was topside and pulled Mark up.

"Chase him," she said. "Stay on him; I'll find you with the horses."

"Okay." Mark ran after Phillip.

The old man legged it. He ran like he was on the last sprint of a marathon, trowel still in hand like a relay baton. Mark couldn't keep pace, and he struggled to keep the old man in his sights. Mark thought deep thoughts – like his time in the sea – and broke into a further sprint without needing to breathe. Now, he was only held back by his own physical prowess at running.

Which wasn't great, so he continued to stay behind.

Phillip turned around with his trowel in hand, held like a throwing knife, and gave it a toss Mark's way. Mark raised his scythe to block it. The trowel hit the pole and then clattered to the floor. Mark checked the surface of his unblemished scythe and then looked up just as Phillip ran around a corner.

Emma flew in from overhead and pursued the man on horseback. He turned to see her coming and ducked into the narrow alley between some houses. She hovered overhead and waited for him to come out the other end, but he didn't. "Damn it," she spat. She went down to the street level and saw that he was no longer in the alley either, despite not reaching the street. Then she saw a shadow moving indoors, on the upper storey of one of the cramped houses, as Phillip exited from one balcony and jumped over to the next.

"Get down from there!" Emma shouted. "You'll break your neck!"

"Not before you do, girl!" he called back.

Emma jumped off her horse and tapped her way through the door, where she received a flying picture frame in the face courtesy of the wily old man. He dashed past her and out the door just before Mark came around the corner.

Now Phillip was young and swarthy, sent back to a halcyon youth as a body-built young man with arms pumped up from years of heavy lifting. His hair was fuller, his face was leaner, and his eyes were alight and alive with a dreadful passion. Mark didn't have a halcyon youth to hark back to, so he just stopped in place as he faced this better version of the former senior.

"Have you ever failed to reap a soul?" the man asked.

"Not yet," Mark said.

Phillip shook his head in disappointment. "Then you haven't even begun to work. You know how many times I failed in my jobs?"

"Not enough to get fired, but too many times to get a decent pension?" Mark guessed.

"Enough to learn that the work is never done," he said. "That one failure cannot put a man down forever. That one bad job is not enough to undo a life of service and effort. If you haven't failed, son, then you aren't working hard enough."

"I'm afraid we cannot afford to fail," Mark said. "For *your* own good, at that."

Phillip threw his arms out in challenge. "I'll untwist your mind for you – a mind that thinks it must always be perfect or be punished. Ask your boss if he's ever dropped his tools and scraped paint that didn't need scraping, and if he threatens to fire you, you'll know it was more times than he could count. The good workers are the ones that fail most often but work hardest to make things right."

"Sir," Emma said. She threw her scythe and cut Phillip from shoulder to rib in an uneven segment that he couldn't recover from. "We appreciate your input. But we really must be going."

Phillip scoffed. His wrinkles returned, and his muscles faded to their age-racked form. "I always swore I'd work all my life. And I still don't feel dead. What am I to build now?"

"Patience," Mark said.

"I've got enough of that as it is," Phillip said as he righted himself and Mark arranged his body parts in a neat pile as Storm-rider galloped down from on high. "I suppose honest work lives in the soul, then."

"That it does, sir," Mark said as he scooped half the soul up.

Phillip patted him on the shoulder – two big thuds from his sledgehammer-weighted hands. He mounted up, rode behind Mark, and gave one longing look at London from above as they rode off to the afterlife.

"I built some of that," he said. "Someone else will have to continue it."

"Yep," Mark said. They slipped through the portal and left the physical world behind, along with a dented trowel lying in the middle of the road and a job finished to an exacting standard that very few would see after its sole worker passed away.

CHAPTER THIRTY-FIVE

They took one hourglass each, left at the same time, and arrived at different times in different sorts of places. When Mark showed up, the world around him was still in glorious Technicolor, his target's time continuing to tick down, while Emma's target's time was up, and the world was already mute grey the moment she appeared in the sky.

"Oh, brilliant," she said with an exasperated breath. "Give me a chance, why don't you?"

Her hourglass pointed to her target's body; she just had to hope their spirit hadn't set off already on a little wander. The location was Sandyford in Newcastle, in a simple set of student flats. And the scene was a bit uncomfortable to face.

Emma arrived at a suicide gone wrong. Not that there was much in the way of what was right in these sorts of circumstances, but it was clear the whole thing had been planned differently. The spirit of the girl was sobbing in the corner, her body was sprawled out, busted up and broken, with bones bulging from under her skin after a drop onto what looked like a hideous piece of modern art, made with angles perfectly aligned to break a body upon impact.

"Polly?" Emma asked. "Polly Harrowsoth?"

"Look at it!" the girl bemoaned, pointing a crooked finger at the disarray. "It's all gone wrong!"

"Yes, that's how it happens," Emma said sympathetically. "One thing leads to another, and you're left with no other—"

"No, no." Polly shook her head. "The setting! The scene! I had it all rigged up, and the bloody rope gave out too soon! Now I've died all ugly and discombobulated, and it was so pretty and perfect before! Must've been..."

"Oh," Emma said. "So, this was..."

"It's *art*," Polly insisted. She huddled against the wall with her knees tucked up to her chin. "It's supposed to be a grand, beautiful statement. Now all they'll say is, 'Look how ragged her body turned when she fell off her perch'. Or worse, 'Look how *fat* she was when she hanged herself...'! I'm bloody not! Clearly!"

"Oh, clearly," Emma said. "It's the hook's fault that it couldn't keep you up."

"Right? I'm not an engineer. But maybe I should've been... for all the good that'll do me now."

"Polly, I'm not an art connoisseur. Can you just walk me through what... you've done?"

Polly stood up and began a short walk around the very pointy architecture. "It's titled, as my note describes, 'the Summit of Woman's Apocrypha'. The various peaks in the formation of this brutal fundamentalist structure, made of stucco plaster with aluminium framing, represent man's assault against the arts for unimpugned practicalism. And to overcome that statement of sheer functionality against all expression, of cold logic and emotionless angular order, it takes the bright, humorous heart of a woman."

"Uh-huh." Emma nodded.

"But to merely add to it is not enough," Polly continued. "One must sacrifice all to stand over the end-all of statements. Thus, martyrdom is necessary as women ascend above man's hard-hewn world of cold stone to bleed colour down from above as their images are elevated and thus sanctified."

"...So you hanged yourself," Emma summarised, more literally, "so that your presence, as such, would leak down over the build-ings of man." She turned to Polly for a confirmation but got a snobby, glib sigh.

"If you're going to obsess over the unimportant details, then there's not much more I can offer you," Polly said dismissively. "So anyway, you're, what... dom-chic Death?"

"I'm just Death," Emma said. "I'm hardly 'chic' anything. Or dominating, for that matter."

"Yeah, clearly," Polly said. She sighed in defeat and moved over to a bench propped up between two diamond-shaped boxes that balanced on their edges and seemed to make a cleaving dent into the floor. "I just wanted my life to mean something. Because the longer I live, the less it will."

"What on earth makes you think that?" Emma asked. "You would have had a whole bright life ahead of you full of... ideas and thoughts. And reasons."

The irony of the situation wasn't lost on Emma. Arguing with someone suicidal over the myriad reasons to stay alive. Of course, it was never that cut and dry. Hadn't Mark tried to coax her down with much the same reasoning? And hadn't she countered each and every part of it with a similar response? – You don't under-stand me; no one does.

Somehow, because the shoe was on the other foot, it was so clear to Emma that Polly's decision had been extreme, rash, and unnecessary. She was a young, bright girl angry with the world but with a potentially bright future in front of her. Emma felt a lump form in her throat.

"You didn't have to go and do this," Emma concluded.

"Yes, I did," Polly insisted. "That's the whole point. The tragedy of a woman fighting for her place in the world is the point – that she *must* fight for the same place men achieve without any struggle. It's like, for every one woman's suffering, a hundred men find success. And yet, they wouldn't exist at all without the sacrifices of their mothers and wives and all the countless smaller people they must trample over to make their own *marks* on the world." She gestured at the brutalist deconstruction that her body hung limply over.

Emma struggled to keep her shit together. At that moment, she understood, for the first time, how Mark must have felt, desperately trying to keep his balance on the dome of the Liver Building. He'd been fighting his fear of heights and all the while trying to talk Emma down, pleading with her to reconsider. She'd been so cocksure that there was no other solution. She'd convinced herself but hadn't managed to convince him, and she remembered becoming increasingly angry as he waffled on about Tupperware instead of getting out her way. She probably owed him an apology.

From Polly's point of view, she'd only done what was necessary to carry on a message that meant more to her than her own life. It was a noble pursuit but highly, viciously overdone. What impacted Emma the most was how young the girl was. It reminded her of the nasty spots she'd been through in her early twenties, being sent into a world of unfairness, woefully ill-equipped and ill-prepared – always the shy wallflower, forgotten and ignored.

These feelings had escalated over time. There was no single catalyst. No clear crossing of a line or attributable trauma. Rather, the gradual and cumulative encumberment of hundreds of straws that broke both the camel's back and Emma's determination to live, each of which was individually preventable and avoidable but overwhelming in the aggregate. Little moments that informed her of a feeling of hopelessness and despair that eventually enforced an idea in her mind that just turning it all off was preferable.

"Polly," Emma said with a sigh, "I'm sorry, but... this is shit."

"Right," Polly said. "Everyone's an art critic. And you're going to lecture me about my fashion sense next? Go ahead, take a tour of my closet. Take out anything you like, and I can shut you down with it."

"No, not the sculpture," Emma said. "Though, it's not for me. I'm into landscapes. But the situation you found yourself in... it was shit. I agree that living sometimes feels like there's no point and it's not worth it. I went through all of that myself and even having someone telling me not to do it and to try and live through it all didn't work to stop me. I still... I still thought there was more peace at the bottom of a thirteen-storey building, without taking the stairs, than continuing with life. Because there are unsolvable problems in the world that come down on us."

"So, what are we supposed to do?" Polly asked.

Emma shrugged. "Live," she said. "Dying doesn't solve anything."

Polly stood up, offended. "Well, if we're all going to die anyway, we may as well have some choice in how we go out. How we're remembered!"

"You can try," Emma said. She turned back to the scene at hand. "But you'll most often fail. The living don't look at death for any greater reasons. No one will come to your funeral and cry that your last piece of art was misunderstood. They'll cry that you're gone. Even your harshest critics will miss you. Because they know their life, one day, will also end. And the meaning and import they gave to the world may end with it."

"That's shit," Polly said.

Emma nodded. "People make up their own minds to feel better about themselves. That's how art works. A hundred people can see what you've done and come up with different reasons for their own benefit. Not yours."

"There had to be some better way to get my message across," Polly said. "To make it crystal clear why I had to die this way... or, in a better way."

"The only better way to die," Emma said, "is when you're very old and in your sleep. The reason you die is always overshadowed by the life you lived."

Polly shook her head. "Is there really no artistry in death?"

"I don't think so," Emma said. "It's not so open to interpretation."

"Then... then can I change things?" Polly begged. "Can I go back and do it again? Do it better? Make a different statement, with life instead of death?"

Emma put a hand on the girl's shoulder. A cold, factual hand. "Few people like the way they die. But they die all the same."

Polly read the brutalism in Emma's eyes, her cold and angular expression. In the face of the overwhelming statement that represented, she simply shrugged and gave up. Emma led her out and rode her back to the river, where she set her loose to wander. There she met Mark, who was already back with a human backpack looped over his shoulders. Emma's long overdue conversation with Mark would have to wait a little while longer.

"What is that?" Emma asked.

"What's he look like?" Mark groaned. "He's quite a devout Buddhist. Ignored me completely for a good while, so I had to carry him back."

"You thinking about taking him to the monks?" Emma asked.

"Yeah. But I'm not sure I can make it."

Emma went around and took the man's legs. He remained in a perfect lotus position as the two of them carried him further into the desert of the unreal to join his like-minded brethren in their eternal purgatory.

"He really hasn't moved at all?"

"Not a bit," Mark huffed.

"He must be quite happy with how he died," she said. "Lucky chap."

"He must've been quite happy dying *fat*," Mark moaned. The two lugged their rotund, living luggage into the void, then returned to their duties – after a short break during which Mark made short work of the smorgasbord of cured meats Veronique had left out for them.

CHAPTER THIRTY-SIX

Things were going well in the land between life and the ever-after, except for a few unresolved complaints that kept arising in Death's cottage. The air was stagnant with an ever-present film of dust. Veronique's duster seemed to add more to the walls rather than brushing it off. So, she had to resort to the more drastic measure of running a vacuum cleaner up and down the walls. It was noisy but effective.

She had the windows open to air everything out but found her efforts floundering against the constant onset of dust that seemed to come from nowhere. It just appeared. She turned her eyes away, and the perfect, sunny-side-up yellow of the wallpaper turned a shade paler and more beige. With a cross breeze, she could at least monitor the trails of dust snaking their way out into the rest of the garden.

It was lonesome work, keeping things tidy. Never really busy, and not always rewarding. She only had one tenant to take care of in Death, and his activities usually kept him out of the house for what felt like days on end. Her time in the land of death had dulled her sense of time and its passing. She'd been dead long enough to know that time no longer mattered.

But the clutter was still hard to ignore. Her eyes darted to every potential piece of dirt that escaped her prior efforts, and she moved in on them like a soldier stalking the trenches. She crouch-walked to the vinyl record collection near the window, swung a feathery duster to bat away the film of dust over the sleeves, and was hit by a blowback. The sharp edge of a blade of grass nicked her face between her jaw and chin before falling to the floor.

"What?" she said. She plucked it and held it up to the exposed outside. She saw a spray of matter in the distance like a silent explosion that had rocked all the wheat and weeds from the ground. She looked on to see her patron reaping the field, using the tractor gifted to him by War, which carved out wide expanses of short, walkable grass with each pass.

She rarely got to see him working the garden. It tended to be her job. She had her own pair of shears for it and everything. It was almost cathartic to cut weeds by hand, one clump at a time, like shearing the hair of an incredibly large and fibrous sheep. But it was ultimately his garden, and tending to it was his favourite hobby. He finally had time for one with his apprentices now taking care of business across the British Isles. She quite fancied having a little go on the new tractor herself.

For now, she decided to make a pitcher of lemonade to refresh him and sauntered out the front door, leaving it open for the dust to evacuate. There was almost more indoors now than there was outside. She arrived just as Death finished clearing a path along the side of the yard that ran all the way down to the loamy shore of the river. He switched off the engine and struggled to climb down from the driver's seat. Back on the ground, he stumbled forward.

"Monsieur!" she called.

Death caught himself with his scythe. The handle shrunk

immediately, and he tucked the blunt side of the blade under his armpit to make a crutch.

"Ah, hello," he replied. "Done with your chores, are you?"

"Are you alright? I could do that for you," she offered, concerned at how frail he looked.

"I'm just fine," he said.

She'd known him for a century or so, and many lifetimes beyond that in the timeless passage of the world outside of human time, so she knew his tells very well. His breathing was shallow and tired. His posture was slumped so badly she could count his vertebrae underneath his tweed vest. The fact he was leaning on his scythe like he needed it told her far more than he wished her to know.

"Are you sure?" she asked.

He groaned. "Yes, yes. I know I look a little pale but trust me, that's the complexion that works best for me. It is a honed pallor. A very dignified and graceful kind of... calcified exposure."

Veronique assessed his work. He'd cut the whole garden down, front to back, while she was fussing with the dust inside. It did explain why a cloud of scattered dirt now filled the home.

"What is that?" he asked, motioning at the glass she was carrying.

"For you," she said.

He took it and downed it. The liquid disappeared into his jaw, which was hollow and had no throat, so it plainly vanished from sight. "Thank you," he said, before handing the empty glass back and shaking some of the droplets of condensation from his fingers.

"Let me escort you back inside," she said.

He scoffed. "It's just a short walk up the hill. Where are those two, anyway?"

"Emma and Mark?" Veronique said. "I believe they are nearly finished collecting their hundred souls."

"Are they now?"

"Oui."

"Hmmm," he hummed. "It's taken them about as long as I suspected."

"So they are on course to impress you?"

"Bah," he said. "Impress me? Not at all. It is impressive only in the sense that they have done it at all and not fallen from their horses and dashed themselves against the hideous reality of hardened tarmac." He reached into his pocket and held up Emma's hourglass. The patch of sand stuck to the side had now crystalized. "So long as they remain useful to me, I will acknowledge their efforts."

"And when they have made their first hundred deliveries?"

"Then they can make another hundred," Death said. "And so on and so forth, eternally, until they give up."

"And you will fill in to do the rest?" she asked sceptically.

He read through her sarcastic tone and hobbled up the path to the house. "Of course, I will! In fact, I was just about to rest before going on a sojourn through Polynesia to hunt for drowning victims along the seabed. A gripping, bracing excursion to deliver me from all this pollen and dander in the air."

"That you put there," Veronique added.

"Is it not your job to clean it up?" he said. He went inside first and looked around. Veronique followed behind. To her surprise, the house now looked far cleaner than she had left it. No dust was visible in any amount. Not even in the corners of the ceilings that she needed ladders to reach.

"We all have duties to perform," he said. "So long as we keep them up, everything will be fine."

"Yes," she agreed. Death hobbled back to his den and rested in his chair. She left him to it but remained concerned for his health. He was out of sorts, it was plain to see. The usual drive to deliver conclusions and reap life seemed spent out in the garden – and what was left was a rather cantankerous old man with a short temper and a long memory.

After a few minutes, he came out again, using his scythe as a walking staff instead of a crutch as he walked out of the door with a more confident – if still lop-sided – gait.

He turned back to Veronique.

"If those two return while I'm gone," he said, "and have fulfilled their duty to me, instruct them to wait in the den. To *wait*, as I shall have my words with them before deciding upon next steps."

"I shall," she said with a bow. While her head was down, she noticed a trail of fresh, almost glittering dust that followed Death, seeming to emerge from under his robe. Veronique went to work sweeping it up and blowing it out the door. The dust path reached all the way back to his den, where the biggest collection of it was on his grand reclining chair.

It was odd. Dust normally accumulated very naturally. She began to suspect it wasn't dust at all. She picked some up with her fingertips and rubbed it together. The way it ground together and tumbled downwards was not like a common house dust. It was more like a dense powder. She swept it all up together into a mound in the porch and let it filter down through her grip.

The particles caught a breeze she could not feel, which pointed towards the river. All the granules and grit – the dust and remnants still lingering on the stonework – lifted and flew away from her. She gave chase to see just where all this dust was being taken.

A murky film expanded over the River Styx as the dust settled onto it and spread out like a dry oil slick. It reflected a silvery tint from the ever-present light of eternity. Veronique sighed as she watched it go. It wasn't her job to clean it anymore, but it was still a contingency of filth she didn't want to tolerate.

It was in Charon's realm now, and she knew better than to mess with that. Death's service was a far finer fate than being a dinghy-maid.

CHAPTER THIRTY-SEVEN

The two humans returned with yet another soul who, instead of wandering out into the vast distance of the vacant, soulless void, decided to wander inland towards Death's cottage to inspect the grounds. There were no rules against approaching Death's home, nor against visitation, aside from the master of the home simply not wanting visitors.

The wanderer found the grim reaper in a humble garment with coveralls and sleeves rolled up to expose his bony arms, crouched down in the middle of a ploughed garden, humming the notes of Mozart's "Dies Irae".

"Oh," Death said. "Hello."

"Hi," the man said with great timidity. "Um... Sorry. I think I'm a bit lost."

"Yes," Death agreed. "Lost without passage to the other side and left to wander and wonder what eternity may yet hold for you?"

The man nodded. "Y-yeah."

"Well," Death said, "it is none of my business."

He returned to his gardening, continuing as if uninterrupted and leaving the stranger a bit speechless. The man watched Death tend to the garden, planting seeds in the ground with his bony fingers.

"What, uh..." he started, speaking up again. "What should I do?"

"Do as you like," Death said. "I'm not fond of house guests, and there's no work to pass down from those who are already in my service."

"Then why am I here?" the man asked.

Death pointed away to the featureless horizon. "To wander into the void. Until some great reckoning splits this place apart and absconds all lost souls to one place or another in service to greater powers than I."

"Like a rapture?"

"Like that," Death said.

"W-was I not a good Christian?"

"Hmph," Death scoffed. "No one is ever good enough of anything. This is all there is unless you bring gold to cross the river. Nothing else can be bartered with."

"So... *everyone* was wrong?" he asked.

"Wrong?" Death said. He stood up and pushed on his hips to crack his back straight. "Wrong how? Were you inspired to live a life bettering others, and yourself, because of the teachings you adhered to?"

"Uh... kind of?" the man said uncertainly.

"Then would that be so wrong?" Death asked. "Was your life lived with compassion, care, and understanding for your neighbours and strangers alike?"

"It was, I suppose," the man admitted. "Never did anyone any harm. I did share a Netflix password for a few months and never told anybody. But no sins in the Bible about not paying for subscriptions, is there?"

"Theft," Death said. "Though, explaining the systems of wealth that exist in modern days to the biblical scholars of the past would leave them utterly confounded on how to morally police such things, which would surely be beyond their comprehension."

"Yeah," the man agreed. "But... so, what am I here for? What do I do?"

"You're here because you died," Death explained. "And there is nothing left *to* do."

"Oh, well, that sucks," the man said.

"Indeed," Death agreed. A trepidatious silence passed by them. Then, Death went back to his garden and his seeding. At the turn of Death's cold shoulder, the man saw fit to wander back towards oblivion. Death continued to hum alone and finished seeding a row of red spider lilies. He looked up at the river where the familiar shape of a boatman drifted up to the edge of the waters through the fog.

Death hoisted himself up and wandered over to the shore where Charon waited on him.

"Odd to see you getting your wrists dirty," Charon said. "Stealin' me water too, are you?"

"Your water?" Death said. "That aside, the river doesn't grow anything. I bring my water from the living world."

"Oh, la-di-da," Charon sing-sang mockingly. "Death's flower bed gets only the purest of mountain spring juices."

Death chuckled. "Indeed. It's yet another reason to keep ties to the living world frequent and fair travelled."

"Not that you're the one treading that ground much anymore," Charon said. "So few people dying that you've time now to start raising life on your own?"

"Hmm," Death said thoughtfully. "It's those two."

"The rejects?"

"Yes," Death answered. "They've nearly completed their trial run. I was loath to admit it, all things considered, but they have proven themselves more useful than I expected. They have attached themselves well to this duty of Death. And perhaps there is some merit to it beyond this trial period. I may have to expand this relationship in the future."

"Aye?" Charon said. He took out a coin and fiddled with it between his fingers. His arm straightened out, taking the coin away from his centre and away from the catching hold of the boat beneath him, towards the water. "There was a time when you were enthused to see them fail and toss their bodies away into the water."

"And I may yet be again," Death said. "But it would betray my own fairness to punish them for success. Thus far, they've not let one soul slip from their grasp."

"So, they're doing better than you, eh?" Charon said.

Death mused darkly for a moment and considered the words.

Charon held his coin fast in the grip between two knuckles. Then, it slipped and dropped into the water. "Whoops." Charon theatrically put his hand to his mouth. "Oh no."

Death suddenly clutched at his side. He held his hand over his ribs and let out a pained seething gasp through his gritted teeth. Charon sat back and observed as Death doubled over with the phantom pain, seemingly brought on by nothing.

"Break something?" Charon asked.

"No," Death said. He took some groaning breaths and tried to straighten himself up. The pain faded, but the resonance spread through the rest of his bones. His shoulder was suddenly sore, and his leg felt a bit out of its socket. He rolled his arm and neck around to adjust. "I've been knee to the ground a bit too long. My body is too used to working. It thinks relaxation is a deathly throe to be abhorred."

"You'd be more relaxed with more apprentices," Charon said. "You may even die from having so many around. May need to rethink your idea of bringing more in."

"That I may," Death agreed. "Well, I'll be off. You have your own duties to tend to, I am sure."

"Oh, of course," Charon said. "It is so hard patrolling the shore for the weeping, wandering souls bereft of any gilding or good value, who beg and plead for passage over a river they do not deserve to cross. Perhaps I ought to receive my own apprentices and make a fleet of boats to cover the river's length across the void."

"I see no need for that," Death said. "There is only one boatman on the river. And he barely has work enough as it stands."

Charon's wry smile turned to a wrinkled, sunken frown, which was covered by the mist that surrounded him as Death retreated up the hill. Charon used his oar to reach down into the shallows of the water to see if he could fish up his gold coin, but it was lost. Anything that touched the water would sink down until it could not be retrieved.

But it was a worthy loss. Though he ached to part with the coin, the parting caused Death far worse pain. The theory he'd travelled out here to test seemed true, but he needed to test it further. Charon pushed away from the shore and turned upstream, with his back to the void and the myriad of awaiting souls trapped on the pitiless side of post-existence.

Death, meanwhile, struggled even to pull his robe over his head. Every reach over his shoulder came with a twinge of sudden pain he couldn't ignore, like a taut string that connected his arm to his chest was being wound too tight and threatened to snap apart in a bloody fashion.

Veronique heard him grunting and groaning and knocked on his den door.

"Monsieur!" she called. "Do you need assistance?"

"None," Death said. He finally got his arm shrugged into his robe sleeve. "I'm going to work. To shake off this doldrum pain."

"Are you certain you are up for it?" she asked. "Mark and Emma are nearly finished with their duties. They left just now to take their ninetieth-ninth soul."

"Ninety-nine already?" Death repeated. His jaw angled into what Veronique guessed was a brief smile. He rejected it and tugged his robe into proper shape. It felt longer than it used to, and his legs felt lost beneath it. He walked slowly across the floor, worried that his bony legs might get caught and pull at the inside threads of his cloak of darkness.

"Shall I prepare a celebration for them?" Veronique asked.

"No need to be so fancy," Death insisted. "I may still have reason to dismiss them in the end."

"Oh, okay," Veronique said. "But then I will have to throw out all of the specialty mushrooms I managed to get half price."

"...Specialty?" he asked.

"Yes. The kind you like so much. It would be a shame to waste—"

"Matsutake mushrooms don't go bad," he snapped.

Veronique giggled, having caught him in the act of caring when he wanted to stand against her own desire to acknowledge success.

"Just... don't be wasteful. You can prepare whatever you like. It's just a weekday dinner."

"With guests!" Veronique said cheerfully. "And cake."

Death followed her out of the room. Sharing his favourite meal with those doing his job for him...

He didn't hate the idea.

CHAPTER THIRTY-EIGHT

Emma and Mark were over London town once more. They'd grown accustomed to the sight after so many of their trial reapings had been trips to and from the capital. Sometimes the south, sometimes the north, mostly in the west for some reason, and only occasionally to the now trendy east. It was still somewhat of a spectral wanderlust tour of "the big smoke" for them, as well as a what-if moment had Mark decided to pursue the career in screenwriting he'd promised to follow instead of pivoting to design.

"Once we become official Deaths," Emma said, "do you think we'll be sent out to more exotic locations?"

"What, like Llanfairpwllgwyngyllgogerychwyrndrobwllllantysiliogogogoch?" Mark asked, grinning smugly as he nailed the pronunciation with a passable Welsh accent.

"Very good, smart arse. Now spell it." Emma smirked, tapping her foot impatiently.

"Where would you want to go?" Mark asked instead, deflecting the question.

"I've always wanted to see South America," Emma said. "Just get further and further away from society until you're firmly in the midst of an impassable mountain range or jungle, surrounded by nature, on an exclusive trek across its reaches."

"No matter what, you'd end up going to places to find corpses. And whatever poor souls go wandering away from their bodies – right?"

"Yeah," she agreed. "Maybe, occasionally, someone might die in a nice place but that just kind of makes it worse, doesn't it? You'd go to see a scenic landmark or a beautiful bit of nature that you've built up in your mind since childhood, and it'd be grey all over..."

"True."

"And then you'd just be there for work. A sort of busman's holiday. It'd spoil the moment."

"I think it'd be nice to see other countries," Mark said. "See how other people live."

"Like the rich and famous?" she said. "They probably won't be dying at all soon if they have the money to help it."

"Well, if they are still dying, they'd better clutch some hard currency before they do pop their clogs," Mark said. "Or they're not getting across the river."

"Not so rich then," she said mockingly.

"But other people, in general," Mark said. "I can't imagine... We had an okay life, all things considered."

Emma rolled her eyes.

"I mean," Mark continued, "compared to the people living in stone huts and bomb shelters. But they're living, despite all that, finding a way to stay alive. And yeah, seeing fancy mansions is nice and all, but seeing how everyone lives and talking to them about how they were happy with it all. I think it's a humbling experience."

"So Death will come up to them and say, 'You know my flat was a lot bigger than this back in Liverpool. I had it good, innit?'"

"Right, like I'll say it like that," he fired back.

The world turned grey. They'd bickered for just a moment too long. Fortunately, their quarry was well in sight, right over the Thames, off Lambeth bridge. Someone had fallen over the railing and died on impact. But their soul was disjointed from their corpse, and the ghost had been left on the bridge in an out-of-body shock experience to watch herself fall to her death.

"Oh, it's a cyclist," Mark said with a hint of disgust, eyeing the reflective strips wrapped around the soul's ankles. "I'll wrap this up quickly if you don't mind."

"Don't hate her for doing her bit for the environment," Emma said, then squinted as they approached. "Hold on."

"What is it?"

"Hang back," she instructed. She flew down and galloped along the halted traffic up behind the lost soul in her biking gear. The woman turned with a start and then squinted up at the dark rider astride her chestnut-brown horse.

"Emma?"

"Louise?"

Emma dismounted and hopped over, just a little giddy, to the utterly distraught woman she meant to greet.

"Wow," Emma said. "Bad way to meet up again, like this?"

"Wha— It *is* you, Emma!" Louise exclaimed as she unclipped her helmet and threw it to the ground, her long curly blonde hair falling across her shoulders. Louise had barely aged they'd last met. Still tall and slender, her cheeks were rosy from the exertion of avoiding London buses and angry cabbies. She reached up and immediately hugged Emma around her leather-lined shoulders. "It's been years, hasn't it?"

"Since we finished university," Emma said, hugging back. "It's good to see you again!" She stepped back and dropped her smile immediately. "Oh... Bad news, though."

"What?"

"You're dead."

"No!"

"Yeah, sorry."

Louise turned to the slightly bent railing from which her bike hung by its spokes. "I was sure I jumped off in time."

"I think your soul left your body before you fell," Emma said. "Never seen that happen before. But... yeah."

Louise turned, confused, then saddened. "So that's it, then?"

Emma nodded. Louise sighed and sat down next to her bike, her back to the Thames. Emma perched her scythe up against the bridge support and sat down next to her – a picture of calm amid the frozen expressions of horror on the faces of the unfortunate bystanders looking down at the river and the body below.

"Shame we have to meet like this," Emma said. She looked up and waved for Mark to come down. His pony trotted into place, and he dismounted. Louise shrank back at the sight of him until he lowered his hood.

"Mark?" she said, aghast.

"Oh – Louise?" He pulled the hourglass out of his sleeve. "Louise May Grosse! I knew I recognised that name! I mean, I thought I did, but I didn't know your middle name. How've you been?"

"Fine, until now," she said. She turned to Emma in disbelief. "Wait. Don't tell me you two *finally* got together?"

"What? No. We're not a couple," Emma said. "I— We're mates.

"Besties," Mark corrected her.

"Flat-mates," Emma clarified. "He actually tried to stop me offing myself, and then..."

"A lot of complications occurred," Mark said. "We're jobbing for Death until we earn our wings. So to speak."

Louise looked back and forth between them, then got up and held her hands out like she was backing away from an overflowing sink. "Oh my God. I can't believe it."

"What?" Emma asked. "If you're thinking how unlikely it is that we're all meeting like this because we're all dead then, yeah, it's uncanny."

"No, not that," Louise said with a sigh. "I can't believe you two still haven't boned!"

"Yeah," Emma said. "We just don't see each other in that way."

"Actually—" Mark put a finger up to reinforce the point he was about to make, but stopped when Emma shook her head at him.

"*Wow!*" Louise exclaimed. "We had a bet going every year. We thought, 'They're going to get it on. It's just a matter of time before they see what everyone else sees.'"

"And what does everyone else see?" Emma asked, already regretting the words even as they escaped her mouth.

"That you were made for each other. But numbnuts here was too chicken to ever ask you out."

"It's not for want of trying," Mark said, a bit too defensively.

Emma stood up, hands on her hips. "We're mates. Always have been, always will be."

"You keep telling yourself that." Louise shook her head and started laughing. "Oh, Mark. Hats off to you. Must have balls like fucking watermelons by now." The mirth quickly ran out and Louise's laugh became forced, false. It was a desperate, afraid sort of laugh. "I died," she said shortly after. "Alone. And you two died together? How's that fair?"

"Oh," Emma said. She looked over at Mark as if dreading the coming storm of emotions to come.

"I was out," Louise began, "on my way home from a date with a total knobhead who sat at a table comparing me to other profiles he'd matched with. And you know what? That was the best date I had this month. *Ugh!*" She sighed with more than exasperation. There was a life-draining, defeated slump in her voice. Emma tapped her fingers together, waiting for a moment to interject.

"It wasn't all good luck," Mark said. "I mean, the intention wasn't to die. At least mine wasn't."

"And yet here we are." Emma wanted to bring the chat to a close – she'd had enough of reminiscing and really just wanted to get on to the next hourglass. She smiled.

Louise just groaned. "There better be singles in the afterlife..."

"There are," Emma said, "but... well, you'll see."

"Any Christians?" Louise asked. Mark instinctively sniggered.

"There's not much of a dating scene in Limbo," Emma said. "And I'm sure someone's tried starting one up before."

The three of them mounted up, with Louise riding on the back of Emma's horse, and left the scene at the bridge to climb into the sky. Emma swung her scythe ahead. A purple crackle of lightning tore across the open air. Then kept crackling and fizzling.

The portal didn't open.

The lightning just continued to crackle freely in the open air.

"That's odd," Emma said.

Mark sensed something going horribly wrong. He tried his hand at opening a fissure – horizontally instead of vertically. His portal opened, but just barely. It was too narrow to go through. He ducked under it. All the energy collapsed together when he passed by in a muffled explosion with no echo. What remained was a ball of lightning that hung in the air, grey like the rest of the landscape, bleeding over into the momentary reality of the living world.

"Emma?" Mark called. "Try swinging harder!"

"Come up here and swing with me!" she told him. He rode up to match her level. They both swung their scythes at the same time. This time, the tear was big enough, though Mark had to fall behind and follow in single file to slip through. Once they were safely on the other side, they looked back to check the portal from the exit.

The lightning collapsed with a thunderous boom, unlike all other times where it had simply spiralled into itself with a faint fizzle as it shut.

"Cor!" Louise shouted. "That was loud! You do this all the time now?"

"It's usually a bit smoother than that," Emma said. She looked at her scythe. Aa few extra sparks stuck to the blade as she scooped it through a trough of neon sparkles.

"So, where are these dead blokes I can meet?" Louise asked.

Emma disregarded the portal anomaly. Of all the strange phenomena related to her duties as the horseman of death, one out of ninety-nine botched portals seemed like a fairly normal inconsistency. It wasn't worth getting hung up or stopping over. Especially not now that they were just one hourglass away from fulfilling their duty to Death.

Just one lost soul away from their freedom or judgement.

CHAPTER THIRTY-NINE

It was a calm and peaceful day on the riverfront. Just like any other day in the last eternity, it was a day with hardly any business. For Charon, that was all that mattered. His compatriots in the natural forces of destruction and despair for the living world were all satiated by something other than the hard exchange of coin and value. They had artistry to care about, diligence, duty: things that couldn't be measured in ounces of gold.

His whole existence revolved around the unchanging value of gold that mankind clung to. Their material possessiveness carried over into the eternally flowing river of death, which incited him into becoming a collector and a hoarder of the value that lasted beyond the final ending. It was all he had. And he couldn't even spend it.

But it still had value, as he came to discover. He rowed himself down to the homestead of War, furthest up the river, in her egregious compound fronted by a magnificent Viking longhouse. She was the only one who provided him some sort of comfort on the waterside, a dock to rest his ship and a post to tether his chain so he could wander inland just far enough to reach her front door.

The length of his chain, however, had altered. He still had plenty of slack to give by the time he reached the door. Nearly enough to enter and turn into the first hallway, though none further. He made keen note of the recent change.

He knocked on the door. After some slogging and meandering, War answered.

"Charon? How do you do?"

"Fine enough," he replied. "A bit fairer than you, it seems."

War clutched her hand to her side, pressing a white wad of bandages together over a slow, slight bleed. Her right leg had a limp in it as well, and her makeup was faded around the area where she'd once expertly hidden a scar across her eyebrow.

"It's just an off day," she said passively. "Old wounds reminding me of the past."

"Of better days?" Charon asked. "Now mankind has no use for spilling warrior blood, when so much more ground is gained through innocents lost and com-pew-tors carrying out their atrocities without the capacity for sin."

"There is still blood on some hands," she said. "Though, what blood doesn't reach them has ended up on me." She smiled, ever charming and sophisticated, even with blood staining her palm. She walked with Charon down to the waterfront and looked over the dock.

"What's to do about this?" he asked as he poked the loose boards with his oar. Some were creaking from lack of use and maintenance. "It speaks of some parable that I'd need to rip boards off my own boat just to give it a place to rest, wouldn't ye agree?"

"That does sound... parabolic," War said. She carefully leaned herself down and inspected the wood and the rot that overtook it.

Charon hovered back and stepped onto his boat over the

water. He reached for a coin hidden in his sleeve and prepared to place it into the water.

"It is outdated," War said. "Such is the trouble of making use of what man has abandoned in the way of war. But I can resettle this into a concrete dock in no time, try and give it that submarine naval base look."

"And that'll be safer?" he asked. "I'd like not for my boat to be torn from me by the current if I'd ever visit."

"It will most certainly be safer," she insisted. She stood up with a huff and patted her side. It was seemingly well again.

Then Charon cast a coin into the water. He watched from his boat as War doubled over from a stabbing pain that coursed through her body. He raised a tentative hand in sympathy.

"You alright, love?" he asked.

"Oh, just dandy," she groaned. "Nothing a little sit down shouldn't fix." Her breathing was pained and shocked. The wound had reopened and now oozed with fresh blood. Charon watched the scarlet red spread through the bandages and mark her hand through all the fabric.

"I'll see if Death's young miss'll give you a courtesy call," he said. "Perhaps she has a supply of fresh dressings."

"I would appreciate that," she said.

Charon pushed off the creaky dock and kept an eye on War as he drifted down the river. She struggled her way back up the path to her home and even fell over once before the fog obscured him entirely. It was an awful coincidence, but still just a theory. He needed repeat success to prove he had a functional practice at hand. And he had two more coins to lose.

Down the river was Pestilence, out in his field watering neon-coloured plants and tossing shredded food into a stagnant pool with a multicoloured film of bacterial colonies across the surface. He waved to Charon with genuine warmth as he approached, and bid him over.

"How goes things?" Charon asked. "Have you finally found the dark grail to sicken all the waters which flow from it as man's baleful drink?"

"Not yet, no. Thanks for asking," Pestilence said. "I'm getting closer though. Little by little, I'm finding new combinations of life-threatening illnesses. It's how to spread them that I haven't quite adjusted to yet."

Charon nodded along, feigning interest, and then slipped a coin into the water.

"Transmission vectors remain the bottlene— *UNGH!*" Immediately, a violent coughing fit interrupted the flow of their discussion. Charon pushed away from the shore as Pestilence fell to his knees. He coughed so hard that he choked on the air he swallowed and was left a panting, miserable mess.

"Dear me," Charon said. "You ought to lower your own exposure. You wouldn't want to be undone by your own works."

"That'd be—" he started, before coughing again. "...alright by me."

"I'll send Death's young miss your way," Charon said. "She may have some cure for your ails that won't harm the little nasties you intend to harvest."

"Thank you," Pestilence said. He remained doubled over in a painful wretch. His theory had proven correct again. If Charon was a betting man, he would stake a healthy wager on having proved his hypothesis. But he wasn't, so there was still one more control test he had to pass.

Famine's dilapidated all-you-can-eat buffet restaurant and homestead was just a bit further downriver. He too was outside, looking thinner and paler than normal, and inattentive. He was smoking a whole wild boar of some extinct genome near the water's edge. The smoke from his pit mingled with the fog and turned into a heavy, airy sludge-like cloud overhead. Charon caught his attention with a wave as he stepped off his boat, and Famine waved back.

"Feeling peckish, are we?" Charon called out.

"Nothing a little snack won't fix," Famine said jovially. He patted his stomach – flattened from what seemed to be a long fast– and tried to jiggle it but could only grip loosened skin.

Charon tossed a coin into the water and watched as Famine suddenly froze. A sunken look overcame the horseman – a loss of all satiation and an onset of a sickening kind of hunger. He was so preoccupied by the pain and ravenous hunger he didn't notice the ferryman clicking back on to his boat and pushing off from the shore. Charon heard the echoing growl of Famine's stomach as his boat drifted away.

War bled, Pestilence sickened, Famine hungered, and even Death faded. All at the act of a coin being loosed from Charon's grip. There was no doubt in his mind.

He brushed his hand over his robe of gold with a cackle. "'Tis natural, then," he said to himself. "One's nature must not be rejected. Else that rejection shall flow into the river and feed into the lands up o'er the shore. Yes..." He cackled again as he picked up his pace and rowed back to his castle hoard.

Up above, he saw the sharp crackle of purple lightning in the sky. The two apprentices, Death's toadies, were returning from yet another dutiless errand for the old bone golem. Charon grimaced at their presence. Two more nodding heads bringing the miserly souls from one world to pester and propagate another. They, too, were outside the nature Charon knew and understood best.

They, too, were proof of a changing tide.

"Six," he muttered. "Six now. Three pale riders astride their horses, carrying souls cut down from the mortal world in the wake of the rage of the other three. There aren't meant to be six horsemen. And if there are, seniority dictates that one ought to come from the water first..."

Charon grumbled as he rowed down the river to his hoard. To his purpose..

CHAPTER FORTY

I t had been a trying few days – or something. Mark and Emma hovered in the air over Belfast with their final soul onboard, hacked up and stuffed into Mark's bag for breaching one of their concessionary rules. They stared ahead at the face of the Albert Memorial Clock. From their perspective, it had been many long days of work since their deaths, with only a few infrequent breaks to tide them over and recharge.

"What time did you get to the Liver Building that day?" Emma asked.

"Two thirty-ish," he said. "Ish, so maybe two thirty-five or two forty?"

According to the clock, it was 2:51 that same afternoon. At the most generous estimate, not even half an hour had passed on Earth since Mark and Emma were absconded by Death and took the role of maintaining the natural order in his stead. In just that time, across the British Isles, one hundred souls had passed on, and they'd taken every single one to another world of eternal waiting in a vacuous void.

"I've never had a job where it felt like hours and hours had passed before just one hour went by in reality," Mark said. "And I forget – is that supposed to be a good thing?"

"What?" Emma said.

"When time slows down... Is that what that means?"

"No," she corrected him. "It's when you're having fun, and time goes by faster."

"Oh, yes," Mark said. "Well... I can't say this isn't fun."

"Deciphering your double negatives and judging by the nature of work on the mind's perception of time, this must be the most boring, god-awful slog of a thankless mistake we've ever made."

He shrugged. "It could be worse."

"How, exactly?" she asked.

"I mean, we know exactly how much worse it could be," he said, jostling his bag. "About this much worse."

"True," she said. "We could be trapped on the riverbank of Limbo for eternity because we didn't put gold under our tongues."

"At least we'd be trapped together," Mark said.

"We are trapped together. Just together at the same job."

"Yeah, but that makes the time go faster."

She pointed at the clock tower.

"Okay, a little faster," he corrected himself. "And I've been thinking... Well, I'll bring it up with Death when we get back."

"Oh?"

"Yeah," he said. He hoisted his scythe up and held it fast. He was a bit worried after the last try hadn't gone too well. This time he swung, and a portal opened easily. They both sighed with relief and travelled through it, back to the familiar void.

The sky, such as it was, had a slightly greyer tint, as if a storm was moving in. But being a featureless void, it looked more like the contrast had been turned down on the TV set that served as their panorama. A fog covered much of the void where it hadn't before, looming and spreading out from the river and even creeping halfway up the garden outside Death's cottage.

"Must be evening," Emma said.

"And also summer," Mark added.

They flew down and hopped off their pair of horses, ready to reassemble their belligerent spirits so they could begin the endurance of their eternal waiting period.

"Monsieur! Madame!" Veronique called out. The maid jogged down to them with a spring in her steps. "Come, come! Please!"

"For what?" Emma asked.

"The celebration!" she said. "One hundred souls delivered, as you promised. Monsieur Death has agreed to a dinner to give you thanks!"

"Oh, that's rather magnanimous of him," Mark said.

"Or did he just agree to it because you already did all the work?" Emma asked.

"Just come!" Veronique insisted, proving Emma right.

"Uh, what about this?" Mark asked, holding up the sack.

"Leave it," Veronique said. "The food is all ready. Do not let it go cold! It is my speciality!"

"I'm not missing an all-out Veronique buffet," Emma said.

"Well, neither am I!" Mark exclaimed. "When Veronique bigs up her own cooking, I bet it's off the charts!"

Emma went off without him up the gravel path. When he dropped the bag down, a light groan came from within.

"Look, mate," Mark told the soul inside, "you shouldn't have swung at me. And now we're here and... Just— just sit tight. You're not gonna miss anything." As the fog slowly crept up behind him, he left the bag mumbling and jittering about on the short, freshly shaved grass.

The pair were met by an assault of glorious smells when they entered the cottage, all from a brilliantly decorated table in the main dining area. There was a spread of gorgeous-looking foods, from a dressed, roasted hen and a deep pot of cheese-topped French onion soup to a basket of fresh-cut baguettes and a rotating plate of various sweet, creamy cheeses. And there was wine for all, one bottle each, and tall glasses to receive it.

Death sat at the apparent head of the table, dressed down in his casual clothes with a pair of reading glasses over his hollow eye sockets. He looked older, somehow. The hue of his bones made them look almost brittle. His lack of energy was clear from the way he slumped in his chair. Veronique, however, easily made up for the deficit in his energy as she popped a champagne cork which flew up and hit a banner that unfolded into a message:

Joyeux 100 trépas!

"Congratulations!" Veronique cheered. Death raised his hands and tapped his palms together.

"Ah, thank you," Mark said. "This is all very..."

"Lovely," Emma said. "Really thoughtful."

"Thank you," Mark agreed. "I'm glad we've made an impression."

"Yes," Death said. His voice, once booming, felt faded and slight. "Celebrating one's duty is much more of a mortal custom. To encourage continued obeisance to the societal systems which ensure your safety and longevity in exchange for labour. Encouraging that same diligence was never necessary. But for you, I suppose, exceptions can be made. You are, already, exceptions of your own."

With that, Death took the bottle of champagne from Veronique and filled four glasses. He took up a flute and nodded for them to follow suit.

"Skål," Death said as he raised his glass.

"Santé," Veronique replied.

Emma and Mark grinned, pleased they'd won some approval from Death.

"Cheers," they said in unison, and clinked glasses with their hosts.

"So our sand still hasn't fallen?" Emma asked after she sipped at her champagne.

Death shook his head.

"Well... at least that time wasn't wasted."

"We brought one hundred souls to their resting place," Mark said. "This... feast feels like quite a reward already."

"Indeed," Death said. "And one hundred souls, without a single failure... It is worth rewarding." As the two sat down across from him, he pulled himself up in his chair. "Even I do not always bring back all the souls I venture out to get."

"Really?" Mark asked.

Death sighed. "There are so many. And they are so impatient. Some run, some fight. Some resist. And then they leave. And I, in my duty, must venture out to find another. The world cannot remain stopped over just one death. It must persist and move ever onward."

"True," Mark said. "We had a few... runners."

"But we corralled them and made them submit," Emma said.

"It's not always fun," Mark admitted. "Taking the spirit of a child, who doesn't understand what's happening, isn't something I'm dying to repeat. Pardon the pun. It can be quite grim, this reaping business. But... it's very good, I think. In the end, all things considered, what we're doing has been quite—"

Death suddenly groaned, not in exasperation but with great weakness. He fell forward, his skull landing on his plate. Veronique gasped and immediately went to his side.

"Mon Dieu!"

"What's wrong?" Emma said. She jumped to her feet and

circled around the table. Mark joined her shortly after to see what was going on. Death held his hand up to placate their growing concern and pushed his chair back.

His legs were... disappearing. Slightly gone from the ankles down. All that was left was a wispy, foggy trail like a classical free-floating ghost.

"It's nothing to worry about," Death said.

"Jesus fucking Christ, really?" Mark flapped, unsure what to do. "You're disappearing!"

"Can you hear me?" Emma leaned towards where Death's ears would be, if he had any. She slowed down her words, focussing on her pronunciation. "You're okay. Help's on its way. I'm Emma. It's going to be alright."

"I'm not having a stroke, you don't need to talk to me like an infant," Death responded calmly as he assessed the vapour where his phalanges should be. "It's... puzzling."

Emma leaned towards Veronique to whisper, "Is this what happens when he gets on the pop? He's like Marty McFly in *Back to the Future*!"

"Non," Veronique protested. "This has never happened before. Monsieur, what should I do?"

Death reached up and patted Veronique on the head. Then he rested his hand on her, a calm reassuring gesture, like he had done to comfort her after her passing many years ago. He tried to stand, but his feet didn't touch the ground. It was like he stood on blocks of slick ice. His legs shuddered to keep him standing.

Then, as he braced his hand against the table, it too lost some of its hardened physical form. His fingertips became wisps. The bone blended into a quickly dissipating smoke, leaving a dusty residue on the varnished wood.

"I simply need to rest," Death said. "You two... have done

exceptionally well thus far. I hope I can continue to rely on you... in the future."

"Monsieur, please," Veronique pleaded. "Allow me." She took his arm over her shoulder and helped shuffle him back into his den. Mark and Emma were left with a table full of food, and their host, their patron, and their employer fading away in a literal sense just a room away.

"I think," Mark said, as he glugged down his champagne, "it'd be impolite to waste this effort. We should dig in."

"No, this is wrong," Emma said direly.

"Right," Mark agreed. "Right. It's wrong."

They rushed to join Veronique in tending to Death. There were still some secrets of this realm between worlds left to learn. Secrets that Death never planned to let loose...

CHAPTER FORTY-ONE

Veronique helped Death into his favourite recliner chair and immediately rushed out to get something to help him. It was clear she didn't know what exactly, from her flustered, averted gaze. Mark and Emma stood to the side and peered in through the crack in the door.

"He's dissolving," Emma whispered.

"He's not deaf," Mark said. He pulled her aside and around the other side of the hall. "Can Death... die?"

"Is that a riddle?" she asked. "No, wait, it's a line. From a song, right?"

"No, that's— I mean, we're not dead."

"No?"

"Technically, no," Mark said. "Still. Sort of. But the conversation did arise, as I remember, of being ported over to the other side as though we were dead once our time expired – or if we were just abject failures at our task, which thankfully we weren't."

"Yes, we've done quite well."

"Right."

They paused to high-five each other in celebration.

"But my point is," Mark continued, "the spirits here, or out in the void, or ones like Veronique and the other horsemen… what happens to them when they, I don't know, fall down their stairs?"

Emma caught on to his thinking, albeit only just. For all the mythical symbolism and grandeur of their spiritual significance, the horsemen and the wandering souls of the void all had some minor mortal habits in common. Her nose caught a whiff of the food going uneaten in the other room.

"For that matter," she said, "why does he eat?"

"Right?" Mark said. "It's not for fun. He hates that."

"So can Death starve?" Emma wondered.

"And can Famine… trip and break his neck? That's not a very war-like or sickly thing to do, and it's just an accident. Random, accidental, and brutal but intended deaths seem to be Death's main thoroughfare."

"That and age," she said.

"I mean, what happens to us if Death dies?"

The two shared an uneasy look. They felt the drag of time in the world between, despite time not moving unless they were present to observe its passing in the final moments of a fated disposal. They were ageing out of sync with the rest of the world. And so had Death been ageing at an even further accelerated rate since the dawn of human history.

"Would it be rude to ask if we are, in fact, the first and only replacements he's hired?" Emma asked.

"You think he might not be the original Death?"

"I think if we stay long enough, there won't be anything left of us but *our* bones, too."

Just then, Veronique came down the hall with a foot spa and an electric heated blanket.

"What about her?" Mark asked.

"She's French," Emma said. "She's got good genes."

"French women decompose too," Mark said.

Emma shook her head dismissively.

"Excuse me," Veronique called, "could I ask you to please get the door?"

Mark noticed she was barely holding onto her items. Emma took the foot spa from her while Mark held the door open to let them in. Death was ailing in his La-Z-Boy – his feet were completely gone up to his ankles, and his hands seemed very much on their way as the tips of his bony fingers were all but evaporating.

They set up his therapeutic measures and tried to coax him into it. He had no power to resist their caretaking, not even to groan. He just sighed airy, wispy sighs. A thin trail of white dust leaked from his mouth and hovered in the air before it sprinkled down like a slow fall of snow.

"You alright, sir?" Mark asked.

"Oh... no," Death said casually. "It seems I am becoming a wraith."

Mark gave Emma a worried look. "Is that... like dying?"

"Somewhat," he answered. "When a soul is left unattended for too long, it loses form. It loses purpose and identity. It loses the rigidity of its form and fizzles out to naught but a speck, an orb, or a roving skull, until it loses all purpose in one world and fades into the next."

"All these souls," Mark said, "out here in Limbo..."

"Indeed." Death sighed. "It is their fate as well. To join the fog upon the river. To sink below or skim above the water, ever seeking passage from the boatman."

"The fog?" Emma said. "It's all souls?"

"The countless untended to," Death proclaimed. "Without purpose, dead without faith, lost in all directions from the annals of history. Dead long enough to know their judgement is not coming, that their God shall not call them. The only purpose which supports them thereafter is the will to travel to the other side. Those who enter the water do not rise again, they simply sink into the abyss. Those who wait even longer lose their form and travel over the water as a mist that cannot be reformed. That is what it means to be a wraith. To lose purpose, and therefore form..."

"Oh no," Mark said. "This is our fault."

"No," Veronique protested. "Do not blame yourself."

"We've been reaping so well," Mark said, "that it's made you lose your purpose as the one true Death."

"Bah!" Death exclaimed. This sudden outburst was too much for his body to handle. He coughed weakly until his breathing steadied. "You are adequate at best. Though I did expect you to lose one or two souls in your duty. But you have not gone through the chaos of man's destructive age to see what true death looks like. Those roving souls upon the land – ghosts and spectres, as those unfortunate few with the sight to see them have so named them – are the souls I could not find in wars and in genocides. In great disasters of the past. Those who have lost the patience to wait for their God to come."

"And those who are still human in shape," Emma said, "stay that way by a sense of a duty greater than wanting to see the afterlife?"

Mark nodded. He wondered if he'd seen any such misty forms moving around during the stoppage of time when he went about his reaping. Then a new, unique worry crept up and threatened to seize his throat.

"Is the world *supposed* to turn all grey and murky when someone dies?" he asked.

"What?" Emma said.

"Like a fog was stuck to everything?"

Emma just blinked. She sought a answer from Death's fading form. He sputtered and shook his head.

"That is normal," he clarified, and Mark sighed with relief. "Even if you found those unfortunate lost souls, there is nothing you can do for them. That is the cost of failure. It is an eternal mark of a duty lapsed and lost to time... Look at the hourglasses." He pointed to the miles of shelves visible through the open door to the Hall of Time at the far end of the room. Today's harvest, the ones with barely any time left to go, were all elderly people, or unfortunate youths about to meet a perilous end in accidents of some kind.

And they were all splotchy.

Mark took one and turned it around. The top bulb of the hourglass was marred on the inside in several spots by what looked like glassy scabs.

"The sand of your hourglasses remains adhered to the sides," Death explained. "As those do. It is a problem rice could not solve. Death, itself, no longer becomes them."

"How does that make sense?" Emma asked. "People die all the time. We've already carried away one hundred souls on our own in just twenty-odd minutes!"

Death laughed, coughed, and kept laughing. "Do you know how many *thousands* die every hour? What a pittance... What a poor, insignificant collection you have gathered up in a time when you could have travelled the whole world's surface and not seen a single minute pass? And how many *haven't*?"

"Monsieur, breathe," Veronique pleaded. "Conserve your strength."

"So?" Mark said. "It's a slow day at the office. That happens. Everyone has a good day. Maybe all those good days... lined up together?" Even he lost belief in what he was saying towards the end.

"No such thing," Death said. "Not like this. Yours was the first. I dreaded it might not be the last. But until those few grains drop, the events which come to end life will stop occurring. And if none pass…"

"Won't time just stop?" Emma asked. "If time, from this perspective, is just a collection of living moments, and those stop…"

"The End Times," Death muttered. "What we horsemen dread to carry out." He turned to his window, which overlooked the river covered in the fog's moisture outside. "When time itself ends."

Mark realised he was gripping the material of his robe with bunched fists. He had been trying to excel at being Death so he could have another chance at life. He was not yet ready to pass to the other side, but now he feared there wouldn't even be a living world to return to.

Emma reached over to hold his hand. She gripped his fingers tight. She too was worried. Not for herself, but at the enormity of what the End Times might mean. She had made the decision to end her life; she'd had her reasons and she'd made an informed choice. But what of all those other lives, represented by the millions of hourglasses they could see and hear in the Hall of Time. All the lives lived, the lives being lived, and those who had yet to begin their journey towards death.

The mood hung heavy in the den, as if the fog was already in there, weighing down the air they struggled to breathe.

CHAPTER FORTY-TWO

They scoured the shelves of Death's archives in the sitting room for books about his work, about the apocrypha of human invention, and anything that might help them through the strange scenario they were dealing with – a time when Death, himself, may die and when all the other aspects of cruel nature were upended by a sudden souring of fate. They turned to his personal writings and musings, carried over from the centuries in all manner of unreadable ancient scripts.

"I found one in German," Mark said.

"Me too," Emma added. "A lot, actually."

"Death having a German phase makes more sense than I thought it would," Mark said. He squinted at the text and tried to read it aloud. "Oh, never mind – it's actually Polish."

"Even more fitting," she said. "Oh, wait, this looks promising." She pulled out a black leather-bound notebook inscribed with a signature of a skull on the front. The text inside was written in simple handwritten English, with a somewhat Victorian vernacular.

"'The End Times,'" Emma read, "'is not yet realised, though I fear its approach may be imminent. This irreversible change of nature, which man has wrought through iron and steam, is but the first dolorous stroke against his own grim fate.'"

"Damn," Mark said. "The industrial revolution screwed us over again."

"'By my mark and on martyr's blood,'" Emma went on, "'waste not... the immortal tides...' It's very poetic, I'll give him that."

"But what does it mean?"

"Apparently," Emma said, "this 'End Times' the horsemen dread, which we also dread, from our own Biblical context, is *literally* an ending of time. The end of progress and all human history as the facets of nature which dictate and determine the sway of all reality come to a grinding halt. When there are no wars to cause the 'chaos of production', no sickness to 'sieve the souls of the weak and bolster future strengths', when there is no famine 'and thus no struggle to unite all clans and tribes together' there shall likewise be 'a secession of Death and all such moments shall thereby remain eternal.'"

She read out loud another key passage. "'It is the lull and the peace they should fear most, as it spells the most essential beginning of their doom. For the first trumpet to sound shall be found in the silence of their own breathing, and the seizure of their sun which will render the sky grey and no breeze shall shift the clouds in the sky. Where it is night shall be night forever; Where it is day shall also be night. And that final moment shall be reap'd as the final thread of fate is severed and left for all the future to go unborn.'"

"So that's it then?" Mark said. "When the horsemen lose their purpose and turn into wraiths, mankind loses? We *need* War and Pestilence and Famine and Death just to go on living?"

"...Yeah?" Emma said, with an uncertain shrug. "It's kind of a shit fate, a symbiosis, but I get it. With how we act, it's a little deserved."

"I don't deserve that," Mark said. "They don't." He waved in the direction of the endless shelves of flowing hourglasses.

"Well, we were going to die eventually," she said. "Or so it seemed."

Death's ruminations, penned over centuries, hadn't uncovered a cure. They, and the whole of civilisation, were in the shit. The hum from the constant flow of sand filled the room – millions of moments still happening for millions of people as they lived their lives obliviously.

The reality of the existential event Mark and Emma were witnessing was almost too profound to comprehend. Emma combed her hands through her hair, looking at the rows and rows of hourglasses neatly arranged on the shelves. Could all of this simply stop soon? No more sand? No more Death? No more life?

"There's only one thing we can do now," Emma said.

"What?" Mark asked.

"If Death is the only thing keeping mankind moving forwards right now, then we'll just have to keep it going ourselves. Move it all ahead one second hand at a time. At least then there's something going right."

"But we can't reap unready souls," he said.

Emma stood up and took Mark's hand, leading him through the door into the vast Hall of Time. She strode towards the closest shelf, running her free hand over the smooth wood of the hourglasses there. With one hundred souls reaped and many thousands of lives weighed in grains of sand literally in the palm of their hands, they instinctively knew how to measure a life. Emma pulled an hourglass off the shelf and looked at the nameplate – Marcus Gordale.

"Five months tops," she assessed.

"Emma, we *can't,*" Mark told her.

He avoided eye contact as long as he could, but she drew closer and closer until there was nowhere left to look but at her face, which seemed very cross with him.

"But if we did,..." she began.

"It wouldn't be fair," Mark said. "Don't take that from us. Being fair is the only thing we can maintain with this title. If we start killing willy-nilly, there'll be no one left in the country to pluck outrageous property valuations out of thin air."

Emma nodded, acknowledging his point and quite pleased to know that if they had gone on an early-death killing spree, they would both have regarded estate agents as collateral damage. They really did have much more in common than Emma cared to admit.

They paused their discussion when Emma spotted Veronique in the den with a sheet over her back – a sheet that leaked steam like an over-boiled kettle. Running back into the den, they found Veronique marching down the hall towards the front door.

"Where are you going?" Emma asked.

"To the river," she said.

"With what?"

Veronique sighed a timid, dreadful sigh. "Have you eaten any food?" she asked them. "Please do. It is a meal I made for you."

"Veronique, where's Death?" Mark asked.

The sheet moved, and a wispy, translucent hand dropped from Veronique's shoulder. It reached back up to find purchase on her arm again. Death lay against her, covered in a white sheet of mournful passing. Even for a skeleton, he looked unhealthy. Some of his teeth were missing. A deep crack reached from his right eye socket down his cheek.

"Markus... Emelia," he groaned.

The two of them approached, not for a moment daring to correct him.

"You... can return now to your world, unafraid of death. For Death has lost all place in the affairs of mortals."

Neither Mark nor Emma wanted to return to their world right now. Not under these circumstances. Not if the End Times were imminent. They were resolute. They were staying put, and would do anything to help Death not die.

"Don't give up, sir," Emma said. "There's still a place for death in the world. We'll do it! It'll be slow, but we can—"

He held up a hand to stop her. "Your power is only borrowed by proxy. Without me, you shall lose the ability to travel there and hence. You should go now. Be with your own kind. For when I travel across the river and intermingle with its mist, it shall truly be the end of all time..."

"Then don't do it," Mark said. "There must be something we can do, or the other horsemen maybe. Or even—"

He turned to Emma with a shock of realisation.

"But would he help?" she asked.

"He stands to lose just as much," Mark said. "No death means no gold, right? If he knows anything, he should want to tell us."

"You speak of the boatman," Death said. "Do not bother. He, too, will not last. Just as I have lost my form, surely he has lost his boat..."

The four inhabitants of Death's cottage were interrupted by the sound of rushing water, the rumble of a mighty engine, and "La Cucaracha" being played over foghorns. Mark and Emma ran out first into the thick bank of fog. Now that they knew what it was, they tried hard not to inhale too much of the residue of immortal spirits. Using their sleeves as masks, they stomped through the thick air until they reached the shore, where the air was clearer.

A ridiculously large, ostentatious yacht bobbed up and down in the water. It was made of solid gold, with an array of six outboard motors and a crusty old captain wearing more jewellery than clothing – though they could make out a pair of neatly pressed boat shorts and a Hawaiian shirt.

"Well, now!" Charon called. He walked to the edge of the deck and leaned over the railing. He was the same rickety, slouching old man of contemptuous appearance. Only his exterior and equipment had changed.

"Nice boat," Mark said.

"That it is!" Charon exclaimed. "A changing of tides came to order. I fished it up after submitting a precious fare into the waters, and out it came, tribute from the abyss of man's creation!"

"Charon!" Emma called. "The End Times are happening!"

"Are they now?" he said with a sly grin. "You've been taught all about yer job only to see it to its bitter ending, eh? Awful time to land a new job when the company is in bankruptcy!" He laughed a devious, throaty cackle.

Emma and Mark turned to the sound of galloping hooves. The black stallion of War, the chestnut mare of Pestilence, the auburn workhorse of Famine, and even Death's pale steed all came forward and went down on their knees at the shore to unload their riders.

War was a mess of blood and cuts. Her skin ran bright red with the effluence of embattled wounds. Famine was a husk, a starving sack of bones wrapped in thin skin. Pestilence looked one ragged breath from his last, with the blue and green of his veins colouring the paleness of his own skin.

And Death was now just a skull floating in a thickened vapour wrapped in a sheet, like a junior-school child's impression of a ghost.

"Har har har!" Charon cackled. "Look how low ye've been

levelled. No wars to watch? No hunger to sow? No sickness to carry? Oh, and you," he said, pointing a golden cane at Death. "The most pitiful of them all. So weak you had two *children* take up your job, so you could slouch and slump all the way to dust!"

"Shut up!" Mark shouted. He stepped forward and kicked the side of Charon's yacht, hurting his foot against the solid gold hull.

"Don't scuff my boat!" Charon shouted back. "Took me all morning to buff, and I'll need it. This great vessel shall replace *ALL* the horses and their riders! A new order of nature shall flow into the mortal world. And you, all of *you*, will look on helplessly from this side of *MY* river, as the souls flow through it like a flood!"

Charon reached into a golden goblet and threw a rain of coins into the water like he was feeding fish. Each time one of the coins hit the water, the horsemen groaned and were reduced to even more pitiful states. Their bodies recoiled in agony as if raked with bullets. Mark and Emma added the events up immediately. They glowered after the crusty sailor as he spun the yacht's wheel and engaged the throttle, performing a doughnut which splashed them with the liquified factor of countless souls sent to drown. Then he sped off.

"He did this!" Emma said. "It had to be him!"

"Right," Mark said, with a shake of his robe to dry it off. "I've always wanted to trash a rich twat's boat. Now I've got a good reason to. Stormrider!"

"Princess!" Emma called.

Their horses came to them out of the fog, dilapidated, tired, and years older than when they'd left them just minutes ago. But they came carrying the one thing they both needed: their scythes. They mounted up and left the ailing horsemen in Veronique's care.

Over the river and down the stream to Charon's house they went...

CHAPTER FORTY-THREE

Mark and Emma, the auxiliary horsemen of the apocalypse, rode along the river, through the great bank of fog, following the glittering spectacle of Charon's golden yacht. They rode as best they could with the very last breaths of their horses sputtering out.

"Come on, Stormrider!" Mark cheered. "You were never the biggest, but you damn sure are the toughest! The most fatal pony in all existence!"

"Keep going, Princess Die!" Emma shouted. "I won't have you crashing into anything but the skull of that shady bastard."

As they rode on, the two passed an endless procession of souls from Limbo. The great featureless void space they occupied shifted far in the distance. No longer featureless, it became rippled with dunes, like a desert of chalk.

"Everything's changing," Emma said. "For the worse."

"We need to get rid of that boatman," Mark replied. "If for no other reason than petty vengeance."

"He's got to know what's going on," Emma said. "Well enough to be able make it worse at will."

As they rode, they heard the thunder of the yacht's outboard motors up ahead and a rumble of hoof stomps from behind. Mark turned to see Veronique catching up to them on her own steed, armed with a feather duster the size of a poleaxe. Her horse was in much better shape, but every racing step it took seemed to age its fur a shade darker and drier.

"Monsieur! Madame!" she called out.

"Where is Charon's house?" Mark asked. "We never did much touring, and it just occurred to me our first visit is going to be to throttle him."

"Charon is behind all this, isn't he?" Emma asked.

"Oui," Veronique confirmed. "The cavaliers did say so. By rejecting the gold he holds so precious, he has warped the natural order to such a degree that it kills Death and wounds War."

"And summons the End Times," Emma added.

The three riders urged their mounts on, ignoring their spluttering and wheezing.

"And the boat?" Emma asked. "Where's he been hiding that?'

"They do not know where his grandiose boat came from," Veronique replied. "It is too unnatural."

Mark turned to her. "Are we at least on the right track in thinking that killing him may reverse all of this?"

"Yes," she confirmed. "But killing him shall create another problem. You must—"

She halted her speech and pointed to the river. A great wave of dreadful, soul-draining water came their way from the wake of Charon's boat. They all hiked their horses up into the air to avoid it. Stormrider lagged and just barely rose above the tide as it splashed his underside.

"Up and away, boy!" Mark shouted, pulling his reins to climb higher. "Very away!"

"Go!" Veronique called. "Across the river!"

Emma and Mark turned and began crossing the wide River Styx from above, leaving Veronique behind. The fog tangled around them as they went, forcing them to rise above it. From there, they could see the forbidden landscape of the other side.

Far in the distance, beyond the shadowy valley, were two split horizons. One was clustered with storm clouds and fearsome flashes of lightning, like approaching Manchester on the M62. The other side was tranquil and calm, with a veil of soft light filtered through a cloudy haze. But that, too, was altered by the perversions of nature around them. The thunder reached into the calm clouds, and the darkness came to an abrupt end where the tempestuous clouds stood still and drooped down like upside-down ice cream dripping onto the lands below.

"Oh," Mark said. "So, there is a Heaven and Hell?"

"Or there was," Emma said.

"It's weird that they're neighbours," he said. "And close enough that... this is an issue that has to be avoided."

"They obviously don't have building regs here," Emma said. "Anybody can build anything where they claim it. No respect for infrastructure or the surrounding aesthetic."

"Speaking of," Mark said. He pointed to the brilliant beacon of gold down below. Charon's manor stretched into an entire estate. His golden hoard made up a dock, a canal, and a castle rampart all in one, and all made of gold. His yacht had been pulled into a subterranean dock-cum-garage that lowered its drawbridge door. Then, a glint of gold sparked from the castle rampart and a thread of light drew rapidly closer.

"Duck!" Mark shouted.

Emma heard him too late. A golden bolt pierced Princess Die

through the chest. Emma was rocked off the back of her horse as it bucked its last and went limp in the air. Mark raced down to catch her as she fell. Stormrider bore their weight as best he could, but descended rapidly to the ground. More golden bolts flew at them, but their unplanned descent allowed them to safely dodge the attacks from on high and reach the ground.

"How dare he?!" Emma shouted as she clutched her scythe handle tight.

"Ballistics. A classic castle defence," Mark said. "We *are* invading his property, after all. To kill him."

"Don't defend him!" she shouted. "He killed my horse!"

"I'm not. I'm just explaining what's happened!"

They dismounted Stormrider, Mark patting the old pony on the nose. Emma adjusted her hat, and they began to crouch-run through the fog towards their foe.

Glaring search lights came on and spotted them immediately. Mark froze on the spot, mid-run, standing as still as a statue, hoping that they might go unnoticed. But he quickly realised he looked a bit ridiculous. A speaker system crackled on and filled the air with a whining noise.

"Where'd he get all this?" Mark wondered.

"What ho, ye sorry sand dodgers!" Charon chided them. "There be no place for fareless ferries across this river of the damned. If you seek your chance to enter into paradise, you must surrender what was once valued in life to attend the life hereafter."

"Haven't you got enough gold, you old miser?" Mark asked.

"Har har!" Charon cackled. "If you've no gold to offer, then I shall make ye a deal!" At his words, a door opened nearby, which seemed to lead below. "A deal that would allow for every wayward soul lost and wealthless to travel across this river to their promised eternity beyond. A new deal for a new nature! Come inside and wander through this humble labyrinth of torment. If you can endure the pains of your worst fears, the entertainment I derive from your suffering shall be payment enough!"

"You proper knob," Mark said. He held his scythe up and swung it to create a portal in the air. The lightning crackled, folded into itself, and imploded with a static discharge that knocked him and Emma backwards. "Okay... looks like we can't do that anymore."

Charon cackled again. "I'll consider that a down payment on your future torment. Now! Pay the boatman's toll, and rack horror unto yer soul!"

The way through the door lit up with dim, blue lights. Emma pushed Mark forward, her hand on his shoulder. She was confident. They just get through this and then deal with him later, she thought. Mark seemed to read her mind and nodded. They walked in and down the stairs, scythes over their shoulders and at the ready. Stormrider followed, weak but still ever faithful.

Within was not so much a maze as it was a direct line into a sunken haunted house. The walls were lined with stucco plaster and painted a nauseatingly deep shade of blue, like they were walking through an underlit aquarium tunnel.

"I don't feel filled with dread yet," Mark whispered.

"Me neither," Emma said. "But if those monks can make a monastery out of sand, anything is poss— EEK!"

Emma wrapped her arm tight around Mark's neck as they approached the first alteration in the hallway's structure. While up to now the walls had been simple brickwork with a line of exposed lightbulbs strung along the ceiling, the head of a hairless, big-eyed doll hung just ahead of them.

Then the very walls themselves became made of interlocking dolls that swivelled their heads and popped out their misshapen eyes. The floor began to move, carrying them along with it. It became an automated tour through a graveyard of Barbie offshoots from end to end as the hall passed by them. Emma remained close at Mark's side and shirked away from the reaching plastic hands of the doll army.

"Right," Mark said. He reached his free arm over and held her. "Don't let him get to you, Ems."

"God damn it," she whispered. "How does he know this about me?"

"Figures he'd know all about us," Mark said. "Acts like the judge of the damned, because he is one."

"I'm not closing my eyes," she said, her head pressed against Mark's shoulder, "but tell me when we're past this bit, okay?"

"Uh..." Mark drew out the word as they continued, then finally said, "We're past."

"Really?"

Emma looked up and saw the environment had changed. They were in a primary school, flanked by desks on all sides. The floor continued to move forward on an automated tram track, taking them further within.

Then suddenly the room was filled with colourful, gaily laughing clowns.

"PaAaAaAsSsS your AnswEr SheEeEeEt to the FroOoOoOnt, Marky!!!"

"What?" Emma looked around at the long line of white-faced, red-lipped figures, baffled that this could in any way be a terrifying descent into someone's darkest fears.

"Yeah..." Mark sighed. He instinctively shirked away a bit when the clowns reached for him or threw papers their way. He was more annoyed than abjectly terrified. "Clowns and retaking failed tests are common fears, I guess."

"Common-ish," she said.

"But putting them together," he continued, "it dulls the terror, you know?" He looked up as if he was addressing a hidden camera where Charon was watching. "You can't just layer fears together and have them intersect like this. They must compliment each other, not compete. Test-taking clowns don't make me feel fearful because I'm not taking the test, and the clowns are just... standing there. You've failed me! You've lost a customer. In fact, I want a refund! You ought to pay *me* for walking through this—"

Mark fell. Emma did not. She watched from her solid piece of track as Mark sank into a semi-soft pit of pale gunk up to his waist, which churned around him.

"The fears of yer nightmares," Charon declared over his speakers, "are but one part of the suffering I intend to pull ye through. The body has its own fears, its own poisons, which are common to all of humanity. The isolating dread of allergies is yer next trial. Now sink into your own worst fear!"

"Emma!" Mark shouted. "It's Brie! I'm intolerant to cheese!"

"Don't you just get a bit gassy if you eat it?"

"Yeah, but I don't know what my arse will do if I'm *submerged* into it! Help!"

"A-alright." She positioned her scythe to try and pull him out of his sinkhole of cheese while Charon, unseen, laughed at their plight.

Yet more trials awaited them, all far worse than what came before.

Charon spun a coin in his fingers and then clutched it hard. When he opened his hand, the coin was crumpled and crushed.

CHAPTER FORTY-FOUR

Blizzard winds blistered past the trench where Mark and Emma were hiding. A little further into their journey, things had taken an unexpected turn for the worse. Charon's industrial refrigeration hallway sent a wave of frost across the gold-lined walls and floor to create an uninhabitable frozen landscape. It was like Sunderland in February.

"Bloody hell," Mark groaned. "This is excessive."

"I hate the cold," Emma said, "but I'm not allergic to it."

"Yeah, what's fair about this?" Mark shouted. He had to turn away from the wind or risk getting a throatful of stinging cold air. He checked on Stormrider, his faithful pony, ever the struggler against the batterings of old age and the cheese pond he had lapped up. He was on his last, shaky legs.

"If we're in this any longer," Mark said, "we may not survive."

"Why aren't these robes suitable for four seasons?" Emma whined. "Death must go to the most frigid places on Earth just as often as the most temperate ones. The robe should account for all of them."

"If we need warmth in an emergency," Mark said, "then we may have to..." He nodded at his steed with a grim look on his face. "Well, it'll smell a lot worse on the inside."

"What?"

"I mean..." He looked forlornly at the frost-covered pony. Stormrider wasn't even looking ahead to where he was going. He just walked dutifully after his master, a horse following its carriage. "I can carry you, but... I can't carry—"

"Mark, you're not killing your pony."

"I don't want to!" he exclaimed. "But we've been in this long enough. I think we might not walk out of it. He's got no reason to let us through! He knows we're after him!"

Emma grabbed Mark's head and forced him to lock eyes with her. "That's just what he wants! He wants us to despair enough to abandon what we're doing."

"Honestly... I'm getting close to that."

Emma too could tell they were in dire straits. Not just from the cold, but the whole arduousness of their venture. She spotted an alcove away from the wind tunnel and pulled Mark into it. They were safe from the wind, but were then subjected to another, more gruesome torment. Mark watched as his beloved pony trotted its last, fell to its front knees, and braced itself against the harsh icy blast. Its eyes slowly shut. It accepted death and fell onto its side, stiff.

Mark sighed. "I had a dog once."

"Oh, Mark," Emma cooed, nuzzling into his shoulder.

"It got hit by a bin lorry," he continued.

"Oh, god."

"Yeah. No, he was fine, strangely. But he backflipped twice and when he landed, he was stiff like ice. I had to pick him up and carry him back."

"Was that Bosco?" Emma asked.

"Yeah, Bosco," Mark confirmed. "He was fine after we thawed him out in the front room for a bit but he always shit the carpet when the binmen went by."

"Why bring him up now?"

"...Stormrider looks like Bosco did," Mark said. "Just... legs all locked up. But he was shivering."

"Oh..." Emma hugged him. They endured the cold with one another's warmth and took the opportunity to assess the situation a bit more comprehensively.

"So, we're screwed then," Mark said. "This track will go on forever, or we'll hit a hallway full of radiators and hair dryers to finish us off."

"And sun lamps," she said. "The light alone would be enough to suffocate us in these things."

"He wants us to get rid of them. Lose the robes. Then next, our scythes."

"No chance," Emma said, clutching hers tightly. Mark gripped his scythe and looked over once more at the very still and very dead pony. Not even a minute had passed since he last checked on Stormrider and his pony was already frosted over and frozen up, desiccated like a mummy by the arctic chill.

"Well, it's definitely not warmer in there now," he said.

"Don't desecrate the body of your horse," Emma chastised him. "Look. There has to be some sort of logic to this."

Mark looked at her like she'd made a far more grotesque decla-ration. "Logic hasn't really worked for us recently," he said. "If logic could dictate our course of action... we wouldn't have lost our horses to golden ballistas because they wouldn't have been able to fly. And we'd be stuck on the wrong side of the river looking at a golden castle through a patch of soul smog."

"Even if things don't make sense," Emma said, "there is a logic behind them. A madman's logic, maybe, but there's a sense and order to what's going on. Charon is one of these... primordial orderly beings too. He has his own objectives beyond just seeing us suffer."

"He's a right prick," Mark said. "That doesn't mean he has to be smart."

"Well, give me something!" Emma demanded. "Give me some hope to cling to or some way to succeed! Give me any reason to hold out hope against all this or... or we may as well give up and—and I don't even know what happens after that! What's next? What happens to reality when time stops working and death no longer matters? What even *is* death?"

"Emma, hush," Mark said. "You're going mad."

"Going? Mark, I was about to jump off the roof!"

"That was then..."

"It's still now! It wasn't that long ago!"

"It was long enough. I wish you'd move on from it. We survived. That's what—"

"We!?" Emma repeated. "It was supposed to be my decision! My choice!"

"But it was the wrong one!"

"Oh, how inconvenient for you! You know how easily you could rebound with a dead flat-mate under your belt?"

"No! Who'd want to move in with me after that claim to fame? Even if they didn't think I was the cause, they'd still wonder 'what if?'. I'd never hear the end of it... and I'd never find a flat-mate I liked enough to replace you."

Emma scoffed but bumped her head against his chest. "I really thought we would make something of ourselves with this. We were doing well..."

"We did great."

"We were finding our purpose. We were finally moving

forward..." She shook her head into his robe. "Why'd we have to die to find someone who valued us?"

"They say the middle-class dream is dead," Mark said. "No wonder this is where we found it."

She scoffed out a laugh and leaned away from him a bit. "I'm just mortified that I've failed at *everything* life threw at me, and now that death is the thing throwing challenges, I can't help but struggle just a little bit more."

"Better than lying down and... uh," Mark stuttered, "not trying. Can't really die. Or we can, but it's a whole different phase of—"

"You," Emma said, pointing her finger right against his chin to stop his mouth moving, "should have followed your dream and just written your damn screenplays. Instead of pretending to be satisfied with working in advertising."

He shrugged. "I *was* satisfied. I just wanted—"

"You wanted to do the right thing. Wanted to not piss off your parents," she said. "It's admirable, but you should have stuck to your guns, gone to London, and kept writing your sitcoms."

"It wouldn't have worked. It was a pipe dream."

"You didn't even try," she retorted.

"Well, the sort of material I was writing isn't even a thing anymore. The television industry's moved on. And I saw you suffering at that job, dead tired and *actually* suicidal over it..."

"I wasn't suicidal from work. I was suicidal because I was lonely. Work was supposed to be my escape and I was fed up with being handed loss after loss for my best efforts."

"Pfff. I never thought of jumping from the roof after getting rejection letters from production companies," Mark said.

She nodded. "That's why I needed you to keep trying. You never let yourself fail. You were always one step away from success."

"One giant leap, more like."

"But I believed in you," she said. "And you believed it too. Or you would have stopped talking about it a long time ago."

Mark sighed. "I wish you hadn't tried to jump."

She smiled. "But I'm glad you tried to stop me."

"Really? You've been quite pissy about it since we got here."

"I know. And I'm sorry."

"Wait? So, you regret it?" Mark ventured. "Would you still go ahead knowing what you know now?"

Before Emma could answer, she caught sight of something above them in the blistering wind. "Look!"

A crystalline butterfly hovered overhead. It was one of the few signs of life and motion inherent to the void, the nascent fluttering wings of an ephemeral spiritual being that guided the souls of the dead to their everlasting peace. One of the strands of illogic that became a familiar, if fleeting, sight to behold.

"Maybe," Emma said, "it wants to help."

Then, an amalgam of hideous baby doll parts snatched it out of the air and chomped it to bits. Emma shrieked, and Mark reached for his scythe.

"No!" he shouted desperately.

The doll-monster's many eyes clattered and focused on them. It moved to pounce and then suddenly vanished. A great burst of air carved a clearing through the snow above them and sliced through the ice-covered walls that surrounded them.

They were encircled by the stomping hooves of four dread horses. One was red like fire, and upon its back was the bleeding visage of a warrior who wielded a sword turned red with aeons of rust. One was brown like the most fetid dirt. Its rider's skin was green, and in his hands he held a bow strung with long golden hair and knocked with an arrow made of a sliver of bone. One horse was black and emaciated, nearly naught but bones, and its rider was a pale and sunken man with sallow skin who held a brassy scale that never tipped its balance.

The last one was a pale horse, its rider far paler and wrapped in a deathbed cloth of white, an ephemeral skeleton holding aloft a reaping blade of harvest. The pale rider extended his hand down to them, offering to lift them from the hell they found themselves in.

"I'm confused," Mark said. "Aren't you all dead already?"

"No," Death said. "It's... complicated."

CHAPTER FORTY-FIVE

Charon relaxed on the deck of his shiny yacht. He had all sorts of consoles filled with dials, levers and gauges, various wheels – all the gadgets and attachments he'd ever want to make navigating the one-way waterway of eternity a game rather than a doldrum churning chore. He even had a room with all the accoutrements of nautical life and a soft bed made of golden threads, mounted on gold pillars and golden bricks. And above that was a mantle where he stored his oar, an artefact of his prior life and the hardships he'd endured before success was his to make.

He sighed, but he didn't feel empty. On the contrary, he felt more invigorated and enthused than ever. Downright victorious. The horsemen he envied had been deposed and left in a despicable state. The nature and order they maintained were in disarray, and a new era had begun. A new nature was beset over the living world, and it was his to control.

He looked down at his leg. It was no longer shackled but still bound, the thick iron lump which once secured him to his duty had been reduced to an edgy piercing through his ankle bone and

a thin, almost thread-like chain that extended to the engine platform at the rear of his boat. It still bound him to the river, only
able to disembark his yacht far enough to indulge in some of the
grand mansion he'd established, but not all of it.

He sighed. "Still not enough. How much more...? What more
must I cast aside and *pay* to be free of this curse?"

He picked up a golden chalice filled with gold coins and
walked over to the edge of the deck. He poured them into the
water. They cascaded down into the pale syrupy waters below and
there came a rumbling in the distance as the space in the void
quaked and changed. Each coin caused a tremor, each splash a
shift, each loss of value into the abyss would form a mountain or a
sinkhole beyond the fog. Yet he still did not care. His chain
remained tight and clamped to his own body, an even more invasive reminder of his bondage unto eternity.

He sighed again. "Damn. Wasted."

He also tossed the chalice overboard, which summoned a
distant roar of thunder. The clouds that swarmed over the
distant passage beyond the valley continued to swirl together,
blending the dark and light with threads of lightning between
them.

"Looks like nasty weather ahead. No time to be on the water."

He walked off his boat and hobbled onto an escalator that
took him up to the top of his castle rampart. The chain was just
long enough for him to get to the edge, where his newly modelled
throne sat. He turned, fell back into the cushioned seat, and let his
leg hang up as the chain pulled taut and suspended his foot in
the air.

He had nothing left to do now. Not until the horsemen were
all well and truly dead.

Then he saw a glint in the distance – four dim lights which
darkened the sky and sucked the life from it. A procession of four

dour omens, and astride their backs were their riders – and two extra passengers holding on from the rear.

"Intruders!" Charon growled. He sprung up and limp-sprinted over to his ballistas. They were coin-operated, coin-loaded, and magnetically charged for firing his gold as ammunition. He fed in a few coins, cocked the primer, and aimed to kill. "Namby-pamby pony parade!"

He fired. The coins zipped through the air like gleaming rays with the velocity of bullets.

Though decrepit, the horsemen were not weak. Their agility and expert manoeuvring outpaced their own lack of vitality. Death led the charge and swung his scythe to cut the coins in mid-air as they came. Famine caught some in his set of scales, which then decayed – the gold itself was replete of all value, equalised to the nothingness which Famine carried, for one could not eat their own wealth as the world starved. Then War came, with a dread horn in one hand, blasting a wailing echo into the sky as her sword hung low in the other.

"Fall into the abyss!" Charon shouted. "Wail into eternal darkness!" He fired a rapid burst of coins, one after another. His gold shattered out of the barrel into flak. The horses scattered. Pestilence was hit. He tossed his bow to War, and Mark caught it. Then Famine was struck. He tossed his scales. Mark caught those too.

"Hang on!" Mark insisted. "I can't get to my pockets!"

"Take this," War said, her voice distant and weary, a tired call of a myriad voices in a rebel chant. She held her sword out to him. "Go."

"I only have two arms," Mark complained. They were next to be rocked from the sky. Mark reached for the sword and took it before jumping from the back of the blood-red mare and landing on the pale horse's stiff, bony hide behind Emma.

"We have to jump," Emma said. "Just like normal."

"Normal where we die on impact?" Mark asked. "Or the new normal?"

"The new one."

"Right!"

Death was the last one still in the air. The others fell and their bodies drifted – pulled by inexorable forces towards the water. The horsemen sank into the river, and their horses followed. Death could tell he would be next, but his apprentices could survive the encounter.

"Charon has gone mad," Death proclaimed. "The order has been disturbed by his rebellion."

"So we have to kill him," Emma said.

"Yes," Death said. "And then—"

BOOM.

Flak rocked them out of the sky. Mark and Emma were suddenly airborne. Death was shredded. Bones went everywhere. They watched as he fell away from them, shards of white against a dim, grey skyline, falling all the way into the murky darkness below. Emma turned down and tried to aim to land on feet on Charon's rampart, next to his throne. When she succeeded, he hopped off his mounted gun and faced her.

Mark landed nearby, on his stomach, overburdened with the tools of the other horsemen. He was mostly unharmed, but not at all ready to fight.

"You two," Charon growled. "You two stumpy little nippers come to chase me from my own castle, eh? This ain't like yer other jobs, lass. This is one soul that won't come along quietly."

"You're not a job," Emma said. "You're an existential threat to the fabric of existence itself."

"Pah!" he scoffed. "The stagnance of this wretched order is worse than death as you know it. What suffering is caused at the widest scale by famine anymore? Your medicines have beaten back all pestilence. And war? Has any war ever truly been fought on the lines of ideals and virtues of opposing men? Or has there been another incentive?" To that end, he rubbed his fingers together and produced from them a coin. "There has been a higher order lurking over the thin veil of your perception for millennia. The plagues of man are now man-made, but no horseman rides to reap them. Death is the only constant, but there is one more sure thing than death in life. Do you know what that is, lass?"

"Taxes?" Mark asked.

Charon grinned a dark, wicked smile. "Aye."

Emma attempted to reach out to him with reason. "You're destroying the world."

"The world's fine!" he said. "It'll go on without War, Famine, Pestilence – even Death may be stayed in favour of this, another ending wrought by man's own making." He held the coin up once more in reverence. "The natural order has long since changed. You've lived it yourself; you know the weight this carries. It's more than life. More than food or blood or illness. This – *value* – is what people live and die for."

"That's not a good thing," Emma said. "Just because it's common doesn't mean it must become part of nature."

"Oh, but it does," Charon said as he flipped the coin. "Why preserve what old ways remain if they can't catch up to the ever-running race to oblivion? People *pay* to starve themselves in a world overrun with food. They pay to inoculate themselves with a sickness so their own body can resist it. They pay and earn to fight, a stance agreed upon by all sides of conflict, and those few who benefit from war speak louder than the millions who cry out in a prideless death. And people will pay to live. Debt will be the new death."

Emma gripped her scythe hard. "What did you say?"

"Behold!" Charon declared, arms out and waves crashing

behind him. "The Fifth Horseman – DEBT! He sat astride a golden chariot to charge across the sky and reap the rewards of a life well lived!" He held his hand out to her. "And the toll is non-negotiable."

Emma swung. Charon hopped back, far spryer than he looked. He reached down and summoned his wooden oar into his hand. It was now sharp and new with a bladed edge like a toothless, long-handled saw.

"If debt is to become part of the law of life and nature," Emma said, "then screw it. I'm killing you out of principle!"

Charon spun the oar artfully around his body and brandished it, countering Emma's stance. "The principal interest to begin fighting me is too high for the likes of you to pay!"

With that, their final battle began at the golden peak of oblivion's edge, the epitaph of apocrypha, where money conquered all.

CHAPTER FORTY-SIX

Blades clashed at the peak of Charon's golden empire. The River Styx swallowed up his golden dock, one building at a time, sinking the wealth he'd gathered over eternity into the abyss as he fought his hardest for his new course of nature.

Emma held her own against his mad swings. His oar, with its bladed paddle, was like an agile polearm, with a blade twice the length of her scythe's. And he was strong, far stronger than he looked. The years of rowing had given him a strength that defied his decrepit age. His gnarled fingers, barely more than bone, were practiced at holding the weight of his oar. For millennia he had stroked the blade through the resistance of the river. Now, battling to ascend as the Alpha and the Omega, the bladed oar danced and sparkled as it jabbed, parried, and spun. He came after Emma, swinging left and right, rowing through the air with the singing of metal as it sliced towards her. All she could do was block and retreat. He left no openings.

Mark, meanwhile, was committed to helping. His best friend and fellow reaper – his one and only love – was fighting for her life against the end of all life as they knew it and the propping up of a new natural order, built from gold and coin, in place of life or death. He knew the full consequences of failure and couldn't accept it. Wouldn't accept it. He ran in, scythe at the ready, only to be deflected from the side.

"Did anyone ever tell you it's *rude* to cut in between a man and a lady?" Charon said.

"She's my lady," Mark replied.

The ferryman-cum-oligarch smirked and then guffawed. "Unrequited, methinks."

Charon poked him with the blunt butt of the oar, and Mark was thrown back into the rampart wall. Despite gold being classified as a soft metal, his body hit the smooth bullion bricks, and the wind was knocked out of him. Emma swung down at the ferryman, but Charon caught her scythe. Then he swung his whole body back, tucked down into a backwards roll, and threw her against the opposite wall. He sprung up and flourished his paddle-blade as Emma slowly rose to her feet.

"Come now!" Charon mocked. "You still fighting off yer sea legs? I thought you young sprats could scrap for hours at a time!"

"Our generation," Emma said, "can't even watch Netflix for hours at a time without getting tired."

"What a waste," Charon said. He rushed in and continued his assault; Emma was forced to return to a desperate defence. Mark was equally desperate to help. His scythe was no good – all wrong in shape and length in the confines of the ramparts. So he picked up War's sword. Or he tried to. It was heavier than it looked, and he'd never wielded one in earnest before. The handle was too short for both hands, but the blade was too heavy for just one.

"Bastard," he cursed as he hoisted it up to his shoulder. He ran forward, ready to drop it down like a sledgehammer when Charon was least suspecting. "From Hell's heart, I swipe at thee!" He dipped his body forward. The blade left his shoulder and swung down hard enough to pierce the gold brick floor below.

Charon dodged deftly away, using the oar as a pivot. Once he regained his footing, he smacked Mark in the chest with the broadside and sent him tumbling back to the pile of discarded horsemen's weapons.

Emma went on the offensive. Now Charon was the one reduced to blocking, which he did with little effort. "We don't have a choice!" she shouted at him. "We can't afford to do anything else!" Their weapons clashed and she pushed herself closer, between the two tangled blades. "Money can't buy everything!"

"But what if it could?" Charon said. He pushed her away and spun his blade behind him. "If it could buy *time*. Wouldn't that be lovely?"

"The same problems would just get worse," Emma said. "Eventually, only a handful of people would be left alive. The rest—"

"Yes!" Charon said, gesturing to the broken horizon. "Just as it is now! But reversed! As it is here, with the ever dead and the unliving left to waste away and dissipate into the mist that clings to the surface of the river of death, the same fate can befall the living! The few will pass on, and the many shall suffer to find a worth equal to those who left them behind. Not war or famine or sickness, not even death will be there to stop them from finding purpose and worth!"

While Charon stood and pontificated over his mad perspective, Mark strung up the bow that belonged to Pestilence with the two gnarled bone arrows he was left with. He decided to knock them both together and drew it back. "Smile, you son of a— *hurk!*" He'd also never fired a bow before in his life, and let go of the arrows before the string, which snapped forwards and whipped back at him as the bone bolts clattered to the ground. He went to pick one up to try again but a hole opened in the floor and the arrows slipped through the crack.

The tower was collapsing around them. All the gold of Charon's hoard was bound for the water and the two shorelines. Even his boat had started to sink. The last precipice they had to stand on was left shaking and uncertain.

"The more gold you lose," Emma shouted over the chaos, "the worse this all gets."

"Good!" Charon said. "What good did that gold ever do me? *This* is the exchange it was meant for! Every piece of value brought from the world of the living was to change the status of the world! They willingly gave their money to me, not in honour of their death, but to dismiss it! To end the ceaseless cycle!"

"Justice is blindsided!" Mark shouted. He ran forward and tried to swing Famine's scales like a hammer. Charon just side-stepped him and let him fall to the ground.

"You total ponce!" Emma said.

"It's really heavy, actually," Mark said, with the scales still in hand.

The tower continued to crumble, and the spray of abysmal water spat up at them in a misty cloud.

"Only the boatman can stay above the water," Charon said. He looked down at his ankle chain. The thread had become thinner and thinner, now nearly fine enough to be dental floss. "See! My bounds weaken! My freedom is near! All the gold and order of life will be worth it! And I shall be FREE!"

"Free of your body!" Emma said. She swung. Charon blocked and spun his oar around. He nabbed the scythe by its crook and twisted it from her hand. She was left completely unarmed. Mark immediately jumped for his scythe and passed it to her. She reached for it, but Charon caught it first.

"What is this, even?" he said. "It's meant for hauling crab pots, not taking necks." He tossed it over his shoulder, off the rampart. The apprentice reapers were left without the only tools of their trade as they faced down the mad ferryman with his bladed oar, surrounded by dashed and depreciated golden furniture.

"Accept change," Charon told them. "Embrace it, as I have. If change had come to your life earlier, would ye not be happy?"

Emma looked at Mark. They shared the same sense of desperation. They stared the very embodiment of debt in the face and it smiled a snaggle-toothed, rotten, "die now, pay later" grin at them, anticipating victory with glazed over eyes of narcissistic import.

Then Mark spotted something else. A glimmer of hope.

Just off the side of the leaning tower was a shaft of wood, curved and burled, like a smoothed branch, which stuck out of the wall behind Emma at an angle.

He picked himself up and charged over to it. Charon stepped away and let him run clean off the edge.

"Mark!" Emma shouted. She rushed to the edge and looked down to where he fell.

"Har har!" Charon cackled. "He raced head-first into oblivion. Neck deep into debt! Cast away into the forgotten tides of the unearned! The fate of all the poor souls – poor in every sense – who live too long and find no worth in themselves! This be the brutal truth of this new nature. Those who can't find value in living ought to be cursed to pay for their own demise!"

He continued to laugh as Emma reached down over the edge.

"You should know all about it," he told her. "Wasn't it you who wished to meet a similar fate? Willingly leaping to the warm embrace of death? And you couldn't even do that properly!"

Charon's laughter died down as Emma stayed still. He wondered what she could be reaching for. What was so intriguing down there that she willingly turned her back to her most fear-some foe? He stomped across to the other side and peered over.

Mark had not only survived but also stood with his feet planted onto the wall and hands gripping the handle of Death's true scythe, just under the blade, which was lodged into the tower wall.

Mark plucked the scythe from its resting place at last and tossed it up. He tucked his robe into the cracks in the wall and stayed suspended, semi-attached to the exterior, as Emma took Death's scythe in both hands. Charon tried to rush at her, but she was already mid-motion when he arrived, and brought down a mighty swing.

His oar split in half. His shirt burst open. His beard was unevenly trimmed. Just the rush of air created by her attempt to hit him sliced through everything he held dear. She stepped forward, eyes ablaze with fury.

"I'm slashing your interest rates," she growled. "IN HALF!"

Charon was cleaved in two from shoulder to hip. From the north wall to the south, his tower was split the same. The top of the rampart drifted downwards into the roiling abyss below. Charon's top half followed it into the river with a plop, and he watched the rest of his body go limp as he bobbed on the surface. And then he laughed. He sank down into the abyss, laughing.

"Free!" he called. "I'm free!" His final words before disap-pearing under the water were a revelry.

Emma stood over his lower remains on the last solid piece of the tower left, knowing it was just one stiff shake from toppling down in the other direction.

"Uh, Emma?" Mark called up from below. "Did you do it?".

"I did," she said as she kicked the rest of Charon's body away. Her leg snagged on something as she did, and the floor beneath her shifted. She looked down at her ankle.

"What was that?" Mark asked.

The tower finally fell, and the river swallowed it up. All the gold Charon had gathered throughout eternity was spilt into the river and scattered across the shore.

But with no conductor to usher in a new order for nature to take, the tides levelled out, the plains went flat, the skies returned to normal, and the world of Death was once again quiet. The river ran calm once more. And glittering gold icons washed up on shore, just within reach of the precipice of the void, where lost souls lingered ever waiting for their meeting with the ferryman.

A new order was established, and yet the old order was still required.

CHAPTER FORTY-SEVEN

A figure wearing a scarlet toga crawled from the river. The first being in existence ever to exit the River Styx departed the churning waters with a sputter and a cough. War reeled her head back and wiped the water from her eyes. A graceless exit, but a welcome one. She headed onto shore and turned to see Famine and Pestilence crawling out after her with soaked loincloths and wrappings.

"Have a nice swim, did you?" she asked.

Pestilence coughed up black water which landed on the riverbank and immediately slithered back to the river like it was alive. "I haven't had to swim since I went fishing for... brain-eating amoebas."

"And I haven't swum ever," Famine said. "Not bad for my first time."

"Think of all the fish you could have eaten," War said, "if you'd ever learned."

He dismissed her with a wave of his hand.

Then the fourth horseman returned from the void, a vision of white wrapped in a loose-fitting sheet which hung from his hip bones in a rather revealing way.

"Oh, for shame. Cover yourself!" War shouted.

Death huffed and wrung out his saturated garb. "We're far past shame, I think."

"True," Famine said. He brushed himself off and walked up onto drier land. "Charon's dealt with, then?"

Death nodded. "His obsession with duty and his discovery of a second path combined into this tempest of change. We ought to take this lesson carefully. As times have changed, so too must we."

"What about them two?" Pestilence asked. "Your apprentices or whatever?"

Death sighed grimly. "Had I told them the truth, I doubt their choice would have changed. They are... duteous."

"Always nice to have enthusiastic help around," War said.

"Wait, look." Famine pointed at a shape that had appeared over the river. The fog was much reduced, a mere trace of what it once was, and a boat was just about visible through it. It was a long, spacious gondola with one figure at the bow and one pushing the boat along with a gaily painted wooden pole. Both figures were hooded in dark garb and were initially hunched forward with the slouch of defeatism. Their ankles were chained to opposite ends of the boat. They both stood taller as they approached.

"Hello, there!" Mark called out. "One at a time, I'm afraid."

"And no song requests or jokes about ice cream," Emma said. "Not until we fish up a golden fiddle to play."

Death stepped forward as they neared the shore. His apprentices were smiling through their own confusion, wanting an explanation even if they seemed to know the answer already.

"There must always be a boatman," Death said, "to carry the spoils of the four horsemen's march."

"Well," Emma said, "the old one is dead. And against all common sense, he *did* take his wealth with him."

"No," Famine pointed out as he picked a coin up from the riverbank. "He just lost it."

Death nodded. "The return of coin to these shores shall ensure a great many of the souls still stranded may yet have their fare to cross over. And thus, the balance of life and death will remain intact."

"But when we get the gold," Mark said, "what do we do with it?"

"Start an economy," Famine suggested. "There's no rule as to what the gold is for. Only that it's needed to cross."

"I'd start a competition for it," War said. "Make the lost souls fight for their rite of passage."

"Maybe start a business with it," Pestilence said. "Become rich."

Mark and Emma exchanged an uncertain look.

Emma said what they both were thinking. "If we were any good at that, we might not have died in the first place."

"We'll figure this out," Mark said. "And we won't do it in a way that, you know, kills you all and commences the End Times and all of that."

"There shouldn't be any need for that," Death said. "You've done far more than was ever expected of you. You have achieved a greater standard than I could have set. And for that—"

"Hey!" a man called. A wandering soul ran up to the water's edge waving a coin over his head. He saw the walking, talking skeleton giving him a gleaming side-eye and shuffled away from Death slightly as he approached the boat. "Hey. You guys doing this whole 'trade coin, go across the river' business?"

When Mark nodded, the man flipped a coin at him. He caught it and looked it over as the man trod through the marshy bank and clambered into the gondola. The man then clapped his hands and pointed his fingers shoreward.

"Let's go!"

"Righto," Mark said. He put the coin up his sleeve and then commenced rowing. "Make sure you give us five stars on the app, please."

"Or we'll dump you overboard," Emma said.

The boat, and those on it, disappeared back into the mist with their passenger-cum-hostage for the other side of the river. Death watched the fog swallow them as the other horsemen gathered themselves up. He stroked his chin thoughtfully and reached into one of the folds of his wreathed sash to pull out a pair of hourglasses. *Their* hourglasses.

And they had changed...

———

Mark and Emma quickly grew accustomed to their new duties. Lost souls found coins scattered from Charon's great hoard. They plucked them from the ground and met the boat as it passed, or fought over the coins found on the shore – as War had predicted – until one won or the gold slipped from their fingers and disappeared back into the depths, ending the conflict before it could escalate past slapping and rude names.

A new order was established, a change to what was known but nothing so new that it broke the world. Coins were now a happenstance of fate. A soul who wandered at peace could stumble across a hundred coins in the time it took a desperate seeker, obsessed and drastic, desperate in their deepest heart to leave the limbo of uncreation to even see one. Only those with settled souls and clear, calm minds would readily find their passage across. Those who were worthy would find the path forward, and those who needed repentance would be left to wander a little longer.

Just like Mark and Emma were told, things worked out alright. Only it was their own doing to make it that way. As far as they could tell, the rest of the world was the same. They still saw the purple flashes of Death traversing the veil between worlds. He'd picked up his pep and was rejuvenated back to his prime, carrying souls whole – and sometimes in bits – to the shore, where he would assemble them and send them on their way. Those who came with money were rare, but pleasant. Those who found it on their travels were much more frequent and thankful. Some even dared to bring more than one coin on their voyage, hoping for some better chance at a more pleasant afterlife, but in the end, it was just a tip for Mark and Emma to discard back into the waters.

Mark had transitioned into his new role with characteristic ease. He understood the rules, understood why he was now a ferryman, and understood that their sacrifice benefitted the whole of the human race, both living and yet to be born. He felt good about it, and didn't mind that their heroism would never be the stuff of books, movies, or even myth. Their actions were, and would remain, the most underappreciated act of selflessness ever committed.

Emma too was quite sanguine about their new circumstances. In one respect, she was now just one step away from her end goal of making it across the river to the afterlife. Unfortunately, that final step was prevented by the iron shackle wrapped around her ankle. The old Emma would have rued how, yet again, she'd over-delivered at work – smashed it out of the park, in fact – only for her actions to be barely acknowledged in her annual appraisal.

But their actions had been appreciated. At least by the small contingent of horsemen that made Limbo their home, along with one very French, very good housekeeper.

Finding themselves literally bound together in eternal servitude to the world's dead came with something neither had particularly much of during their lives, and none at all as Death's assistants: time to talk. Really talk.

"I owe you an answer," Emma said, after they'd waved off another happy client.

"Good luck, because I've been trying to figure it out since I was about seven."

Emma considered Mark for a moment, pretty sure they weren't quite on the same page.

"I'm not talking about why you never see a baby pigeon." Emma clarified.

"Please! Put me out of my misery. I can't figure it out! Wait... An answer to what then?"

Emma took the red, white, and blue pole from Mark and rested it across the gondola, motioning for him to take a seat. Then she sat down herself and took a deep breath.

"On the Liver Building. You told me that you loved me."

Mark shuffled a bit in his seat, caught unawares by the conversation topic. He'd been working hard to keep his feelings for Emma subdued since their arrival in Limbo and hadn't planned to open that Pandora's box again.

"I did," he eventually responded.

"Did you mean it? Or were you just trying anything to stop me from jumping?"

"I meant it." Mark looked across to Emma, his blue eyes almost sparkling. "I still do."

"Why though? I was a miserable cow. Suicidal, in fact."

Mark had prepared for this moment for most of his adult life. The conversation had played out a thousand times in his mind – every night since he'd met her in freshers' week, all through their university years, and their working adult lives. But right now he couldn't remember a word of his carefully crafted speech. Not one of the heartfelt pleas he'd planned or any of the solemn pledges he wanted to deliver. All he could think about was accidentally walking into the bathroom half-asleep and catching her getting out of the shower when they'd first decided to share a flat. How his heart – and let's face it, his loins – had yearned for her. Every molecule of his being wanted her. To be with her. To love her and cherish her.

"Because of your beautiful, perfect arse," Mark blurted out.

"I see." Emma nodded. "So it was just a case of forbidden fruit. I'm the booty call that never called."

"No. Not at all. Fuck... Let me go again."

Mark knew he was blowing it. He centred himself, gripping the sides of the gondola so hard his knuckles were white.

"I love you with all my heart, body, and soul." He shuffled towards her on his hands and knees, pausing to roll the pole out of the way. "I've never loved anyone else and never will. You are my life. And that's why being on this boat with you is both the most wonderful and most painful twist of fate imaginable."

"Why painful?"

"Because you don't see me the same way I see you."

Emma smiled and reached for one of Mark's hands. Holding it in hers, enjoying the shared warmth. "But what if I did...?" she started, not sure if she was ready to finish the thought. "What if... I love you too."

"Is that a question or a statement?" Mark asked, mouth wide open. "It's really important you clarify."

Emma leaned forwards and kissed him. It was the lightest of pecks, their lips barely touching. But they both felt it like a bolt of electricity.

"I love you," Emma stated. "Not a question."

"Shit," Mark replied before he leaned in to kiss her again.

This time there was more than just a glancing meeting of their lips. There were tongues, saliva, and freely roving hands as they finally consummated their love for each other in a disappointingly brief but wondrous union.

Emma and Mark set up home in a little hut on the north shore – the one where Charon used to stay before his gold hoard became his new home. They spruced it up with hand-me-downs from the horsemen's homes, and made it a place to rest in the doldrums between long shifts at the water. But when work summoned them, they had no choice and no way to sleep through it. Their alarms were bolted to their ankles. When the boat left, they would either be on it or dragged under the current by the legs. Mark learned that once the hard way, and swore never again to try to hit the snooze button.

It was work. It was necessary. And best of all, it was appreciated. Between ferrying souls and passionate lovemaking, they still met Veronique infrequently as she rode along the shore and shared her latest cookery from Death's abode. Their chains were not long enough to enter any other house. It was a solemn, pensive existence. But at least they now had each other.

They did this for what felt like years: thousands of ferries, thousands of trips, thousands of journeys to the ever-after that they themselves could not reach. And a feeling of unease finally began to settle in.

"This is utter shit," Mark said.

"Mmmm... yeah," Emma eventually agreed. "You want me to paddle instead?"

"No, not that," he said. "You did it yesterday. I mean the whole... the whole thing. This."

"It's not any worse than being a hired driver taking people to fancy parties and then coming home to a single room in a flat or something," she said. "It's a job."

"I'm just saying," Mark began, "while I feel no compulsion at all to seek a grand disruption of the worldly order on a cosmic scale, I think I can see how this could drive a man mad after an eternity or so."

"Yeah, well, give it an eternity. Maybe the pension is fantastic."

"It *was*," he said. "We sank it."

"Oh, right." She laughed. "We did, didn't we?"

Their gaiety rang out over the lake and reached the shore, where four figures stood awaiting their arrival. Mark leaned the boat in and faced down Death, along with War, Famine, and Pestilence.

"Uh, no group discounts," he said.

"None of you are planning to cross today, are you?" Emma asked.

"Not at all," War said. "Quite the contrary."

Death put his hand up. It was his place to speak now, and his matter to start. He pulled a pair of hourglasses out of his black robe and held them up as he approached. Mark and Emma gathered together near the middle of the boat and looked at them with their now skilled eyes.

"Your time," Death declared, "is not yet over." He held the hourglasses aloft and handed them over.

Mark took them and checked the names. They were Emma's and his.

"The error of your death is not yet resolved," Death continued. "The moment of your death is still yet to arrive."

"Well," Mark said, "that's fine by me. I suppose."

"They make a nice souvenir," Emma said. "We can pop them on top of the mantlepiece!"

"Oh, that'll look lovely." Mark nodded.

"No," Death said. "They are yours to keep. Into your... next venture."

"Our what now?" Mark asked. "I thought we were just doing this because of the..." He leaned down and jiggled the chain around his ankle.

Death turned to War with a nod. She hoisted up her sword, reclaimed from the river, and the other two horsemen waded into the water towards the boat. Famine held it still with his girthy frame while Pestilence gathered the ankle chains up in a bundle between the two ferrymen.

"We have concluded," Death declared, "that you are no longer fit to bear the burden of the ferry-persons. Not for any failure on your part, nor any issues of judgement passed unfairly to those you have taken on their final journey. But because you still have life left to endure and moments left to capture. An unknown future awaits you. It cannot be spent here, in the same moment, repeated forever."

"Wait, what?" Emma asked. She suddenly became incensed and clutched at her chain possessively. "Are you firing us!?"

"Yes," Death said. "I believe you are... *overqualified* for this position."

Emma looked hurt. She turned to Pestilence, up to his chest in the lapping waves between her and the water.

"I'm going to drown myself!" Emma exclaimed. "Overqualified! This bollocks again! After everything we've done!"

"Death, please don't fire her," Mark begged. "She'll kill herself. And I don't think I can stop her twice."

Death sighed. He nodded War over with her sword. Emma ceased her struggle and slid away from the centre of the boat. War's blade came crashing down and stopped just short of the wooden hull, leaving the shattered iron links of their chains as debris along the bottom of the gondola. With the chains broken at the root, the rest of them seemed to wither away and the braces around their ankles unlatched.

They were free.

"Drift into the void," Death told them. "And you shall return to the life you still have. When you return here, it shall be with me. And you shall enter the natural cycle as intended."

"…Thank you," Emma said. "But then, who will replace us?"

Death held his head up as Veronique walked out from behind him.

"Bon voyage, Mark et Emma!" She waved them off as Famine pushed their boat out into the increasing current. Sensing freedom adrift on its surface, the River Styx accelerated to flush the still living souls from its course and send them back to their own world. Mark and Emma held hands as the speed increased until all around them was but a blur of mist and darkness…

And at the shore, a new boat surfaced from the water. A sleek and sporty little dinghy, marked with a red cross on the side and padded with cushions all over. Veronique happily hopped into it and pulled out a long trench coat from the storage.

"Ahem." Death cleared his throat. "I… am glad that you have taken charge of this."

"It is my pleasure," she said. She held up a tatty World War One–era gas mask and prepared to strap it on. She held it up to her face to test it against her mouth. Her voice warped into something demonic, like the chatter of a hellish fiend intercepting a radio broadcast. "PAY THE FARE OR SUFFER THE WATERY GRAVE!" She pulled it away and looked at the horsemen. "Too much?"

"Just enough," War replied.

"It is unnecessary," Death said. "But… this is your duty now. Perform it as you see fit."

"I have two great examples to guide me," she said proudly. "I will not let them down!"

"Yes," Death said. He looked off to the distance. A faint flash was cast far downstream, further than any soul could ever venture. "Adequate, at the very least."

CHAPTER FORTY-EIGHT

It was night-time and the reflection of the Liverpool waterfront twinkled and danced on the inky black waters of the River Mersey. Grade I listed buildings sat proudly next to their much younger and sleeker steel and glass siblings, a melting pot of architecture that matched the cultural mix of the population. The girls wore short dresses and long lashes, and the lads sported figure-hugging T-shirts. The streets weren't busy, but the pubs were filling up and the cabbies and rideshares were bustling along. It was Saturday night, and having fun was top of the agenda.

Two dark figures emerged from an unseen alley, a shadowy space where no eyes were ever cast. They walked down Matthew Street with an accompanying mist that clung around their feet with each step. They stood outside an office building just off the city centre, which appeared to be closed for more than just the night.

"That's a shame," Emma said. "I didn't think they'd go under in just a day."

"I didn't think we'd be gone just a day," Mark said. "Didn't it feel like years?"

"Well, it was a boring job. It feels like you're doing it longer than you actually are."

"Yeah." He nodded. "That's just how it goes... But it was a good one."

"Paid well," she agreed.

They sighed. They were back to life. All those souls they'd taken, and all who Death later reaped, still amounted to little more than a day passing in their own life. They had been released from the bonds of death and the duties that reached beyond it, leaving them to enjoy their lives again for the few precious moments they still had to see. And now they had a way of tracking exactly when those moments would come.

"This is a sad gift," Mark said, as he pulled out his own hourglass.

"Is it?"

"It's kind of wrong to know when you're going to die, isn't it?" Mark said. "Takes the excitement out of it knowing you've only got... is that six good moments left?"

"Well," Emma said, "what's important is making those moments count. A thousand years of boredom can pass and only one grain may fall from it."

Mark nodded. "True. Well, I know what one of my moments will be."

"What's that?"

"That story I've always wanted to write," he said. "I've got a hell of an idea."

"No one reads books anymore," she said.

"I'm thinking screenplay," he said. "Might even give myself a cameo."

She smiled. "Fancy a drink at the Albert Dock?

"In that get up?" Mark asked.

"Oh, god," she muttered. She still had on her grim leather jumpsuit. "Can this even come off in this realm?"

"It better," Mark said lasciviously.

"Oh, hardy har," Emma mocked.

"Come on then. Pint." And then he had sudden, worrying realisation. "Have you actually got any money?"

Emma reached into the tight-knit crop of her collar and pulled out a coin – minted with the profile of Julius Caesar and hand-carved with Latin lettering, an authentic relic of a history once thought eternally lost to time.

"So no..." Mark said. "Because that's not cash."

She laughed and grabbed his wrist. He followed and caught up with her, and they wandered side by side into their future together. However long or short they had, they'd both make the best of it, knowing full well what awaited them in the end.

Their second chance at life would be better. And the second time they died, they'd be ready and – certainly in Mark's case – much more willing.

ABOUT THE AUTHOR

Jon Smith is the bestselling author of 14 books for children, teens, and adults. His books have sold more than 500,000 copies and are published in seven languages. In addition to writing books, Jon is an award-winning screenwriter and musical theatre lyricist and librettist with productions at the Birmingham Hippodrome, Belfast Waterfront and London's Park & Waterloo East theatres.

Jon enjoyed a happy childhood—making daisy chains, holidays in the sun and an obsessive interest in all things fantasy. No brace, few spots, only one broken bone and one broken heart (not his). It all went swimmingly.

Father of four, he lives near Liverpool with his wife, Mrs. Smith, and their two school-age children. When he grows up he'd like to be a librarian.

www.jonsmith.net

twitter.com/jonsmith_author

instagram.com/jonsmith_author

goodreads.com/jonsmith_author

amazon.com/author/jonsmith

facebook.com/authorjonsmith